THE
LADY
LIGHTHOUSE
KEEPER

A HISTORICAL NOVEL

MARY KORPI

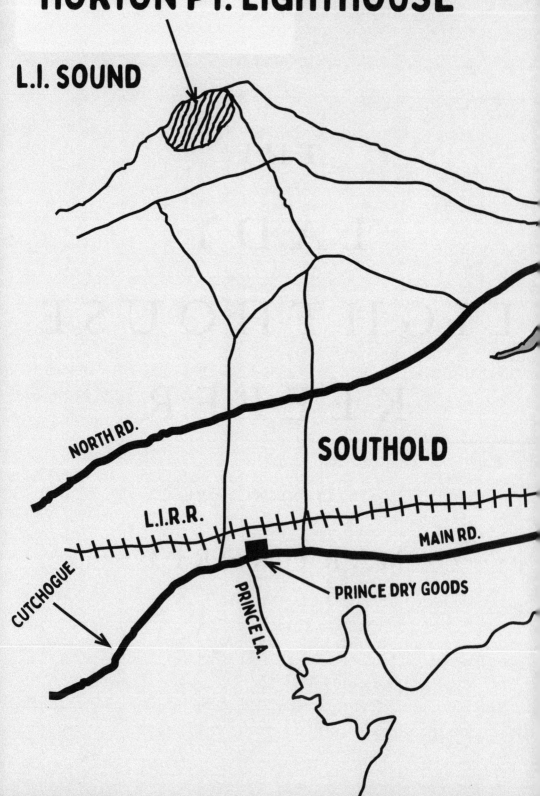

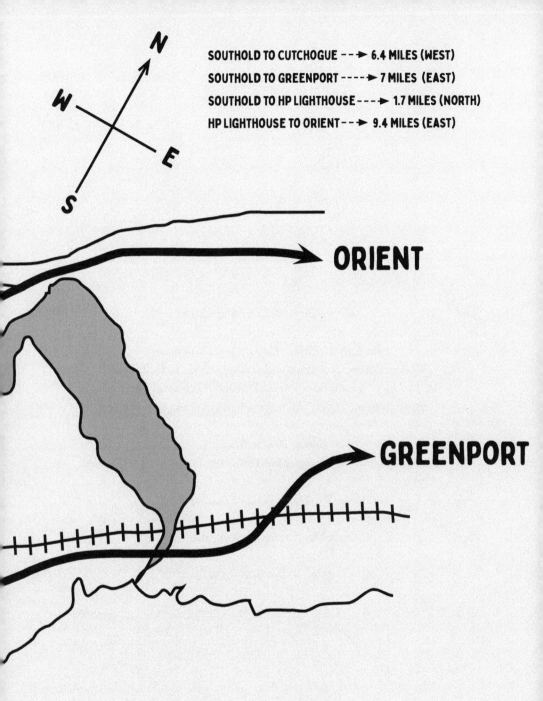

N

W · E

S

SOUTHOLD TO CUTCHOGUE ‑‑► 6.4 MILES (WEST)

SOUTHOLD TO GREENPORT ‑‑‑‑► 7 MILES (EAST)

SOUTHOLD TO HP LIGHTHOUSE ‑‑‑► 1.7 MILES (NORTH)

HP LIGHTHOUSE TO ORIENT ‑‑► 9.4 MILES (EAST)

ORIENT

GREENPORT

PECONIC BAY

Editor: Helene Munson
Cover Design/Interior Design/Map: David Ter-Avanesyan/Ter33Design

Published by North Fork Publications, 2022

Contact Mary at maryko50@gmail.com.

ISBN: 978-1-6781-0579-2

*This book is dedicated to the memory of mother—Isabel (1921–2020)
who, like Stella, dutifully performed her life's work without fanfare.*

INTRODUCTION

At the end of my shift at Horton Point Lighthouse, I walk around the museum turning off the lights that illuminate each display cabinet. In the small room with the images of the former keepers, I stop and take a long look at the photograph of Stella Maria Prince Terry. I wish she could speak to me. Stella, the only woman to serve at Horton Point, known as Hortons Point in her day, remains a mystery. Stella lived at Horton Point longer than anyone else, more than half her life, yet there is little factual record of her time there.

I searched the archives of the local historical societies, the Prince family genealogy records, and family journals, gaining knowledge about how people lived and worked on the North Fork of Long Island. Over many months, I pieced together the remnants of a life that was at times ordinary but also extraordinary—making the honor roll in school, learning to row a boat, all the while tending to the vital work of keeping the beacon lit.

As I learned about the arduous lives led by lighthouse keepers' in the late 1800s, the harsh realities of battling mother nature replaced the romantic myth I held about life as a keeper. The struggle to stay warm, dry, and nourished dominated their every waking moment. Even the simple act of washing clothes was a laborious all-day affair, let alone the work required for a once-weekly bath. And, of course, one mustn't ever forget the endless steps to the top of the tower, all-night vigils, and the terror of storms blasting at the windows as they stand guard, ensuring the lantern stays lit. The hours of isolation were perhaps somewhat offset by the natural beauty of their surroundings.

HISTORY OF HORTON POINT

The lighthouse property was part of the original 1656 land grant purchased by Barnabas Horton. The northernmost piece resides along the Long Island Sound. The Sound was an early superhighway transporting goods and passengers from the hard-working harbors of New York City and ports along northern Long Island to Connecticut and Massachusetts. Due to many shipwrecks, the water around Horton Point was known as Dead Man's Cove. In 1790, George Washington commissioned a lighthouse at Hortons Point. Sixty years later, in 1854, the federal government purchased the 8-acre parcel from Charles Payne for 550 dollars, and the building commenced in May 1857. Five months later, on October 15, 1857, Keeper William Sinclair lit the beacon for the first time.

The lighthouse stands 58 feet tall and is set back from the edge of the bluff, approximately 60-feet above sea level. In clear conditions, the beacon is visible for 14-nautical miles. The tower's white concrete exterior comprises a 13 foot square at the base, and the inside is a brick cylinder with a 28-step metal circular stairway leading to the first of two 7-step metal ladders. The attached keeper's house is a 2-story Federalist-style building. Perhaps the only distinguishing feature of the tower is the ten decorative gargoyle head rainspouts that jut off the domed roof. During the Civil War, the change-over from clean-burning whale oil, which became too expensive due to overfishing, to the smokier but cheaper lard oil, required two keepers to ensure that the lens and windows stay clear and soot-free.

STELLA PRINCE'S FAMILY HISTORY

Stella Prince is a direct descendant of Captain John Prince, a whaler who settled with his wife in Southold in the 1780s. As a whaling Captain's family, the Princes would be something of local royalty, yet Stella's side of the family doesn't appear to share in the rewards of this birthright. Stella's grandfather, John Prince, died in 1859, leaving a pregnant wife and three children. George, the eldest, was just 17-year-old when his father died. George's mother remarried and relocated up-island and was not involved with George's children, Stella and Lucy.

George enlisted in the Civil War in 1863 in part to escape the poverty of his home life. He was wounded twice and returned to Southold, a reluctant hero, relieved to be free from the rigor of the military. Building his home on Prince Lane in Southold is his proudest achievement. Working as a carpenter, George takes pride in working with his hands. But, he appreciates having the freedom to choose when and which jobs to take as he also enjoys spending time with his buddies, particularly on his Cousin Waitley's fishing boat. George accepted the appointment of Assistant Lighthouse Keeper at Hortons Point with reservations. While he recognizes it is an honor granted because of his military service, he dreads working under someone else's command. However, he knows that the regular paychecks that the appointment to Hortons Point will provide are necessary to support Caroline and their daughters.

His first year at the lighthouse, George was the Assistant Keeper under Theron Squires, a local farmer and a fellow Civil War veteran. The two men had an amicable relationship and did not feel undue pressure to maintain the lighthouse. In 1871 renovations were completed, and

Captain Goldsmith took charge as the new Head Keeper. The Captain, accustomed to commanding whaling vessels, is quick to direct George in their day-to-day responsibilities. He tackles deferred maintenance with zeal and expects George to do the same. George resents the Captain's directives. The close living and working conditions add to George's bad temper as there is little opportunity for escape.

Caroline Merrill Prince, Stella's mother, grew up in Greenport in comparative wealth. Her father was a hard-working butcher who became an affluent landowner. Although she was one of six children, her family prospered. So what brought Caroline, this daughter of comfort, to marry George Prince, a local carpenter? Perhaps, the dark good looks of the returned war hero from the esteemed Prince family added to his mystique. The mismatched couple could not foresee that Caroline was ill-suited to the requirements of life married to a troubled man who struggles to provide for his family. However, when they set off for the lighthouse, she is hopeful that this new opportunity will turn their fortunes around.

CHAPTER I

June 1, 1871

Thar She Blows! -
the call when a whale is spotted.

T he big day is finally here. Little Stella Prince rushed through breakfast to watch Da loading the last of their belongings from the cottage in Southold. They're moving to the light-house. When she sees Da tie the rocking chair on the wagon, she runs back inside and calls, "Hurry, Ma! Da's ready!" Caroline takes one last look around their home on Prince Lane. They've had their share of troubles here, with George's struggles to find steady work. But she has happy memories too, both her girls were born here. Caroline will miss the close ties she's forged with her neighbors but hopes this move will allow George to grow into the man she believes he's capable of becoming.

George comes inside, sensing Caroline's hesitance; he cajoles her saying, "Come on, Mrs. P., you'll have a bigger garden at the light-house." She searches his eyes for reassurance that this is the right move, the new beginning he's promised. He turns away, not wanting to face this virtuous woman who chose to marry him despite her family's reservations.

"Will we get there today?" Stella asks, dancing around her parents.

"Yes, Stella, now settle down," Da says as he checks one last time that they're not leaving anything behind. The Lighthouse Service provides furnished quarters, so they only need to bring their personal belongings though, Caroline insisted they take the rocking chair George made during her confinement.

Stella follows Da outside, ensuring he doesn't go without her. Da lifts Stella onto the wagon's high front seat and then takes baby Lucy while Caroline climbs up. He hands the baby back to Caroline, walks around the wagon, checks that all is secure, and climbs onto the front of the overstuffed wagon. Uncle Waitley comes out to say goodbye and wish them a safe journey. Stella notices a tear in Ma's eyes as they drive down the familiar dirt road with houses and stores on both sides.

Ma says, "I hope we will be back for Sunday services."

"Of course, you will," Da barks, his limited patience exhausted by Caroline's hesitance.

They are heading to a new life, lighthouse keepers, at Hortons Point. Caroline is apprehensive about living so far outside of town, isolated from family and neighbors. Living with George in Southold, she has grown close to his family and enjoys the short train ride to Greenport to visit her mother. She never learned to handle a horse and wagon; growing up, they relied on Old Jonas, their driver. Sometimes, he told them stories of the hardships his family endured before they were freed. Caroline loved Old Jonas and was sickened to think that his family was treated in this manner. No doubt, some of her attraction to George is the pride she feels about him volunteering to fight to free enslaved people.

Stella sits up tall between her parents, leaning forward; she waves to people walking by along the Main Road. She feels special in the new bonnet Grandmother Merrill, Caroline's mother, bought for her.

Stella insisted on wearing the bonnet, explaining with childish logic, "So, the lighthouse will be happy to see me!" Da scoffs at her foolishness, but Ma gives in, and they set off with Jenny, their mare, straining to pull the overloaded wagon.

They ride past Cousin Henry's store, then turn left and continue to the North Road. The jostling of the carriage lulls baby Lucy to sleep in Ma's arms, but Stella struggles to stay awake so she doesn't miss any part of the journey. As the carriage lurches across the train tracks, Caroline remembers taking the train into New York City to shop for her trousseau not so many years before. Cuddling little Lucy, she admires the delicate woven wool baby blanket her mother purchased at the brand new department store Arnold Constable & Co. The soft pastel colors stand out against Lucy's dark hair and eyes. The wagon lurches forward, and Caroline is propelled back into the present as they approach the well-traveled North Road. They stop and watch as several carriages pass, heading east, bringing summer guests to one of the many boarding homes in Greenport and Orient.

Across the road, they stop at a gate. There's a path behind it that leads through a field of potatoes. Da climbs down, opens the gate, herds the horse through the opening, then secures the gate behind them before climbing back into the wagon. They repeat the tedious process at several gates, moving towards their goal through rows of sprouting vegetables. George rubs his shoulder, feeling a familiar ache in his back as they jostle along the rutted path, reminding him of his war wounds.

"Are we there yet?" Stella asks.

"Stella, sit still! If you don't settle down, Da's going to make us get out and walk." Stella's eyes widen in fear. She turns to Da and relaxes when she sees him smile.

"She's excited, Mrs. P."

"I'm worried she'll fall with all her wiggling on this rutted trail," replies Ma.

"I don't see how she can get loose." Da reaches over Stella with one hand ensuring her tight fit between him and Ma.

When they stop at the next gate, Ma says, "Stella, listen! Do you hear the birds calling?" Stella holds still. She sees an osprey overhead and points to it.

In the quiet, baby Lucy sits up and points towards the sky and says, "bir-bir."

Smiling, Ma says, "that's right, Lucy, b-i-r-d," she repeats, exaggerating the sounds for the little one to learn.

"Ma, she's talking!"

"Yes, Stella. Lucy is learning to talk." Da climbs back up and urges Jenny through the opening, taking no notice of the family's high spirits. Rested from her nap, baby Lucy chortles as the wagon jerks forward.

At the next field, a herd of curious cows ambles over. Stella jumps up for a better look and knocks her bonnet off. It blows down, lands in the mud, getting caught under the wheel.

Stella cries out, "My bonnet!" Da jerks on Jenny's reins and climbs down to free up the soiled bonnet.

He pulls the hat out from the mud, thrusts it at Caroline, says, "I told you she shouldn't wear it."

"I'll wash it out when we get to the lighthouse, but Stella," she continues turning to the small child, "now you have to wear it dirty or not."

Stella turns to Ma, ready to protest but seeing the serious look on her face, she stays quiet. The bovines clear a path as Da urges Jenny forward.

"Are these our cows?" Stella asks.

"No, Stella," Da replies. "They belong to the Tillinghast's." He points west at a farmhouse and barn in the distance. "Looks like they keep a tidy place. They must be hard-working folks. They will be our closest neighbor, except for the Goldsmiths, the head keeper, and his wife." Ma shudders at the thought that their closest neighbor will be so far away.

"Whoa, Jenny," Da says as he pulls on the reins and stops the horse at the next gate. He climbs down and repeats the steps, and returning to the wagon, George points straight ahead and says,

"See, there's the lighthouse."

Stella doesn't see where he's pointing. She doesn't know what a lighthouse is, but she is excited about going to this new place where Da says they will live at the edge of the world. The slow rhythm of the wagon lulls Stella to sleep. She wakes when Da stops, and the first thing she sees is a vast expanse of water. Stella catches a glimpse of the rolling waves on the Sound.

"Ma, what's that?" Stella asks, pointing at the water.

"That's the Long Island Sound, Stella," Ma replies.

"Why is the water bumpy?"

"Those are the waves," George says as he and Caroline exchange a rare warm look over the tops of their daughters' heads.

Da lifts Stella out of the wagon, places her on the ground, then walks around to the other side to assist Caroline with the baby. As soon as her feet touch the ground, Stella takes off full tilt toward the edge.

Ma yells, "Stella!" alarmed that she is running towards the end of the 60-foot high bluff. Stella doesn't hear her mother's calling.

Suddenly, she's scooped up high in the air, and a rumbly voice says, "Slow down, little lady . . . mustn't get too close to the edge."

Stella tries to squirm out of the tight grasp of the stranger's strong arms. She turns her head and looks into the eyes of the big man who stopped her perilous run. Frightened tears run down Stella's cheeks as Ma rushes over and takes her from Captain Goldsmith's arms. Stella presses her head into Ma's shoulder.

"Stella Prince, Don't ever do that again!" Caroline scolds her.

Stella pulls her head off her mother's shoulder and looks out over the bluff at the water below.

She stretches her arms wide and exclaims, "But it's so grand!"

CHAPTER 2

1871

Establish -

To place an authorized aid to navigation in operation for the first time.

George hands the baby to Caroline and places Stella on the ground, grasping her hand. Captain Goldsmith points to the tower behind them, and as Stella turns, she says, "It's BIG!"

The Captain chuckles and says, "I guess George told you the history of the tower?"

"Not really," Caroline replies.

George calls from the wagon, "I'll pull up in front so we can unload."

Captain Goldsmith ignoring the interruption, continues, "Well, George Washington commissioned a lighthouse at Hortons Point back in 1790. Sixty years later, the Lighthouse Service built it."

"Hmm, took them quite a while," Caroline says. "I guess other projects got in the way?"

"Seems so," he says with a shrug.

They walk across the field and into the breezeway that connects the tower to the house—Stella darts to the circular stairway that leads to the top. Caroline rushes over and pulls her back.

"Not now, Stella. We need to help Da unload the wagon."

Caroline steps inside the house and inhales the earthy scent of freshly sawed wood, eliciting memories of the sawdust-covered floors in her father's butcher shop.

The Captain following behind says, "This side will be for your family gesturing to the parlor. Your bedrooms are up these stairs in the back."

Caroline looks around the well-proportioned room, with a chunky wood table and four chairs centered in front of the large hearth.

George comes in the front door carrying the rocking chair, "Where do you want me to put this?"

"It doesn't matter," Caroline responds and gestures to the corner, then continues, "And you and the Mrs. are your accommodations suitable?"

"Yes," the Captain says, leading Caroline into the entryway of the front door and to the other side of the cottage where Mrs. Goldsmith is tending the fire in the hearth. A wall runs down the center of the living quarters creating mirage image living spaces.

"Nice to meet you," Caroline says as the older woman turns to greet them. Stella hides behind her mother's skirt while Lucy snuggles against her mother's shoulder. Mrs. Goldsmith approaches and reaches out, touching Lucy on the cheek, saying,

"Aren't you sweet?" Then, turning to Caroline, she says, "And this must be?" gesturing to Stella.

"Stella," Caroline says, trying to extricate her from her skirt.

"Stella, is it? I think we're going to be great friends. She just needs time to warm up," the older woman says, looking up at Caroline, "You go get settled. Please let us know if you need anything."

Caroline relieved to return to her side of the cottage, hears George grumbling upstairs. Taking Stella's hand, she heads to the back stairs and climbs up into the bedroom that she and George will share heated with a small black coal stove. Caroline walks through the room, observing the sturdy wooden bed frame with a small table on each side and a large wood chiffarobe. She sees a door leading to a second smaller bedroom for the girls. The wall that divides the parlors downstairs also separates the bedrooms from the Goldsmith's side of the house.

Caroline admires the newly completed living quarters but worries about her ability to keep it up to standard. Growing up with household help, she is not conscientious about tending to household chores. However, George warned her she must keep their quarters at the lighthouse spotless as the twice-yearly inspections from the Lighthouse Service includes the families' quarters. If the inspector finds anything out of place, George will get demerits that may impact his continued employment. While Caroline unpacks, Stella and Lucy explore every nook and cranny. Stella is fascinated with the circular stairs that lead up to the tower. Their home in Southold only had a ladder to the loft.

"Up," Stella says, pointing to the stairs.

"Not now, Stella; Ma is busy," Caroline scolds.

George comes down from the tower and, finding Stella at the bottom of the stairs, says,

"Look, Mrs. P. Stella is ready to get to work."

"Let's not get ahead of ourselves, George. She's only three." Caroline admonishes.

❧

Caroline wakes to the sound of George tossing coal on the grate of the hearth downstairs. She enjoys a moment of quiet before going down to start breakfast. By the time she gets down, George has gone to the outhouse.

Mrs. Goldsmith taps on the door, and Caroline calls, "Come in." The older woman enters and places a basket of eggs and a bottle of fresh milk on the table. Caroline thanks her. Just as Mrs. Goldsmith steps out, Ma hears baby Lucy babbling. She smiles and climbs back upstairs to gather the girls for their first day at Hortons Point.

Caroline sits the girls at the table just as George comes in. He pats them on the head while they sip the fresh warm milk Mrs. Goldsmith brought.

George asks, "Where'd you get milk?" Caroline gestures towards the Goldsmiths' side of the cottage. Holding up an egg then she cracks it into the frying pan.

"Eggs too?" he asks. Caroline nods.

Stella eats her porridge while Lucy tries to feed herself, making a mess in the process. George sits down next to the baby. He tries feeding her but is not very successful, as Lucy is determined to keep hold of the spoon and do it herself. Caroline serves George eggs and puts a bit in front of each of the girls. She takes the seat on the other side of Lucy and distracts her while feeding her.

Caroline takes a rag and dips it into a bucket of warmed water next to the hearth. She wipes the girls' mouths and hands to get the sticky breakfast off, then places them in the corner farthest from the hot stove. She lays three kitchen chairs on the floor around the corner where the girls are sitting to block an easy escape while she starts to clean up from breakfast. George heads up to bed, reminding Caroline to keep the girls quiet as he's been up all night and needs to sleep. When Caroline recognizes that request's futility, she abandons her cleaning and gets the girls' sweaters to go outside. Mrs. Goldsmith told her the former keeper was not much of a gardener, and since it's already June, they're going to have to work fast if they expect to have anything to put up for the winter.

Caroline lays baby Lucy on the floor and pulls a sweater over her head, "You are getting so big, my sweet baby," Caroline murmurs. Then, turning to Stella, she holds up a new sweater and says, "Grandmother Merrill sent this to you, Stella. Isn't it pretty?" She buttons it, then takes her hand, scooping up Lucy, they head out the front door. Caroline takes in the refreshing, cool breeze off the Sound. As she steps off the porch, Stella jumps and takes off towards the bluff. Caroline grabs her by the arm.

Stella implores, "I wanna see the water."

"No, Stella," Caroline admonishes, "We're going to work in the garden first. I'll take you and Lucy down to the beach later." They walk around to the back of the cottage, and Caroline sees Mrs. Goldsmith is already in the garden hoeing.

"Morning," Caroline calls, "Sorry, it took me a while to get out."

"That's understandable," Mrs. Goldsmith responds with a smile.

"Let's see what we can do to keep these two busy while we work." Caroline looks on as Mrs. Goldsmith pulls out a rope.

"I think, for now, we're going to have to secure them to the wheelbarrow."

Caroline hesitates and mutters, "I've never tied them up."

"You've never lived on a 60-foot bluff, I imagine. Better to keep them safe, and we can get some work done. I asked the Captain to request the government put up a fence, but that could take some time."

"Thank you, Mrs. Goldsmith; I appreciate all you're doing to make us welcome."

"We're going to be living mighty close here. Best we be neighborly, don't you think?"

Caroline nods. Taking the end of one of the ropes, she wraps it around Stella's waist. Stella looks confused and pulls it.

"Stella, leave that alone, sweetie; it'll keep you safe. Ma is right here in the garden."

While Ma ties the rope around Lu, Mrs. Goldsmith places a pile of shells of various sizes between the girls.

"Let's see what you two can do with these," she says while demonstrating digging and dumping dirt from one shell to the other. Stella and Lu are intrigued by the novel playthings and start digging. Lucy puts a shell into her mouth.

Pointing, Stella yells, NNo, dirty."

Mrs. Goldsmith chuckles and says, "What a big helper you are, Stella." Stella smiles at her warm tone.

Caroline is not comfortable tying them; she realizes they must keep them safe. She looks up and feels the warmth of the sun on her face. Here, on the south side of the lighthouse, they are protected from the breeze off of the Sound. It is a beautiful day, and Caroline reminds herself how fortunate they are to have this new opportunity. She remembers how hard her father worked to support their large family and provide them with the finest things. But George doesn't seem to have that kind of drive. She hopes he is better suited to life at the lighthouse, and she won't need to ask her parents for financial help again. At least they'll receive a regular paycheck.

Caroline is roused from her thoughts by Lucy's cries, pulling on the rope, frustrated she can't get loose. Stella is also tired of being in one spot and is trying to untie the rope.

"Caroline, if you'd like, I can take the girls inside with me."

"Oh, that is very kind, but I can't impose."

Mrs. Goldsmith walks over to the girls and unties them.

"It's no trouble. You stay out and work as long as you like. I enjoy little ones. I miss the time when my own were babies. I'll clean them up and bring them inside while I'll start the Captain's dinner."

Stella looks back at her mother as Mrs. Goldsmith pulls her towards the water pump. Caroline raises her hand, pushing it in a gesturing, 'go ahead—it's fine'—while nodding her head to reassure the child.

Caroline loses track of time as she moves on, prepping the next section of the garden. Before she realizes she's getting hungry, the Captain comes out and says,

"Caroline, Mrs. Goldsmith has prepared dinner for a crew. Would you and George care to join us? The girls are already digging in." Caroline feels a little uncomfortable at the generosity of these kind people who she just met,

"Thank you. I'll be right in and see if George is up."

As she climbs upstairs, she hears him snoring. She wakes him and explains the Captain and Mrs. Goldsmith asked us to join them. He rolls over with a growl.

She persists, "George, I think it's best if we accept their hospitality.

"What you ain't gonna cook no more?" he grumbles.

"Of course, I am, but I've been working in the garden, and Mrs. Goldsmith went in first and prepared dinner. She said Captain has his big meal mid-day."

"Where are the girls?" he asks, opening his eyes and scanning the small room.

"They're eating with the Goldsmiths."

"Let me see if I got this straight; Mrs. Goldsmith took the girls and made dinner while you relaxed in the garden?"

Caroline blushes but responds with control, "No, George, I didn't relax in the garden. I was turning it over for planting. Mrs. Goldsmith and I did quite a bit this morning, but there's much to do. It's already June, and nothing's been seen to."

"Ok, ok," George says, climbing out of bed.

Day by day, trust grows between the two women, and confidences are shared. Tending to Stella and Lucy's care builds a strong bond on which both women come to rely. George and Captain Goldsmith don't ever develop a natural give and take but rather maintain a more formal supervisor/employee relationship despite the close quarters they share.

George goes fishing with Cousin Waitley off his boat. Caroline offers to cover his shift in the tower, but Captain Goldsmith refuses. Caroline worries that George will come back empty-handed, making it evident that his absence is little more than an excuse to over-imbibe in the local brew. While George is away, Mrs. Goldsmith insists that Caroline and the girls eat with them. Even as her affection grows for the old couple, Caroline feels a bit claustrophobic, not seeing anyone outside of their little group for weeks on end. The girls thrive in their new home and benefit from Mrs. Goldsmith's loving care. But Caroline feels isolated. The walk to Southold with the little ones is too arduous. She realizes they are more fortunate than most wickies, who live on islands only accessible by boat. She relies on letters for news, cherishing the correspondence with her mother and sisters whom she longs to see.

George returns with many bluefish and a large number of bay scallops. He also brought gifts from Uncle Waitley for the girls - a corn husk horse for Stella and a cow for Lucy. The girls are delighted with their new playthings and act out little stories with the toys while the women prepare a feast on fried scallops with roasted potatoes and squash from the garden.

After the abundant meal, a relaxed and satiated Captain Goldsmith reminisces about his travels as a whaling captain.

"We sailed around Cape Horn and up the west coast into the Arctic. Sometimes, we would be at sea for three years."

The Captain explains that Francis, the Mrs., accompanied him on his last voyage, "What did you do with the children while you were away?" Caroline asks.

"That was the spring of 1860; Daniel, our youngest, was fifteen, so he came with us. Chary Ann, David, and Bess were all married by then. Though I did miss out on the birth of my second and third grandsons, it was the adventure of a lifetime." Captain Goldsmith smiles at his wife.

"Did you catch many whales?" George asked.

"Yes, we did." Captain Goldsmith continues. "Frances stayed in San Francisco at a woman's boarding house."

"Quite respectable," Mrs. Goldsmith chimes in at Caroline's startled expression.

Captain Goldsmith continues, "The crew and I headed up towards Alaska. We got us a 17-foot Narwhale, a couple of Belugas, and, of course, Bowheads. Bowheads are the only baleen whales up north. They are much prized and were plentiful in the Arctic."

Caroline, not familiar with baleen, looks confused.

Captain Goldsmith explains, "Some whales have baleen instead of teeth. They are spikes that filter their food. Baleen is in great demand. They use it in many everyday things, even women's corsets."

"Whaling is hard work," he continues in another vein. "You don't come back till all the

barrels are full of oil." George, shoulders raised, bristles at what he interprets as a slight comparing it with the easy job they have here at the lighthouse.

"On the way back," Mrs. Goldsmith continues, "They picked me up, and we sailed to a Hawaiian island so the men could have a shore break then back around the Cape."

"Oh, my! That must have been so frightening."

"I knew we were in good hands with the Captain at the helm," Mrs. Goldsmith says with a nod and a smile towards her husband.

"But what about your son, Daniel?" Caroline asks.

"He had the time of his life, yes it's hard work, but there's nothing better to help a young man grow up. Time to go, Frances, we've all got things to attend to, I expect." Rising, the Captain and Mrs. Goldsmith retreat to their side of the cottage.

George lights the bedroom stove for Caroline and the girls. He returns downstairs, sits close to the stove, and reads the newest updates in the *Keepers' Information Sheet*. He tries to read during his night watch up in the keeper's room but often dozes off on the bench next to the stove, although he knows it can lead to disaster as the lantern requires constant watching and frequent cleaning to prevent the build-up of soot.

George reads an article about the invention of the Fresnel Lens. The inventor, a French physicist, Augustus Fresnel, discovered that bending glass magnified the light from the wicks burning inside. Fresnel lenses improved visibility for ships at sea. There are six different sizes or 'orders' of Fresnel Lens. The tallest lighthouses, such as Montauk Point, have first-order lenses that project light over 20 nautical miles. George is pleased that Hortons Point's 3rd order Fresnel Lens is far smaller though it still requires meticulous care. The light at Hortons Point can be seen for 14 nautical miles across the Long Island Sound and is visible on the Connecticut shore to the north and Shinnecock Lighthouse to the south.

George reflects that although he's never been to Connecticut, he saw plenty of the south during the war. Thanks to the aches that never leave his shoulder and back from his wounds fighting in the 'Battle of the Wilderness,' he can't forget the war. Yet, he smiles, recalling the kindness of Mrs. Lincoln, who visited each soldier's bedside and thanked them for defending the cause. "Going to war makes a boy into a man, not sailing around on a whaling ship with mommy and daddy," George grumbles to himself, recalling the conversation earlier that evening. He banks the fire and goes up to join Caroline in the now warmed bed, knowing he has to rise at 1 a.m. to assume the watch.

❦

As winter descends on the lighthouse, Caroline is sure she's never been so cold. She struggles to keep up with what feels like never-ending chores – preparing meals, keeping the cottage clean, and tending to the girls. They wage a constant battle to keep the damp and drafty house warm and dry. She never finds even a moment to herself.

A December snow makes traveling impossible at Christmas, so they gather around the small pine tree the Captain cut down and placed in the parlor. Caroline helps the girls hang shells and pine cones to decorate. Daniel Goldsmith comes by in the afternoon bringing a couple of oranges which they share. Lucy and Stella enjoy their first taste of this tantalizing fruit.

A quick thaw later in the week frees the Captain and Mrs. Goldsmith to visit their daughter. They offer to bring Caroline and the girls to Southold for Sunday services and join them for the noon meal at their daughter, Chary Ann's. Caroline quickly packs up the girls and is thrilled when they arrive at the church just as the service begins. Once inside the sanctuary, Caroline is happy to see so many familiar faces. At first, the girls fidget, unaccustomed to the restrictions of sitting and being quiet but soon enough, they doze off in the warm sanctuary. When the service ends, they enjoy running around the churchyard along with the gang of little ones while Caroline catches up on neighborly gossip. She is delighted to speak with Mrs. Tillinghast, whose twins, Belle and Bertie, are the same age as Stella.

Captain Goldsmith picks them up after services. The girls snuggle close to Caroline against the cold. Away from the relentless grind at the lighthouse, a relaxed Captain Goldsmith tells Caroline that he married Frances after his first wife died. Charry Ann is named in honor of her as she was also Frances's sister.

Caroline is flattered that the Captain reveals their personal history and says, "that must have been a difficult time for you both though it is grat-ifying that you have forged a satisfying life despite a painful beginning."

CHAPTER 3

Winter 1873–Autumn 1874

Prism -
a transparent piece of glass that refracts or disperses light.

Stella and Lucy struggle to carry a bucket of water across the icy field back to the cottage from the well when they spot the S.S. Cactus, the Lighthouse Service supply ship, moored off the coast. Stella spots the flag of the Inspector flying at the mast and knows this means that Inspector Finneas Fanning is here to conduct the twice-yearly review at Hortons Point. Every aspect of the keeper's work is open to scrutiny: the daily logbook, the tower's general maintenance, even inspection of the keepers' personal quarters. These unscheduled visits are a source of enormous concern to all keepers as their very livelihoods rests on the inspector's report.

Stella and Lucy know they have to stay out of the way during inspections as the Captain and George follow the Inspector around the lighthouse.

"Hurry, Lucy," Stella exclaims, "the government inspector's here!" They try running back to the house to alert Da and the Captain while carrying the bucket full of water, Stella all but dragging Lu and the bucket.

Stella stops and says, "Lucy, you stay here with the bucket; I'll go tell Da."

"No," whines Lucy, "It's too cold to stay here by myself. By the time

Da wakes up, they'll be here!"

"Lucy, I have to alert them!" Stella runs across the field towards the house.

She spots Captain Goldsmith coming out of the barn and starts yelling, "Captain, Captain!"

"What's the fuss, Stella? Is everything alright?"

"Yes, but," she continues gasping for breath, "the 'spector's here."

"The what?"

"Inspector Fanning is coming! Lucy and I saw the ship."

"Ok. Wake your Da, quick! And Stella, good job." He says, giving her a quick squeeze on her shoulders. Stella heads towards the back of the cottage, feeling proud of herself.

She runs in and tells Ma, "the inspector's here."

"Stella, go wake Da!"

Stella dashes up the stairs yelling, "Da, Da . . ."

A sleepy George asks, "What's going on?"

"The inspector is here."

"Oh, that's ok, just tell him I'm napping."

"Daaaa! You gotta get up!" she yells, pulling the quilt off him.

"Ok, ok, don't get all in a conniption. I'm up. You go down and sweep the bottom of the stairs. They love to find us working."

"Ok," Stella responds, happy to have a role in this important event. She dashes down the stairs and over to the tower, grabs the broom, and begins sweeping, causing dust to fly, with no discernable improvement. She hears Captain Goldsmith greet Inspector Fanning outside the tower's door and starts up the steps, sweeping from the first landing down.

As the two men enter the tower base, Captain Goldsmith calls up, "George, is that you?"

"No, Captain, it's just me."

"Ok, you can stop now," the Captain calls as the inspector coughs, clearing his throat from the dust. "That's our Stella, George's eldest daughter; she's a hard worker."

"So I see."

Stella descends the stairs, broom in hand, eyes downcast.

"Go get your Da." the Captain says.

Stella nods and heads out the door, grateful to escape the attention of the two men.

The Inspector checks out the condition of the lighthouse, making notes for his report. When he and the Captain reach the top of the tower, George joins them. Captain Goldsmith is not pleased with George's relaxed demeanor. He would like to see him show proper respect. The long hours of physical work and the constant battle with the elements are increasingly challenging to the Captain, as he's not getting any younger.

The three men carefully remove the black cloth that is draped around the Fresnel lens each morning to protect the glass from the sun. While Mr. Fanning closely inspects the lens, the Captain silently considers what to do about George's inconsistent work habits and reliance on spirits. He has seen this dependence ruin men at sea. While he respects the man's military service, the Captain believes George lacks the discipline needed for civilian life. Often George doesn't thoroughly clean the lens in the morning, requiring the Captain to go back over what George should have done.

The Captain and the Inspector go to the office while George stays in the tower, cloth in hand, putting on a bit of a show wiping and re-wiping each piece of glass. The Inspector reviews the Keeper's Logbook. Behind closed doors, Inspector Fanning queries Captain Goldsmith about George's performance. Although his frustrations with George are ready to combust, his concern for Caroline and the girls overrule these sentiments, and, in a measured manner, he says, "George does require close supervision."

Mr. Fanning sees that the Captain is getting on in years and wonders how much longer Captain Goldsmith will be able to handle the demands of the job.

The following week, after a few too many swigs from the jug of spirits, George passes out next to the warm stove in the watch room, and heavy winds blow the beacon out. Ever vigilant during George's watch, Caroline startles awake in total darkness. She bundles up and heads to the tower.

Climbing the circular stairway, Caroline calls, "George," but gets no response. She yells louder at the bottom of the ladder and is alarmed when he doesn't respond. At the top of the ladder, she sees the dark shape of George's body collapsed on the small stool against the wall by the woodstove, a jug of spirits at his side.

Shaking him, George comes to, opening one eye, and smiles up at her.

"What you doin' up here at this time of night?" he asks, smiling lasciviously. "You need something?"

"George," Caroline draws her wrap close, and pointing, says, "the lantern."

"Good Lord!" George exclaims, getting up from the stool and climbing the ladder to the top of the tower. She hears his thrashing around in the dark and more muffled cursing, then the sound of the match strike, followed by the ebbing glow of the lantern as he lights each of the wicks.

As the light of the beacon guides her back down the ladder, she calls, "Do you need anything?"

"No! Go back to bed," George admonishes.

"And you stay awake!" she commands.

George yells back, "Don't you get sassy with me!"

Caroline wishing to avoid further unpleasantness, rushes down the circular stairway, careful to secure her bulky nightclothes, and after checking the girls, she climbs back in bed.

At first light, she adds coal to the fire for breakfast and is disturbed by banging on the outside door; George rushes in from the tower, opens the door, and sees several wet and half-frozen sailors. George assists the weaker men, moving them close to the fire. Captain Goldsmith, alerted by the noise, enters and quickly assesses the situation and commands:

" Caroline! Get Frances and bring blankets and emergency supplies."

While George and the Captain distribute extra blankets and dry clothes, Caroline and Mrs. Goldsmith retreat to prepare hot coffee and porridge, returning when the men are covered.

In accented English, one of the men says, "I am the First Mate from the Lewis Welch. On route to Providence with a cargo of coal. Weather conditions deteriorated, and the schooner started to take on water. We headed for shore as the vessel started to sink. We didn't see the light and ran aground just west of here."

George glances over at Caroline, who averts her eyes, wrestling with her conscience.

"Do we need to get the doctor?" Captain Goldsmith asks.

"No, I think it's just the cold. Now that it's light, I'll go back and assess the damage. The ship's Captain and the rest of the men are in better shape. They stayed on the beach to salvage the cargo."

"Then, I'll go back with you. George, see to the men here and the lantern," Captain Goldsmith directs.

Stella and Lucy descend the steps from their bedroom, shy but curious about the unfamiliar noise from the parlor.

Mrs. Goldsmith shoos them from the bottom of the stairway, " Get some porridge for yourself in the kitchen."

Caroline hesitates, and one of the men observing her confusion smiles and says, "Take care of the little ones. We are fine."

Caroline gives each of the girls a small portion of porridge.

"Girls, eat this, then go out and collect the eggs. Be quick now."

Looking over at Mrs. Goldsmith, Caroline continues, "I'll kill a few hens to stew. We have vegetables in the root cellar and samp to stretch it."

The girls eat their small portions. Lucy holds up her empty bowl, pleading, "More, please?"

Stella snatches the dish out of Lucy's hands, full of self-importance, says, "Not now! We have to get the eggs!"

❀

By the fall of 1874, six-year-old Stella and five-year-old Lucy are big helpers. Like most children of their time, they do many chores. Before breakfast, they go out to the chicken coop to feed, water, and gather eggs. Then, they bring the eggs into Mrs. Goldsmith, watching how many eggs she puts aside, as they've learned when she keeps more than four, she will bake later in the day.

Mrs. Goldsmith is stirring the porridge when the girls come in.

"How many today, little ones?" she asks. Lucy, proud to show off her new counting skills, takes each egg from the basket and places it in the bowl on the table.

"One, two, three," she begins counting up to 12.

"Oh my," Mrs. Goldsmith says, "that is a good day. Hmm, I'll have to see how much sugar I have and come up with a treat to bake later today."

Lucy, her dark eyebrows raised, exchanges excited glances with Stella. Stella struggling to contain herself says, "that would be nice if you find the time?"

Smiling, Mrs. Goldsmith says, "Maybe you girls could come back later and give me a hand?"

Stella's face lights up with pleasure as she says, "I'll check with Ma. She may have some things we need to do first."

"Ask your Ma and let me know after breakfast."

As the girls gather the eggs back into the basket, Stella continues, "Um, how many eggs would you like?"

Mrs. Goldsmith responds, chuckling, "How about you leave six here? That way, you all will have a nice hearty breakfast before we put you to work."

Lucy chimes in, "Da says it's time we start working in the tower." Stella gives Lucy a threatening look.

"Wha-a-t?" Lucy whines, "he did!"

Mrs. Goldsmith looks concerned but refrains from commenting, knowing it is not her business even though she feels these two are like her own. Working in the tower is hazardous, and the girls never are idle, what with the gardening and animals to tend to and, of course, wash day and keeping the cottage clean.

Stella explains, "He just wants us to sweep the stairs."

"Well, that's not so much. It might even be fun," Mrs. Goldsmith says.

Stella and Lucy go back to their side of the cottage, eager to tell Ma that Mrs. Goldsmith asked them to help her bake. Caroline smiles at the close bonds the girls have forged with Frances. If only George would settle into his job. The work is challenging, but Caroline believes he is up to it. The winters are harsh with longer hours and storms, but it's hard on all of them.

Lost in thought, Caroline wonders what George was like before he went to the war. She was just 16 in 1863 when George enlisted; she didn't meet him until he returned. Caroline's pride in her husband's service will never waiver, but she wonders how the war might have changed him. Caroline knows many other men who served and returned ready to embrace adulthood, while George prefers spending time with his cousins. She believes he is a good man but is embarrassed by his harshness and predilection for spirits. She loathes that George hides a jug of local brew, and she's sure that the Captain is also aware of this.

"Ma-a-a," Lucy yells.

"Where are you?" Stella adds.

"Just having a moment to myself," Ma replies.

Lucy continues, "Can we?"

"Can you what?"

"Can we bake with Mrs. Goldsmith today?" Lucy asks, then notices the stern look Stella gives her. "What?" she mouths. Stella is worried that if Lucy becomes too insistent, Ma will say, "No, just because. . . ."

"Ok, girls," Ma continues, "time for breakfast" she looks up as the front door opens, and Da comes rushing in from his morning visit to the outhouse.

"Brrr, starting to feel like winter," George continues, "better get the last of that garden in." Now Stella is distraught. She tries to get Lucy's attention to tell her to stop pressing mom to allow them to bake in front of Da. Stella knows that he will go up and sleep after breakfast, and they will be more likely to get a yes from Ma.

"Where's breakfast?" George asks, looking around.

Ma cracks each of the eggs into the melted lard. "Porridge is ready. Start with that. Eggs will just take a minute." Da is annoyed. He likes his breakfast ready as soon as he comes in.

"Did you girls spend time over with Mrs. Goldsmith instead of bringing the eggs right to Ma?" Lucy looks from Stella to Ma.

"Don't even answer. I can see from your faces that you've been holding Ma up with some foolishness. I have told you, girls, too many times; you need to pull your weight around here."

"George," Ma says patiently. "they're still so young."

"That's what you always say, but I think it's time they learn what's expected of them."

"We do, Dada," Lucy says in her best baby voice. Da's expression softens as Caroline places the hot eggs onto his plate alongside the porridge. George wolfs down his eggs and heads upstairs to sleep. The girls sit, and Ma joins them, giving each a bit of scrambled egg. They take their time eating, eyes cast downward, wishing to avoid any more fuss. In short order, they hear the rhythmic growls of Da's snoring. Ma says gently, "Ok, girls, let's go get to work on the garden. You can help Mrs. Goldsmith later."

"Yeah!" Lucy yells.

Ma and Stella turn to her with identical gestures—pointer fingers to the front of their pursed lips, "Shhh!"

"Don't wake Da," Stella whispers.

"I'm just excited. I love to bake with Mrs. Goldsmith."

After a few hours in the garden, Mrs. Goldsmith stretches and says, "I think it's about time to start dinner." With a twinkle in her eye, she turns to the girls and asks, "Would you girls care to join me later?"

Both girls look up at Ma with pleading, "How can I say no to those faces. Let's finish this row first."

Caroline and the girls' have a quick dinner, then they head over to the Goldsmiths while Caroline returns to the garden and wonders if she's wrong to hold Stella back from school. She worries over how difficult it would be to get her to town each day and resigns herself to holding her back till next year when the girls can go together. She decides to teach them their letters and numbers during the winter.

George is looking forward to hunting. Bringing back venison helps to supplement the supplies the government provides, but it also gives him an escape from the routine and Captain Goldsmith's endless demands. The week before he leaves, Caroline asks him to take her and the girls into Southold to pick up some items at Cousin Henry's store and drive past the little schoolhouse to show the girls.

They set off on a beautiful fall afternoon. Stella and Lucy are big enough to ride in the back. George gets down to open the gate at the end of each field, leads Jenny through, and closes it behind him before climbing back up. Caroline enjoys listening to the girls naming the cows as they meander towards the wagon. The Tillinghasts large fields dwarf their garden at Hortons Point. Caroline sighs, grateful that the harvest is over for this year and they have plenty stored.

They turn west on the Main Road and slow down in front of the little schoolhouse. Ma asks Da to stop there and let the girls listen to the children singing the alphabet song.

Stella says, "Ma, could you teach us that song?"

"Of course," she replies, wondering what more she should be teaching the girls to prepare them for the start of school next year.

They turn left onto Prince Lane and drive past their former home. The cottage is small compared to the Light House and falling into disrepair. Stella and Lucy don't even remember living there. Caroline hopes that someday they'll be able to return to their cottage in town, but for now, she's glad that George's work at the lighthouse brings in a steady paycheck. They continue down to the end of the road and see Cousin Waitley at the dock. Da stops and chats, then turns the wagon around to go to Cousin Henry's store.

Prince's Dry Goods is chock full of inviting and essential items. The girls press their noses against the tall glass cases filled with colorful ribbons, pencils, and candy. George's Cousin Henry, Uncle Henry to the girls, comes out from the back when he hears Caroline and George greeted by his wife, Jennie. She often helps out with tiny 4-year-old Anna on her hip at the store. Uncle Henry comments on how big the girls are getting. Jennie asks if Stella started school, and Caroline hesitates, then explains how hard it would be to get Stella to school each day from the lighthouse. She explains that they will send the girls together next year, and she will do some lessons at home now that the hectic summer season has passed.

"Oh," Jennie says, turning to George, "Did you have a lot of visitors this summer?"

"Yeah," he grunts as he carries a box of supplies out to the wagon.

Caroline continues, "The garden keeps us quite busy, but now that we've got most of that put up . . ." she trails off.

Henry says, "I'm sure they'll pick up with you teaching them, Caroline."

"Anna will start school next year too," Jennie says, gesturing to the little one on her hip.

Listening to the adults' conversation, Stella places both hands on her hips, looks with disdain at little Anna, and calls out,

"Is it a baby school?"

"Stella," Caroline rebukes.

Henry, chuckling, kneels in front of Stella and says, "Anna won't always be a baby, you know. Next year when she's five, she can go to school too."

Looking over Anna, cuddling her mother, Stella says, "She looks like a baby to me."

Jennie grasps Anna closer as if to protect her from her cousin's wrath.

George calls from the door, "Time, we get back."

As Caroline collects the girls, Henry comes out from his office and hands Caroline a stack of magazines.

"Since you're thinking about homeschooling, I thought these might be of interest." Caroline looks down at the pile of magazines in surprise, then glances over at George.

"Thanks," he mutters, "let's go."

Caroline takes the bundle from Henry and says, "Girls, look. These are periodicals for children. We can read them together." The cover of 'The Little Corporal" features a young boy's photograph in a 'Zouave' military uniform.

"Why is he dressed like that?" Lu asks.

Uncle Henry says, "Why Lu, that's a kind of soldier's uniform. Hasn't your Da told you about being a soldier?" The girls look at the picture in awe.

"Da was a soldier?" They say in unison.

Caroline explains, "George doesn't talk about the war, Henry."

Henry leans close to Caroline and whispers, "You didn't know him, but he was different before. There's no telling how service will affect a young man."

George calls from the doorway, "Mrs. P., you ready?" A flustered Caroline hugs Jennie and Henry.

Lucy catching up to George, asks, "How come you never told us you were a soldier?" George picks up each of the girls and puts them in the back of the wagon.

"Guess I didn't think you'd be interested."

"We have a picture. Uncle gave us."

Lucy continues.

George looks at the stack of magazines in Caroline's hands.

"We better put these under the box of dry goods for safekeeping on the trip back." Caroline releases the magazines to George, grateful for Henry's generosity and George's acceptance of the gift. Jennie and Henry come out of the store and wave them off.

With a quick jerk of the reigns, George calls, "Yah, Jenny." Lucy covers her mouth and starts giggling.

Stella asks, "What's funny?"

Lucy whispers, "Aunt Jennie is named after our horse!"

Stella's eyes widen, then she joins Lucy laughing uproariously at the idea that fancy Aunt Jennie and the horse have the same name.

When they get back to the Lighthouse, Captain and Mrs. Goldsmith greet them and invite the girls in for some hot cocoa.

George says to Caroline, "You think we were gone for a month. The way they fuss over those girls."

"Oh, George," Caroline responds, emboldened by the pleasant day in town, "It's good for the girls to have older people in their lives who care for them." It's also good for the Goldsmiths to have the young ones to fuss over, Caroline reflects as she puts away each of the precious goods they purchased at the store.

Mrs. Goldsmith invites them for supper. Caroline accepts after checking with George. The warmth of Mrs. Goldsmith's kitchen and the enticing smell of venison stew cooking over the fire welcomes them. After dinner, the Captain heads up to tend the lantern while George goes out to bed the animals down. Mrs. Goldsmith sits in her rocker beside the hearth, knitting. Caroline snuggles with the girls and takes out one of the magazines.

The girls are delighted to look at the pictures. They select a short story for Caroline to read. The story's theme is that one must complete one's chores with good cheer. Stella and Lucy exchange disappointed looks and ask Caroline to read something else.

George stops in and says, "I'm going up." Caroline nods, grateful for this man who has given her their daughters, despite his many flaws. Her mind wanders, reflecting on Henry's generosity, but she reminds herself, 'even Henry isn't perfect.'

"We'll be up in a little while," Caroline answers, then says to the girls, "Let's pick out the letters in this poem." The girls look at the picture of lambs frolicking while Caroline points to each letter of the alphabet. "A," Caroline says.

Lucy and Stella repeat, "A."

Then she points to 'B' for baby lamb.

Pointing, Stella says, "Look, Ma, there's three 'A's right in a row."

"That's right, Stella," Caroline says with pride, "Ba-a-a," she repeats for the girls to copy.

"Smart girl," Mrs. Goldsmith comments from her chair next to the fire.

They continue through the alphabet. Caroline finds every letter except 'X.' Even 'Z' as the poem ends with the baby lamb sleeping at her mother's side, while 'Z's' are circling their heads.

"Why does it keep saying this one?" asks Lu.

"What letter is that?" asks Caroline.

"That's the last one," Stella says.

"What's the name of that letter?" Stella is starting to get sleepy, so she just shrugs.

"That's the letter, Z," Caroline responds.

Lucy chimes in, "Z, Z, Z."

CHAPTER 4

September 1875–June 1876

Pod -

the common name for a school, herd, or shoal of whales.

Stella and Lucy anticipate the first day of school with an equal measure of excitement and fear.

"What if nobody talks to me?" Lucy whines.

Stella says, "What if they want me to talk? I won't know what to say."

Ma reassures both the girls as best she can. She recalls her school days and hopes the girls will overcome their fear and shyness. She has worked diligently, and they are both now able to read and write their names and a few words. They can count to 126, thanks to the stairs to the beach, and do simple sums with shells. Mrs. Goldsmith helped Ma sew each of the girls' new school clothes. She and the Captain went into town and returned with bright red ribbons for Stella's braids and soft blue ones for Lucy's. Ma is pleased that they are excited but also glad she held Stella back so they can start together.

Caroline walks with them through the fields.

As they approach the North Road, Mrs. Tillinghast calls, "Hello," with Belle and Bertie at her side. Stella runs over and gives her friend a quick hug. Once they cross the road, Mrs. Tillinghast hugs the twins and walks back home. Henry Boisseau jumps out from behind a bush, yelling, "Boo," scaring poor Lucy. Caroline gives him a gentle reprimand, taking Lucy's hand to calm her. Stella and Belle wag warning fingers in his face, and Bertie guffaws at Henry's prank.

They continue along the road without incident. When the group gets closer to the school, children rush past, some with parents in tow, others on their own.

At the schoolhouse, Caroline stops at the bottom of the stairs, hugs both girls, and reminds them, "I'll be here when school is over."

"But, how will you know," Lucy asks, blinking back tears.

"I'll know," Ma replies confidently. She guides Lucy towards the stairs, and turning to Stella, says, "Stella, look out for your sister."

Stella grabs Lucy's hand, still holding onto Belle with the other, and the three girls march up the steps; Belle leading the way, Lucy looks back longingly at her mother. Caroline lingers, waving as the girls disappear inside.

She enjoys a pleasant morning walking through the village, stopping at local shops, and chatting with former neighbors. At dinnertime, the sounds of children calling each other as they head home catch her attention. She walks over to the school and peeks inside. She sees the teacher, Miss Glover, sitting at her desk, enjoying her repast. In Caroline's view, Miss Glover appears young to be responsible for educating the town's youth. She is tall and slim. Her brown hair is collected in a bun, although tendrils have escaped the top knot falling around her face even just halfway through her day. The three girls sit at their desks, eating from their dinner pails and whispering. Miss Glover looks up when she hears Caroline at the door and rises from her desk chair, pulling herself up to her full height as if gathering up her courage. She smooths down her straight brown skirt and marches toward Caroline.

"Good afternoon, Mrs. Prince, is it?"

"Yes, I was close by and thought I'd check how the day is going."

"I guess that's ok for the first day, but please don't make a habit of it. The girls are doing fine," she continues stepping into the foyer with

Caroline. "They are both shy, but all and all, they seem to have mastered the basics."

Caroline responds, "I hope they will find their place."

"I expect they will."

Lucy, unable to contain herself any longer, comes rushing over and grabs her mother around the legs.

"Now, Lucy," Miss Glover rebukes, "That's an unnecessary display for the schoolroom. Please return to your seat." Lucy inhaling the familiar scent of home on Ma, trudges back to her seat, head down. Caroline smiles at the girls as she retreats, backing out the schoolhouse door.

Caroline is waiting outside the building as other parents gather at the end of the day. Miss Glover emerges and, standing at the top of the stairs, rings the handbell releasing the children for the day. The girls walk out in single file, little ones first. They hurry down the stairs, with the boys thundering right behind. The children scatter in all directions while Stella and Lucy grasp onto Caroline and immediately chatter about the day. It feels as if they've been gone for a year instead of just one day.

Stella pipes right up, "We learned so much today, Ma. Thank you for taking us to school. Miss Glover is very nice," startling Caroline by her immediate devotion to this young woman.

Belle chimes in from behind Caroline, "I think she's the best teacher in the world."

"No, she ain't," says Henry.

"She's just the only teacher, you know," Bertie retorts.

Lucy insists, "She is the best teacher. Ma, do you know that the world is round?"

"Yes, I do," Caroline responds, amused by the question.

"I told you, Lucy, that Ma and Da would know that," Stella reminds Lucy.

"Miss Glover has a–a big round ball."

"A globe," cuts in Henry.

"Oh yeah," Lucy continues, "a globe, and it has all the places in the whole world, and we're gonna learn them."

"Not all the places," Bertie interrupts.

"Yes," Lucy insists, "all of them!"

Stella and Belle lock eyes as they walk ahead of Ma, Lucy, and the boys, not allowing the silliness to ruin their happy mood. As they approach the North Road, Caroline greets Mrs. Tillinghast, waiting to assist them in the crossing. Bertie runs off through the bushes towards his house to the east while Caroline fills Mrs. Tillinghast in on her dinnertime meeting with Miss Glover as they walk towards the Tillinghast's farmhouse.

The girls listening in on their mothers' conversation prompts Belle to ask, "Ma, can I stay at school for dinner with Stella and Lucy?"

"I guess . . . if it's alright with Miss Glover?"

Caroline and the girls continue their walk through the Tillinghasts' fields, opening and closing each of the three gates to keep the grazing animals inside.

"Boy, the Tillinghasts must be rich," comments Lucy as they trudge along.

"Why do you say that, Lucy?" Ma asks.

"They own all this," she says, gesturing with her open arm.

"And animals," Stella adds, looking around at the herd of cattle on the far side of the field.

"How come they have so much, and we don't?" asks Lucy.

Caroline responds thoughtfully, "We do have a lot compared with some folks. But what's most important is that we have our love and our faith in the Lord." The girls look up at her, confused. Caroline continues, "Girls, it isn't how many things people have; it's how we live our lives that matters."

"That's what the Reverend says."

"That's right, Stella," Caroline continues, "some people have a lot of things, but it doesn't mean they are any happier or closer to God. And being close to God and following his teachings is important. And, girls," Caroline pauses as they walk around to the front of the lighthouse, "Just look at this view. We have the whole world right at our front door." They climb onto the porch taking in the panoramic view of the Long Island Sound.

"It's beautiful! I never want to leave this place," Stella says with reverence.

Caroline looks up, surprised; "I've never heard you say that before, Stella."

"Why would I leave? Everyone I love is here."

"I'm glad you feel that way now, but I think someday you may want to see other places." Lucy adds, "When I grow up and get married, I'm gonna have lots of babies. Ma, will you have more babies?"

"I don't know Lucy, but right now, I think you two are all the babies I can handle," she says, teasing. Stella and Lucy look up, insulted.

"We're NOT babies!" they exclaim.

"Ok, ok, if you aren't babies, then maybe you'd better go get your afternoon chores done," George says, coming out of the cottage.

Lucy runs up to George and says, "I love school, and Miss Glover is the best teacher in the world!"

"I'm glad to hear that you like school so much, Lucy. Stella, how about you?" Stella continues to gaze out at the horizon on the clear, crisp day. She notices the smoke rising from the train that runs along the coast of Connecticut on the other side of the Sound.

"School is ok, Da, but I like it here best." Caroline tells George, "Stella wants to live at the Lighthouse all her life."

"Maybe if she started doing more of the chores, she'd see it's not just fun and pretty views. Maybe I'll have her come up and help me on my watch tonight."

"George," Caroline says, dismayed, "she's just a child."

"She'll be eight soon."

"Not till October," Caroline counters.

"Oh Ma, please could I go up and help in the tower?" pleads Stella.

"Maybe when you're eight, but for now, you have enough to do down on the ground.

True to her word, after her birthday in October, Stella begins helping Da on his watch. She rises before the sun comes up and climbs up to see if George is awake in the watch room. Stella continues up the ladder to the lantern room, where she searches for light from any ships then stands witness to the first streaks of sunlight. Once the sun rises, George comes up and shows her the morning routine extinguishing the flame, removing soot build-up from the lenses, wiping down the windows, then draping the lens with the heavy black cloth. Stella reaches as high as she can to clean the glass. When it's all squared away, they go down for breakfast with Ma and Lucy. Stella warms her hands in front of the hearth after the cold in the tower.

❈

When heavy rain or ice makes the fields impassible, Caroline is glad to keep the girls home. Nevertheless, the girls thrive in school and are glad when the weather allows them to go. March arrives, bringing a mid-day snowstorm. Caroline is cleaning the cellar and doesn't notice the sudden change in the weather until George comes down and says, "It looks like winter's not done with us yet."

Caroline peers out the window and exclaims, "The girls! How will they get home from school?"

"I don't think they'll get back today." Seeing that Caroline's upset, he continues, "Don't worry, Mrs. P.; they're sensible girls."

Caroline speaks with Mrs. Goldsmith, who reassures her that the girls are safe at the schoolhouse. As heavy clouds close in, George and the Captain light the lantern. Caroline ventures up to the tower to see if she can spot the girls coming home through the snow.

George says, "The girls are safer in town. They'll be home tomorrow."

Caroline sits up all night, and at first light, she sees the bright sun glistening on the pure white snow. Snow is melting off the edge of the roof. Caroline sweeps the snow off the front porch. She stops and listens for the girls tromping through the snow, but there's only the sound of the melting snow dripping off the edge of the roof.

When George comes down from his night's watch, she says, "I want to go into town and find the girls."

"Now, Mrs. P., I don't think you should venture out across the field just yet. If they're not back when I get up, I'll go look." Eyes averted, Caroline nods, but the minute she hears the rhythmic sound of George's snoring, she bundles up and heads out, first telling Mrs. Goldsmith she's going to search for the girls. She'll at least go as far as the Tillinghasts and see if Belle and Bertie are home.

Mrs. Goldsmith understands Caroline's concern and says, "Looks to me like the snow is melting. In another hour or two, it'll just be mud. Easier and a little warmer for walking, I expect."

"I can't wait," Caroline snaps, the strain of the worry and lost night sleep weighing on her.

She goes out the back door and begins the long walk through the open fields. The wind is calm, and the sun is bright; if it weren't for the pain of worry in her heart, she might enjoy the walk. When she gets to the Tillinghasts, she taps on the door, and Mrs. Tillinghast comes right out.

"Are you going into town to get the children?" she asks. Caroline responds with a firm nod of her head.

"May I join you?"

"There's no need for both of us to get wet. I'll look for Belle and Bertie too. Why don't you stay here and have something warm ready for when I return?"

Reluctantly, Mrs. Tillinghast agrees as Caroline moves on. Caroline observes that the snow has all but melted on the hard-packed North Road under the beating sun and frequent flow of horses and wagons. She follows a fresh trail made by a horse-drawn sleigh straight down the road into town. When she gets to the schoolhouse, she sees that the sled is in front, and Mr. Boisseau is loading up the children.

Caroline smiles with relief as Lucy and Stella call out, "Ma!"

Mr. Boisseau says, "Mrs. Prince, please join us."

He extends his arm for her to climb up onto the front of the sleigh, but she asks, "Would you mind if I sat in the back with the children?"

"Of course not, if you prefer, might be a bit bumpy," he warns.

"And noisy!" exclaims Henry.

"That's quite alright," Caroline replies as she climbs up and sits down on the long wooden bench that runs around the sides of the sled, snuggling between Lucy and Stella. "All set," she calls as Lucy and Stella hold on to Caroline more for comfort than warmth.

The sun blazes across the countryside as they travel at a good clip up to the North Road then across the fields on the other side. At the farmhouse, Mrs. Tillinghast greets them.

"Thank you, Mr. Boisseau; I see the Lord took good care," Mrs. Tillinghast exclaims with a big smile.

"Would you care to come in for some warm cocoa?"

"I think we'd better push on. No telling what we'll encounter to get to the Lighthouse."

Caroline calls out, "We can walk from here, Mr. Boisseau."

"No need," he responds as he flicks the whip across the horses' flanks, and they take off. The girls lean against Caroline, eager to tell her all that transpired. Caroline holds them tight and breathes in their scent with a sigh of relief,

"You can tell us all about it at dinner."

Stella nods, and Lucy adds, "I can't wait."

❖

On the last school day, Ma joins other parents to see the school play and Declamation speeches. Each of the graduates has prepared a dramatic reading of their choice. Standing tall in the front of the room, Miss Glover introduces the graduating students. They stand and walk to the front as their name is announced. Stella and Lucy sit rapt with attention as they watch their older schoolmates get up and speak. The parents clap as each student completes their oration.

Then they all gather in the cloakroom in the front of the schoolhouse and, with excited whispers, put on costumes. They perform a short play entitled, *While the Cat's Away*. The theme is the importance of being on your best behavior even if no one else will know.

Being the smallest and youngest student, Little Anna Prince plays the cat crawling around and hiding behind various students dressed as trees and bushes while the three oldest students recite the only speaking parts in the play.

Stella is happy to stand still and be quiet as she plays a bush, but Lucy, who plays the part of a boat that just sits on the ground, is jealous of Anna, whose charming manner steals the show as she crawls around the stage. The audience enthusiastically applauds the students' efforts and then stands and chats while the children take off their costumes and pile them into the big storage box for next year. Miss Glover asks the students to return to their desks and announces the award recipients. Stella is proud to learn that she has made the honor roll in reading, spelling, and deportment. Lucy is disappointed that she only made the

Honor Roll in spelling, but she is proud of her big sister. Ma looks on with pride at her girls, knowing how hard they worked to catch up with the other students.

After the festivities, Henry and Jennie congratulate her on how well the girls are doing. She comments on how sweet little Anna was in the play. After reluctant goodbyes to Miss Glover, Lucy takes Ma's hand and walks down the steps while Stella and Belle run ahead. The girls make plans for summer fun, hoping to go swimming at the beach and explore the shore and woods, while the boys look forward to fishing.

When they arrive home, Stella and Lucy greet Mrs. Goldsmith, waiting for their arrival on the front porch with a special treat. They show her their report cards. Mrs. Goldsmith exclaims at the girls' accomplishments.

While Stella and Lucy are happy to be off for summer vacation, they know they will need to spend more time working in the garden and the tower. Though they are not strong enough to carry up the oil to kindle the lantern, Da says they can build their muscles carrying water to the garden. Stella learns to trim the wicks on the lantern each morning and wipes down the windows and the lenses. A small stool is kept in the tower so she can reach the top of the windows. Da wipes down the outside of the windows, navigating the steep metal walkway around the tower with care. This summer, the Captain and George will whitewash the outside of the tower. George expects it will take the better part of the summer to finish, but now that Stella and Lucy are home, they can tend to the animals and the garden freeing him to do the whitewashing.

Once a week, the brass fittings are polished. George has been doing this job himself, but he announces it's time the girls learn how to do this tedious task. Captain Goldsmith looks on with consternation but holds his tongue, scowling; he walks off. Caroline, sensing the tension, touches her hand to her throat and averts her eyes.

Lucy, ever the peacemaker, says, "I guess summer isn't going to be playtime after all." Ma and Mrs. Goldsmith chuckle.

"That's right, Lucy, you girls need to help out as much as you can. You know what it says in the good book, 'Idle hands are the devil's workshop.'"

Da makes good on his promise to teach Stella and Lucy the work of a lighthouse keeper that summer. Each morning, the girls wipe the Fresnel lens with a special soft cloth provided by the Lighthouse Service. They take turns climbing the small ladder and stretch to reach as high as possible to get to the top of the windows.

When Caroline checks on the girls, she is glad to see them being useful but wonders if George doesn't expect too much. She reminds them to come down to feed the chickens and gather eggs for breakfast. Lucy, eager for time with the animals, is relieved to get out of the tower. But Stella loves anything to do with the lighthouse and tells Ma she'll be down as soon as she finishes. She performs each of the jobs with meticulous care. After the first week, Lucy goes down with Caroline each morning and tends the animals, but Stella remains in the tower until the morning tasks are complete. George brings up the bucket of lard oil, placing it on the coal stove in the watch room to melt before refueling the lantern. Stella inhales the familiar scent of melting lard as it permeates the air in the tower. While it melts, George returns to the lantern room and assists Stella with draping the heavy black cover around the lens to protect it from the harsh sunlight. By the time breakfast is ready, Stella and George have finished the morning tower chores, and they go downstairs to join Ma and Lucy.

After breakfast, George goes to bed while Caroline and the girls take care of the house and the garden. Mrs. Goldsmith joins them in the garden each morning, and they work side by side. The girls perform the hot and sweaty task of carrying water from the pump to water the vegetables. The full watering can is too heavy, but as long as they don't fill it all the way, they're able to manage. They welcome the cool water spilling over onto their arms as they struggle back to the garden. As the summer passes, the vegetables ripen. They all understand how vital the garden is, as it will help sustain them through the long winter months.

Most afternoons, the girls go down to the beach. They wade in the cold water of the Long Island Sound and add to their extensive seashell and rock collections. Later in the summer, they forage for beach plums, then help Mrs. Goldsmith make the tart fruit into jam. When it is too hot, even on the beach, they enjoy exploring the overgrown woods just west of the lighthouse property. Here they hunt for berries, wild asparagus, and onions, or take a book and find a shady spot to read.

Sometimes Belle, Bertie, and Henry come over. Stella enjoys showing them the tower, and if it isn't too hot, they go up and look for ships out on the Sound. The boys talk about the adventures they'll have when they grow up and go to sea.

When they come down overheated from too long in the intense sun of the glass-enclosed tower, they find Mrs. Goldsmith sitting on the front porch. Stella tells her that the boys are planning on going to sea someday. Mrs. Goldsmith tells them about her adventures onboard a whaling ship when she and Captain Goldsmith were young.

While the children can't imagine that Captain and Mrs. Goldsmith was ever young, they do love hearing her stories about sailing on a whaling ship. She mesmerizes them with tales of sailing around South America to Hawaii. She relays the excitement of watching when they harpooned a colossal whale.

She explains, "The men hand it up alongside the boat then cut the blubber off to melt in the giant caldrons. It was very unpleasant smelling."

The idea of catching a giant whale delights the children, and they ask, "How big was it?"

"I think about 45-feet long," she responds.

"How big is that?" asks Lucy.

"Let's see if we can figure it out," Mrs. Goldsmith suggests to the eager children. She has them line up across the front of the cottage and directs Stella and Lucy to the fence on the west side while Belle and the boys run over and stand by the fence to the east. When they get to the end of the enclosure, Mrs. Goldsmith tells Belle to stop there and the boys to go further. They jump over the little picket fence that encloses the front yard and run to the end of the oil house.

Mr. Goldsmith calls, "I think that's about right."

"Wait a minute," Henry says, "No way a whale is this big!"

Bertie says to Henry, "You stay here, and I'll pace off how many feet this is. Henry stands still while Bert paces off with giant steps, counting by 3's.

"3-6-9-err…not sure," he says, stopping before he even gets to where Belle waits at the fence.

"Let me do it," Belle commands. "I know my three times table." Stella and Lu giggle at Bert's difficulty. He flops down on his belly, ducking his head in the grass in disgrace.

Henry says to Belle, "but you're steps aren't gonna be big enough."

"Sure they are," says Belle. "I'm just as tall as Bertie."

Belle starts standing in front of Stella and counts – "3-6-9-12-15-18-…," she stops at the fence. Mrs. Goldsmith calls out, "That's the body of the whale. Now you have to count the tail."

"Um, where was I?" asks Belle.

"Twenty-one," calls Stella.

"Wait, this isn't working. Why don't we do one step at a time?" Bertie suggests.

"Yeah, that might be better," admits Belle, a little embarrassed at not having gotten much further than her brother.

"I know says, Henry. Bert, come here." Bertie runs back to where Henry is standing.

"Ok, now you start here and Belle, you start by Lucy and Stella. Count each step and meet in the middle."

Belle starts counting each step "1-2-3," and Bertie does the same in the other direction. When they meet in the middle, Bertie counts 25 steps, and Belle is 20.

Stella says, "That's it! 45 feet long! We did it! Mrs. Goldsmith is right." Mrs. Goldsmith chuckles with pleasure. She enjoyed watching the children puzzle out the problem on their own. She says with satisfaction, "Isn't that something! A 45-foot whale right across the front of our quarters."

"It'd squash that little fence to bits," says Henry shaking his head back and forth as he walks across the yard, jumping over the fence and back on the front porch, "That sure must have been exciting."

"Yes, indeed," Mrs. Goldsmith says, smiling at the memories.

CHAPTER 5

Winter 1877

Interim Light-keeper-
a light-keeper who serves on a temporary basis.

Mrs. Goldsmith comes down with a chesty cough. Caroline tries to make her comfortable, putting additional coal in the stove preparing chicken soup and a hot compress of roasted onions, which she wraps in a towel for Mrs. Goldsmith to place on her chest.

"When I was growing up, cook made this up when we were congested," she explains. Mrs. Goldsmith asks Caroline to make up some yarrow root tea to help with her sore throat.

Over the next few days, Mrs. Goldsmith's condition deteriorates. Caroline prepares meals for them before serving her own family. Caroline doesn't know how old the Captain and Mrs. Goldsmith are, but they are getting on in years. Living in the damp and cold of the cottage is difficult, and with winter coming, Caroline is concerned.

Captain Goldsmith informs Caroline and George that he and Frances are going to their daughter's. Caroline assures him they will tend the light.

The Captain stares at George, and Caroline says, "I'll go see to Mrs. Goldsmith. You two can discuss business."

"That is kind of you. I expect the rest will do us both good," the Captain replies.

Caroline finds Mrs. Goldsmith sitting by the hearth and helps her pack a few personal belongings.

George comes in and says, "I'll drive them. We need the horse here."

"OK, but you'll be back before sunset?" Caroline asks.

"Yeh," George grumbles.

He assists Mrs. Goldsmith up from the rocker and out to the wagon. Caroline waves as they pull away, noticing Mrs. Goldsmith's eyes are closed, blocking out the wind as they jostle along the rutted trail. She chastises herself for not realizing how frail Mrs. Goldsmith has grown and hopes that time spent in her daughter's care will speed her recovery.

Caroline is surprised when she hears the girls' voices as they arrive home from school. The girls are sad that Mrs. Goldsmith left without saying goodbye, but Caroline reminds them that Mrs. Goldsmith needs rest. Caroline starts dinner while Stella and Lu sit at the table and do homework.

Stella asks, "Ma, where's Da?"

"I told you he took the Goldsmith's."

"Oh," says Stella, "but what about the light?" Caroline looks up from the dinner preparations noticing the growing shadows in the room, and realizes they need to kindle the lantern.

Stella volunteers, "I'll do it!"

"You've never lit it yourself, Stella," Caroline says.

"I know how, Ma. I can do it."

"I'll go up with you."

Lucy asks, "Do I have to go?"

"No, Lucy, you stay here and watch the soup doesn't burn." Lucy takes out a rag doll and tells her that Mrs. Goldsmith has gone away but will come back when she's better.

Stella and Caroline bundle up and head through the side door across the breezeway and up to the tower. They are glad to see that George carried up fresh lard, but they have to melt it and refuel the lantern.

Caroline watches as Stella adjusts the oil flow to the wicks and strikes the match. Stella pulls herself up to her full height, gathers her courage, and with a deep inhale, puts the lit match stick to the wick. They both jump back as the wick makes a distinctive 'whoosh' when it ignites.

"Ma, I think I should stay here and keep watch." Caroline hesitates, Stella is only ten years old after all, and fire and oil hazards are always a concern. At the same time, she realizes that Stella has watched this process more than anyone else and seems comfortable assuming this role.

"I'm sure Da will be back soon. I'll call you when dinner is ready," Caroline says, knowing Stella is nothing but pleased to take on this responsibility.

An hour later, Caroline returns and tells Stella to go down and have dinner. Reluctant, though hungry, Stella goes and eats, grabs a blanket and a book, and climbs back up the tower. She assures her mother she'll be fine and settles in next to the stove in the watch room to read the book she took out of the lighthouse's library, *Little Women*. Caroline is grateful that the Lighthouse Service brings a crate of books quarterly to each lighthouse. The traveling libraries are well worth the government's investment as the books provide hours of entertainment for keepers and their families. The girls are avid readers and are excited when a new chest of books arrives. The oak chest is quite heavy. The block and tackle rigging is put into service to hoist it up the 60-foot bluff. The wooden crate is kept in the corner of the Goldsmith's parlor, but the girls are encouraged to explore its contents whenever they wish.

When Caroline goes down, she prepares for bed, and an exhausted Stella returns to the watch room to read. While Caroline listens to Lucy's nightly prayers, she warms a brick to bring up to Stella. Once Lucy is settled, Caroline brings it up and places it at the foot of the little chair.

Stella asks, "I wonder when Da will be back?

"I don't know Stella, but I expect he's fine," Ma replies. "I guess you can stay here until he returns unless you'd rather I do it?" Caroline asks.

"I'd love to stay here, Ma, can I please?"

"I guess it's alright, but first, let me hear your prayers."

Stella says her nightly devotion with a special request for Mrs. Goldsmith. Caroline kisses her cheek and descends from the tower. As the chill takes over, Stella dozes off. During the night, George comes in. He climbs up to the watch room and exclaims,

"Oh, so here's the little lighthouse keeper. I'll take over now, Stella." He booms, startling Stella out of her sleep. Stella looks up at him, confused. Da is not usually so loud and jovial.

"You go to bed, Stella, I'll take over. Unless you want to stay?" he asks, winking. Stella gathers her blanket and makes her way down, through the parlor, then up the stairs to the bedroom. She climbs in close to Lucy, grateful that her sleeping sister has warmed the bed.

Caroline whispers, "Thank you, Stella, you are my big girl." Despite her fatigue, Stella smiles with pride.

A couple of days before Christmas, Captain Goldsmith comes back to stay at the lighthouse. Caroline welcomes him, and he joins her and George for a hearty dinner of venison stew. He fills them in on Mrs. Goldsmith's progress.

"Slow but steady she goes," says the Captain. Caroline smiles at the old seamen's reference to his wife's health as that of a ship. They speak about lighthouse maintenance and, of course, the weather. The Captain thanks, George, for assuming full command in his absence. They recollect how the job was easier when whale oil was available. The smokier but less expensive lard oil requires a keeper to be up periodically through the night, clearing soot from the lens and the windows, so the beacon remains visible. They return to their old schedule, the Captain will take the first watch, and George will relieve him at 1 AM, extinguishing the lantern at dawn. Stella joins him most mornings to clean soot from the lenses and the windows, while George replenishes the oil, so they are prepared for nightfall or in case of a storm that requires them to light up during the day.

The Captain spends the afternoon in his office updating the *Keepers Logbook* while Caroline and George bundle up and go outside to tend the animals. They discuss when Mrs. Goldsmith might be well enough to return. George comments that the Captain looks older despite his time away from the Lighthouse. Caroline suggests that worry over Mrs. Goldsmith's health may have taken a toll on him.

When the girls return from school, they are pleased to see Captain Goldsmith walking around the front yard and rushing inside to greet Mrs. Goldsmith. Caroline, preparing the fire for dinner, hears the girls and checks on them.

"Girls, she reprimands, "Why are you in here?"

"We're looking for Mrs. Goldsmith. Is she upstairs?" asks Lucy, confused at not finding her.

"Girls, come. I'll explain." The girls look at Caroline, worry etched across their young faces. "Everything's fine," Caroline reassures them, "Mrs. Goldsmith is just enjoying spending time with her daughter, so she's not coming back yet; maybe she'll be back after Christmas? Why don't you two go outside and ask the Captain to join us? Supper's ready."

Both girls, while disappointed, are relieved to learn that Mrs. Goldsmith will return soon. They go outside and spot the Captain at the top of the stairs leading down to the beach. Stella strolls in his direction, head down, feeling a little shy since it's been a while since she's seen him, but Lucy races past her, calling,

"Captain . . . Captain, welcome home!" He turns around with a big, warm smile, arms extended. He hugs Lucy and then reaches for Stella, who runs into his open arms.

"It is so good to see you both; I think you have grown bigger since

I've been away."The girls cast their eyes down, embarrassed by the attention, but can't hide their big grins.

"Look!" Stella exclaims a large ship is making its way past them on the Sound.

"It's beautiful," Lucy says with awe.

"What kind of ship is that?" asks Stella.

"That's a clipper. From France, judging by the flag, she's flying," he says.

"Have you ever been to France?" Stella asks.

"Yes, a long, long time ago," the Captain murmurs, memories of his youthful days at sea playing across his face. Stella continues,

"This school break, I'm going to learn every flag in the world so I can keep track of where each ship that goes by is from."

"That's a fine project, Stella." says the Captain, "Come on now, girls. It's going to be dark soon."

"Oh, we almost forgot, Ma, said dinner's ready if you want some before you head up."

"Thank you, Lucy. I am happy to join you. You're Ma is a mighty fine cook."

As they walk back, Stella asks, "Captain, can I go up to the tower with you tonight?"

"Have you worked in the tower a lot while I was away?"

Stella admits, "Sometimes."

Lucy stares at her sister and says with outrage, "Stella! You've been up there more than Da!"

"That's not true, Lucy. Da comes up every night as soon as he can," replies Stella protectively. Stella worries that Da's inattention to the Lighthouse is best not shared.

"Ok, girls," says the Captain, "I've got the picture, but I think, for the time being, Stella, you better sleep at night at least while school is in session. When does Christmas vacation start?" he asks.

Lucy replies, "This is the last week, then we'll be off for two whole weeks."

"Ok then, how about if you help out during vacation. I'm hoping Mrs. Goldsmith will come back after Christmas if she's up to it," the Captain continues opening the door to the cottage. They remove their outdoor clothing and enter the cozy parlor—the welcome fragrance of onions and potatoes roasting on the hearth beckons.

"Mmm, smells good," exclaims Lucy.

"I'm hungry," agrees Stella rubbing her tummy.

"Come and sit down; it's almost ready," Caroline says, smiling at the girls.

❄

Mrs. Goldsmith never returns to live at the lighthouse. She continues to struggle to regain her health throughout the winter. The Captain divides his time between his work at Hortons Point and staying at his daughter's place with Mrs. Goldsmith. Stella is eager to step into the role of the assistant lighthouse keeper. She takes the first watch anytime the Captain isn't available. While she still can't carry up or pour the oil into the lantern, she keeps the tower swept and free of debris, and before school, she and Lucy clean the windows and meticulously wipe the soot off the lens. Da is still needed to drape the heavy protective cloth around the lens and maintain the outside of the windows. He also makes the daily notations in the official Keeper's Logbook.

On the last day of school, the girls are excited to go to Belle's sleepover. Stella, Lucy, and little Anna Prince will all stay with the Tillinghasts for the night. Caroline drops off the girls' nightclothes and a change for the next day. Then she walks to school to escort the excited girls back to the Tillinghasts. She tells them that Da took the Captain back to Chary Ann's, but they will visit after services on Christmas day.

Upon hearing this news, Stella's mood changes from a carefree child to a worried premature adult; when they get to the Tillinghasts, Ma says she needs to get home. Stella hangs back and clings to Ma. Caroline gestures to Mrs. Tillinghast to go on in and turns to address Stella.

"I know what's troubling you."

"Ma," Stella says with more authority in her voice than one would expect to find in a 10-year-old, "You could be alone all night if Da doesn't come back."

"I know, Stella, but that's not your concern right now. I want you to go with the other girls and have fun. I'll take care of the light if Da is delayed." While there is no practical reason that George cannot make it back in time to attend to the beacon, Stella and Caroline know there is a good chance he won't.

"Stella, I want you to have a good time with your friends tonight," Caroline urges. Stella tramps up the steps as if she's marching to her impending doom. How can she have fun when neglecting her responsibility to the lighthouse? If Ma falls asleep, the lantern could go out, and a ship could wash up on the rocks. Stella knows in her heart that keeping the lantern-lit is her responsibility. She believes it with a seriousness not often found in one so young.

Once inside, a quiet Stella watches the other girls as they gather around the table, helping Mrs. Tillinghast make cookies. It reminds her of the fun they had with Mrs. Goldsmith. Ma is a good cook, but she doesn't seem to have time for baking. Mrs. Tillinghast rolls out the dough and gives each girl a portion. A clean pile of seashells sits at the center of the table. The girls select a few to press into the dough and make seashell cookies.

Mrs. Tillinghast noticing that Stella is hanging back, puts a few shells in front of her and says, "These are for you, Stella."

"No, thanks. I'll just watch."

Mrs. Tillinghast cajoles, "Don't miss out on the fun."

The other girls join in, "Come on, Stella, you should make some too,"

Lucy whispers in Stella's ear, "If you make some, we'll have two batches to take home." Stella smiles at Lucy's childish greed and reluctantly begins pressing the dough in front of her with the shells.

Stella keeps looking out the back window that faces north towards the lighthouse. As the sun sets, she sees the light burning from the tower. Relief washes over her young face. While sitting by the fire reading the farm report, Mr. Tillinghast notices the change in her demeanor and asks,

"Stella, is everything alright?" She turns towards the group who have stopped and are staring at her.

Lucy, ever protective and often Stella's explainer, says, "She's just worried about the light. Now that it's on, she'll have fun too." Stella looks at her sister with exasperation.

"Well, it's true," continues Lucy glaring back at her sister with reproof.

Mrs. Tillinghast nods at Mr. Tillinghast; Stella's reaction and Lucy's explanation confirm what they've heard: the Prince girls, especially Stella, are responsible for the light when George isn't up to the task.

Anna tells the girls about her family's upcoming trip to New York City. Anna explains that they will take the train this year, making the trip ever so much faster. Belle and Lucy listen enthralled, trying to picture so many tall buildings.

Stella, tired of Anna's boasting, says, "I bet none of them fancy buildings are higher than the lighthouse." Anna is struck silent for a moment, registering though not fully understanding Stella's angry tone.

Lucy steps closer to Stella while Belle wheedles, "I bet you're right, Stella."

"How would you know?" Anna demands, "you've never even been to New York!"

"Now, girls," Mrs. Tillinghast says as she enters Belle's room, drawn by the sound of their raised voices, "What seems to be the trouble."

Stella, eyes downcast, remains silent, but Anna continues yelling, "Stella says that the lighthouse is taller than the buildings in New York City."

"Hmm," Mrs. Tillinghast soothes, "I don't know about that. Maybe we could ask your Pa when he picks you up tomorrow?"

Anna, accustomed to having her way at home, begins to pout.

Belle being a twin and the girl twin at that, is used to making peace and says, "Come on now, let's not ruin our party. Why does it matter what's higher anyway? You two hug and makeup." With a gentle push from Lucy, Stella goes over to Anna and touches her shoulder.

"You're right, Anna. I haven't been to lots of places like you, but I have been up in the tower, and it is very tall." Anna looking over at Belle, and Lucy's worried faces, decides to let it go. In her heart, she knows she's right, but she doesn't want to ruin their time together by being disagreeable. She is the youngest and wishes to ingratiate herself with these older girls.

She hugs Stella and says, "Someday, you'll get to go to New York City." Stella shrugs. She doesn't have any interest in going to the city. She glances out the window and is calmed by the steady white beacon radiating across the farm.

Stella rises before sunrise, worrying about her mother at the lighthouse; she wakes Lucy and rushes her downstairs to the kitchen where Mrs. Tillinghast is preparing breakfast. Stella thanks Mrs. Tillinghast and all but drags Lucy out to walk home. Lucy trudges behind Stella, pouting at having to leave the party so early but knowing there's no convincing Stella to change her mind. She holds tight to the wrapped cookies Mrs. Tillinghast pressed into her hand as she left.

When they arrive, it is as Stella feared. Da has not returned. Having extinguished the light, an exhausted Caroline is just going up to bed. Lucy complains to Caroline that Stella made her leave the party, but

Caroline soothes her with a gentle pat and says, "They'll be other get-to-gethers. Now, you girls get the fire going in here, warm up some porridge for breakfast. You'll need to tend the animals this morning too."

"What about the light, Ma?" Stella asks, "Did you wipe down the lens and bring up fresh oil?"

"Not yet, Stella," Caroline replies. "Da will be back soon, I'm sure, and he can see to the light. You girls see to the animals. I need to rest."

The girls make fast work of starting the fire and sweeping out the cottage. When Lucy goes out to the barn to gather eggs, Stella goes up to the tower and wipes the lens. With Ma still asleep and no sign of Da, Stella convinces Lucy to help her refill the oil bucket and carry it up to the lantern. Stella knows it's essential to replace the oil each morning. She awkwardly carries down the empty oil can and places it under the spout of the storage barrel. They struggle to open the knob on the nozzle. When they finally succeed, the oil gushes out. They wrestle the handle closed, but there is more oil in the can than Stella hoped. Together the girls drag the heavy can to the bottom of the 28 step circular stairway.

"We'll never do this," laments Lucy, breathless from the exertion.

"Come on. If we work together, we can," Stella urges her sister. One step at a time, the girls lift the heavy can, plunking it down on each step, oil spilling over the top with each plunk. Halfway up, the girls are sweating despite the cold. By the time they get to the top of the stairway, they sit down, exhausted by their efforts.

"How will we ever get it up the ladders?" Lucy asks, staring up at the ladders leading to the lantern room. Releasing long sighs, they rest their heads on their hands. Lucy picks up her head and says, "Do you hear that?" Stella stands and climbs up the ladder to the watch room. Peering out the window, she sees Da leading Jenny and the wagon into the yard.

Leaving the oil bucket at the top of the steps, Lucy and Stella race down and run outside, not noticing how much oil spilled while they were lugging the can.

"Da, where have you been?" Lucy calls.

"What's the problem, girls?" Da cajole. Stella, frowning, commands, "We need to refill the lantern."

"Don't be a scold, Stella," he says, chucking her chin, "I'm here now. I'll take care of it."

Lucy continues, "We carried the oil up to the top step, but we can't get it up the ladder."

George turns to look at them with surprise, "You did? Hmmm!" George ties up Jenny and walks inside with the girls trailing behind.

Ma is in the parlor as they pass through. She glances towards George and says, "Thank you, girls, for tidying up and keeping the fire going,"

Lucy explains, "Ma, we carried the oil up the steps, but we couldn't get it up the ladder."

"You did what?" Caroline asks.

George calls, "It's alright. I'm here." Stella and Lucy continue to follow him to the tower.

He approaches the stairs and yells, "Stella, what's this? On the steps?" He touches the drops of spilled oil. "The Lighthouse Service holds me responsible for every drop of this oil. You spilled it all over the place," George yells.

Stella, shocked and angry, starts to speak, but George cuts her off, "Go get some rags and clean up the mess you made." Stella runs to the oil room and gathers rags fighting off the tears welling up in her eyes.

When she rushes through the parlor, Caroline takes her chin in her hand, looks into her eyes, says, "I know you meant no harm, Stella." Stella pulls away, bursting with anger. She hands Lucy a rag, and together they wipe the steps.

George comes down the stairs and says, "That isn't even enough oil."

"We know Da," says Lucy, "but we couldn't carry anymore than that."

"If you're going to do a job, at least do it right." He barks as he heads out to refill the can while Lucy and Stella clean up every drop of oil off the steps.

❈

Two exhausted little girls fall into bed by 6 PM that night. Caroline lies between them, trying to lift them out of the somber mood, asks, "You girls didn't tell me about the sleepover. Was it fun?"

Stella turns away from her mother and faces the wall, but Lucy tells Caroline, "Stella and Anna argued!"

"What?" cries Caroline. "Stella, what happened?"

"Nuthin'," mumbles Stella.

Caroline looks over at Lucy, "Yes, it did," she continues sitting up.

"Anna said she's going to New York City and that the buildings there are taller than the lighthouse."

"U-huh?" Rubbing Stella's shoulder, Caroline asks, "And you had a problem with that?"

"Everyone knows the lighthouse is the tallest building in the whole world. I've never seen anything taller than it. Have you?"

"I think there could be. When I was a girl, my Pa took us into New York City one time, and there were some very tall buildings. Now, I'm not saying they were taller; but is that any reason to argue with your cousin?"

"She's just such a little 'know it all,'" says Lucy on Stella's behalf.

"Lucy," Caroline entreats, "Anna is your little cousin. You should be nice to her."

"But she's always in the middle of everything like she got to be the cat in the play, and everyone thought she was so cute, and I was just a dumb boat."

Stella chimes in, "better than a bush."

Caroline, smiling, says, "Oh, so is that what this is really about?"

"No, the lighthouse is the tallest!"

"I know that's what you believe because that's all you've seen, but you can't be sure."

"Oh, Ma, why does Anna get to go to New York City, and she's just seven!" Lucy whines.

Sighing, Caroline says, "Girls, there's always going to be some who have more, or at least it might look that way, but only the Almighty knows what's in a person's heart. Uncle

"Maybe I should try and be Anna's special friend."

"Why Lucy," says Caroline, "that is my good Christian girl."

"Good luck with that," Stella remarks.

"Ok, girls. Time for prayers." After she listens to her daughters' earnest prayers, Caroline rubs the girls' backs; as they settle down and fall into a peaceful slumber. She rises from the cozy bed, banks the fire, then climbs into her bed and prays that George stays awake on his watch.

A few days later, the girls are excited about the Christmas festivities. During the morning service, they admire the simple displays of evergreens spread around the altar and exchange furtive glances with friends. As the building warms, the girls fight off sleep, but George, exhausted from being up all night, dozes, leaning on Caroline's shoulder and snoring, much to her embarrassment.

When the service is over, the girls huddle under a deerskin blanket in the back of the horse-drawn wagon, and Da drives them to Chary Ann's in Cutchogue. The festivities have already started when they arrive. Many of the men are spilling out onto the porch. Caroline nods greetings as they walk thru the crowd holding onto the girls with both hands. The large parlor is packed with the Goldsmiths' children, grandchildren, friends, and neighbors.

The girls hang back behind Ma's skirt in the crowded room until Mrs. Goldsmith calls them, "Come over here, girls; it's so good to see you." She gathers them in her arms.

"Now, let me have a good look at you. My, I do believe the Captain is right."

"Right about what?" Lucy asks.

"He said you've been growing again!" she says with a warm smile.

"Now, do you see that big table over there?" The girls nod and look over at the large dining table burdened with holiday treats.

"You go and make me up a plate with all your favorite things." Eyes wide, the girls walk over to the large dining room table covered with special treats. Looking back at Ma for permission, the girls are transfixed by the array as the men come in and stride up to the table, grab empty plates, and proceed to load them up with heaps of food.

Stella and Lu exchange looks of alarm; Ma comes over and whispers, "Don't worry. There's plenty."

Once the men finish, new dishes are placed on the table, while the women make up plates to bring to the elders and then spoon out items for little children and babies. Next, the older children gather around, excited by the variety of foods. With Ma's help, Stella and Lucy make up their plates and take them back to Mrs. Goldsmith. They sit at her feet, enjoying the special treats.

Happy to see that Mrs. Goldsmith isn't sick anymore, Lucy asks, "Are you coming back to the lighthouse today?"

"I'm sorry to tell you I won't be coming back to live at the lighthouse though I will visit you in the nice weather."

Frowning, Lucy asks, "Why not?"

Seeing the girls' expressions, Caroline comes over and asks, "What's wrong?"

Lucy says, "Mrs. Goldsmith isn't coming back to live at the lighthouse."

Caroline pats the girls and says, "I thought that might happen. I guess I should have prepared you, girls."

"But you two can come here and visit with me whenever you'd like," Mrs. Goldsmith says as she gathers the girls into her arms.

As the crowd grows silent, enjoying the food, Captain Goldsmith stands and calls out, "I'd like to make an announcement. As you may know, I've been working for a long time, close to 70 years, I imagine."

"Now, Captain," calls Mrs. Goldsmith, "Don't you be exaggerating." The guests chuckle as the couple exchanges fond glances.

"In any case, Mrs. Goldsmith and I have decided it's time for me to slow down a bit. I've put in for my retirement from the Lighthouse Service. I'll stay on for another month or two to give them time to find my replacement," he continues, looking over at his son Daniel, Jr., a round of applause sweeps through the packed home.

"Congratulations, Mrs. Goldsmith," Caroline says, bending down to kiss her on the cheek. "I'm going to go find George; you girls stay here."

"Of course," Mrs. Goldsmith says.

"Um . . . what's retired?" Lucy asks, stumbling on the new word.

"Captain and I won't be living at the lighthouse anymore." Stella is shocked into silence. She can't imagine how they will manage without the Goldsmiths. After what feels like an eternity, Ma comes back and says,

"Come on, girls, say goodbye. We're going home." Lucy is reluctant to leave the party, but Stella is relieved to escape to think about the lighthouse without the Goldsmiths.

CHAPTER 6

1878

Hamstring -
to sever the fluke tendons to stop a running whale.

George is promoted to Head Keeper, while Daniel Goldsmith, Jr., is named the new Assistant. Daniel and his wife Martha move into his parents' former quarters that spring. Although the girls are excited about their new neighbors, they miss Mrs. Goldsmit. Caroline and Martha become fast friends as they tend to their shared home and put in the garden. Daniel, full of enthusiasm and wishing to prove himself worthy of this new position, jumps in and tackles many of the more demanding tasks George neglected—whitewashing the inside tower and stairs.

Once the warmer weather arrives, Daniel and George spend afternoons whitewashing the outside of the tower. As the head keeper, George is now responsible for recording in the official *Keeper's Log* though Daniel, eager to learn, often joins him in the morning to discuss the entries. They keep the same schedule that his father had set. Daniel lights the lantern at sunset and stays up till 1 a.m., when George is supposed to relieve him. Daniel comes back down during the early evening to say goodnight to Martha. Weather permitting, they sit on the front porch where he can monitor the beacon as it shines across the Sound till the chill chases her inside to bed.

One night a strong gust of wind blew out the light. By the time

Daniel got to the tower, Stella was already there, preparing to rekindle the lantern.

"Stella," Daniel asks, "What are you doing up here?"

Surprised by his harsh tone, Stella backs up against the tower window, "Hurry!" she urges, "The lantern!"

Daniel efficiently rekindles the lantern, then, turning back to her, says, "Why are you here?"

"I was falling asleep, and I saw that the light went out. That sometimes happens with an east wind 'specially." Daniel glares at her.

"Stella," he continues, "I am here to see to the light."

"I'm sorry," Stella murmurs as she descends the ladder.

When she gets back into bed alongside Lucy, Caroline sits up and asks, "Stella, are you alright?"

"Yes, Ma," she whispers.

Rising from her bed, she walks over to the girls and touches Stella's forehead to check for fever.

"Are you sick?"

"No, Ma," Stella murmurs, "The light was out, so I went up to relight it."

"Isn't Daniel here?"

"Yes, Ma, but I-I just thought he might have fallen asleep."

"Oh, was he?"

"No, Ma, he came and lit it, . . .but he was angry at me."

Caroline hears her sniff and sees a stream of tears running down Stella's cheeks in the reflection of the light.

"I'm sure he didn't mean anything. He was probably just surprised," Caroline says as she wipes Stella's cheeks with the edge of her shawl.

"Go back to sleep. You're not responsible for the beacon." Stella turns her back away from her mother and pulls the covers over her head, angry at the injustice. Even Ma doesn't understand. Disquieting thoughts swirl through her head, but she soon falls asleep deriving comfort from the glow of the beacon out her window.

❀

Daniel invites them to help him paint the picket fence during spring break. The girls embrace the job with glee and spend every morning painting a section once the dew is dry enough for the whitewash to stick. When he sees how committed they are, he asks George about the possibility of paying them.

George looks at the girls working and says, "You got so much you want to throw it at kids? Everyone has to pitch in."

"They're just kids," Daniel continues.

"And that's why they get to go to school all day, but that's gonna change. How much learnin' do girls need, anyway? They both read and write better than most adults I know."

Stella and Lucy, working nearby, overhear the two men speaking.

Lucy runs up to her father, pleading, "Oh, Da, please let us go back to school."

"See what I mean, they know where it's easy for them. You've both had more schooling than most." Stella, crushed at the thought of not going to school, marches to the oil shed to put away the supplies.

Lucy hurrying behind her, says, "Stella, did you hear what Da said?"

"Yes, Lucy, I did!"

"Don't you want to go to school?

"I certainly do, and I intend to."

Lucy gives her sister an appraising look filled with new respect.

"What if he doesn't let us?"

"Just let him try," Stella says with newfound steeliness.

❀

On the way home from Thanksgiving at Uncle Henry's, the Prince's pick up Martha and Daniel. Ma fusses over Martha, insisting she and Daniel sit on the bench in the front of the wagon while Caroline joins the girls in the back. Lucy notices other small changes in how Ma treats Martha.

Lucy whispers to Stella, "Do you think there's something wrong with Martha?"

"What do you mean?" a confused Stella responds.

"Don't you see how Ma won't let her do any of the heavy work? She keeps telling her to sit down, and she's cooking for them too, just like when Mrs. Goldsmith was sick."

"Oh, you know, Ma, she's just nice."

"I think there's something else," Lucy states, not in the least dissuaded by Stella.

On Christmas, the Prince family goes to Charry Ann's after services. They enjoy a pleasant day with friends and special treats. Mrs. Goldsmith tells the girls that she will stay at the lighthouse in the spring. While the girls are happy that Mrs. Goldsmith is returning, this announcement adds to Lucy's worry that something is wrong with Martha. During Christmas vacation, she notices that Ma suggests Martha take a nap in the afternoon.

Once Martha leaves to nap, and the men go out to do chores, Lucy asks, "Ma is Martha sick?"

Smiling, Ma says, "No, Lucy, but I guess you noticed that we've been taking special care of her."

"Yes, and Mrs. Goldsmith said she might come back to the lighthouse in the spring. That would be so nice, but where will Martha go?"

Caroline smiles, saying, "I guess you girls are big enough to share in the news, but you have to keep it to yourself."

Stella looks up from her book. She is reading Part II of *Little Women*, her best Christmas present. She is up to the part where Amy and Aunt March came to see Jo in NY on their way to Europe, and Jo's heart is about to be broken. But Ma's serious tone catches her attention.

"What is it, Ma?" Ma pulls the rocker near the hearth and invites the girls to come and sit by her.

"You both are getting so big." She says, adjusting their braids as they sit at her feet.

"There's no need to worry. Martha isn't sick, but she does need to be a little extra careful. You see, she's going to have a baby."

"A baby!" squeals Lucy jumping with excitement. "I told you something was going on," Lucy says with a fierce stare. "I knew it, I knew it, I knew it!"

"You thought she was sick!" Stella says, "Stop jumping around like a frog."

"A baby," continues Lucy, her enthusiasm not the least bit tempered by Stella's reproach.

"Now, girls," Caroline continues, "calm down. Although this is a special time, it doesn't always go as expected. It's in the hands of the Almighty, so you must keep it to yourselves." Stella and Lucy exchange long looks.

"We can't even tell Belle?" asks Lucy.

"This isn't our news to tell."

That winter, the months pass much quicker than usual. When the girls come home from school, they ask about Martha. Ma assures them she is fine and often comes up with a chore they can do to help out. The girls get in the habit of bringing in the coal and building up the fire in the late afternoon for Martha. Daniel and Martha appreciate the girls' help, and the girls blossom under their kind approval.

By early March, Martha is slowing down. Ma includes the Goldsmiths' laundry with their own, and the girls take over the garden. Daniel does all he can to help, but he is exhausted from being up at night. He isn't as quick as the Captain was to wake George when he doesn't show up at 1 a.m. for his watch. Perhaps he dozes off himself, but Caroline often has to rouse George to take over so Daniel can go to bed.

The second week in April, the midwife comes and checks on Martha.

She announces, "Time is near." Daniel brings his mother and father to stay at Hortons Point, and the wait for the new baby begins in earnest. When the girls come home from school, all four Goldsmiths sit on the front porch. They run right into the warm embrace that Mrs. Goldsmith extends.

"My, my look at you both. You're getting so tall and grown-up. Where did my little girls go?" Captain Goldsmith picking up on the game, says,

"Mrs. Goldsmith, I don't believe I've met these two young ladies. How do you know them?" For a second, Stella and Lucy stare up at the Captain, then he breaks into a hearty laugh, and reaching out, scoops them up together onto his lap.

"I thought you forgot us!" Lucy moans. Stella, nose in the air, sniffing, says, "Mmm, something smells good." The adults laugh and explain,

"Your Ma has been busy making a special welcome supper for us to share tonight.

Caroline calls, "Girls, bring in more coal."

They go down to the coal bin, fill the can with coal, and then carry it back upstairs to the stove.

Ma says, "Lucy set the table, and Stella, you come here and stir the stew."

Mrs. Goldsmith comes in and says, "It's such a pleasure to be here with all of you. What can I do to help?"

Ma looks over, smiling, says, "You just sit and enjoy your visit. You never know when you're going to be needed."

"Caroline, we are so grateful to you and the girls. You are like another daughter to me." Stella notices Ma's eyes are wet with tears.

"You all right, Ma?" she asks, confused.

"Yes, sweetheart. I'm just happy and hopeful that the Almighty will look over us during the next few days, and we'll have more to celebrate soon."

Stella returns to her job, stirring the stew and suddenly realizing, says,

"Oh, I see. The baby is coming." She turns to Lucy, who nods at her sister.

Caroline says, "Girls go ask everyone to come in." Daniel helps Martha up out of the chair and into the Prince's parlor. Martha is given the seat closest to the fire, usually Lucy's chair, but Lucy is happy to give it up. A delicious meal is had by all except Martha, who eats little and appears to be distressed.

Daniel assists Martha to their side of the cottage. Martha lies down on the mattress by the hearth, and the Captain and Mrs. Goldsmith settle in by the fire; while Daniel returns to the tower.

Mrs. Goldsmith says, "It is nice to be back, but I can't say I miss it."

The Captain looks out the front window watching the light as it glistens over the Sound, and says, "Hmm, I'm glad you're happy at Chary Ann's Frances, but for me, there is nothing compares to the rhythm of the sea. I know it's a hardship in many ways, but it feeds my soul."

"Come to bed now, Captain; we may be up during the night."

On the morning of April 10, the burden of early labor takes over. Heavy rains flooded the fields around the lighthouse, and the girls could not go to school. Daniel rushes out with the wagon to get the midwife in the driving rain but turns back at the first gate as the field is impassable.

They are all concerned about Martha's safety, but midwives didn't attend any of Mrs. Goldsmith's births, and she's had four healthy babies. A stack of clean cloths sits close to the hearth, and the girls bring buckets of water to heat over the fire. Lucy can't keep her eyes off Martha and finds every excuse to be close by, but Stella, uncomfortable with all the commotion, goes up to check on the tower. Caroline recognizes the signs that Martha's time is near. She shoos everyone out while she and Mrs. Goldsmith take over.

Daniel goes up to the tower and lights the lantern just as the sunsets. The sounds of Martha's labor are audible throughout the cottage, reverberating up and down the tower's brick walls.

Hearing an ear-piercing cry, Stella exchanges a frightened look with Daniel, who says, "You take the watch, Stella." She nods as he rushes down just in time to hear the bleating of his new baby.

Daniel peeks in, "All's fine, son," Mrs. Goldsmith assures him, "Go wait inside, and we'll call you when we're finished." Daniel paces back and forth in front of the door until his Mother calls, "Ok, son. You can come in now." Squaring his shoulders, he enters and looks at the new baby resting in his mother's arms, then at his wife, the new mother, not knowing who he should go to first. Caroline finishes ministering to Martha and props her up.

"Daniel," Martha murmurs, "Would you like to hold your daughter?" Daniel lifts the tiny bundle out of his mother's arms. Engulfing the wee babe, he walks to his wife's bedside.

"Do you like her?" Martha asks.

"Yes, she's beautiful. Kind of small for all the trouble she's caused." The baby starts to whimper, and Daniel hands her to Martha to nurse. Martha lowers her shawl and puts the baby to her nipple. The baby squirms in her mother's arms. Caroline suggests, Martha rubs the baby's cheek and lips with her nipple, and she grabs on and begins to suck.

"Looks like she's getting the hang of it," Caroline encourages. The baby releases the nipple and makes a few whimpering sounds, and then in a soft whoosh, out comes the first baby poop.

Caroline says, "Let me take her and clean her up." Martha hands her over. Turning to Daniel, she asks, "What shall we name her?"

Gently stroking the newborn's brow, he says without a moment's hesitation, "Martha, of course. Someday, she'll be just as beautiful and strong as you, my love," he adds as he kisses his wife on the top of her head.

"I guess I better get back up to the light. Though I left it in the expert hands of young Stella."

Early the following morning, Lucy, missing Ma, goes to the Goldsmiths' side of the cottage and whispers, "May I come in?"

"Yes, come and meet baby, Martha," Martha says. Delighted, Lucy goes over to Ma, who is changing the baby. Lucy gazes at this new life in wonder.

Mrs. Goldsmith comes down the stairs and tuts, "Do you think she should be in here?"

"Oh, Mother, it's fine," Martha says.

Not wishing to make the older woman uncomfortable, Caroline tells Lucy,

"Go start breakfast." Lucy walks out slowly, eyes fixated on the sleeping bundle.

Mrs. Goldsmith stays on for several weeks, and the girls enjoy having her close though she is kept busy tending to both Martha's – new mom and new baby. Stella is put out and complains to Ma about the amount of fuss this new baby causes everyone, but Lucy is enchanted.

"When I grow up, I'm going to have ten no 12 babies!" she announces, holding baby Martha in her arms and staring into her blue eyes with pure wonder.

The women laugh, and Mrs. Goldsmith says, "You better marry well little one. Maybe a doctor or a whaling captain."

"No, whalers," Lucy declares. "I don't want my husband gone to sea for years at a time."

"Why, Lucy, you've given this some thought," Mrs. Goldsmith continues.

"You are wise beyond your years," says Martha, "And where do you plan on finding such a man?"

"Hmm, I haven't quite worked that part out yet," Lucy murmurs.

❖

The birth of baby Martha without a midwife adds to the urgency for a road to the lighthouse. George holds the unpopular position that a road is unnecessary. At a town meeting held just ten days after Martha's birth, the Highway Commission votes to build a road to the lighthouse.

Following the vote, George takes off on an extended fishing trip and returns in high spirits with several dozen eels and hundreds of moss-bunker. George sells the fish to the Orient Guano Fish Factory, where the fish oil will be extracted and sold for lantern fuel. He feels triumphant with cash in his pockets and buys several jugs of the local brew, which he hides in the outbuildings.

Although she is pleased to have George back home, Caroline struggles to ignore his growing reliance on spirits despite her disdain for partaking in alcohol. Caroline accepts this unhappy compromise as long as George attends to his duties as the keeper. In her daily prayers, she asks the Lord to help him find the strength to salve the wounds that continue to fester in his soul and for her forbearance to remain a dutiful wife.

While George is away, the girls are off from school for spring break, and Stella takes his watch in the tower. While she isn't strong enough to carry a full oil can to replenish the lantern, she can complete the job with 1/2 full cans, replacing the oil for the lantern each morning.

Captain and Mrs. Goldsmith reluctantly return to their daughter's home in town as concerns for their health weigh on everyone's mind. Caroline tends to baby Martha, so the new Mama has time to get back on her feet. Lucy is an able helper, but Stella is far more interested in working in the tower and barely notices the baby while Lucy and Caroline jump to soothe her every whimper.

CHAPTER 7

Spring 1881

Make a Passage, to-
to pass from one whaling ground to another.

On the last school day before spring break, Belle invites the girls to a sleepover. Anna again insinuates herself into the little group as they discuss their plans before the school bell rings. Anna tries to impress the girls with promises of a new type of treat that just arrived in her father's store—'candy corn.' Her description of this new candy wins over Lucy and Belle, but Stella frowns and turns a cold shoulder to Anna.

Uncle Henry observing Stella's attempts at excluding his dear Anna, pulls her aside and reminds her how important it is to her Ma that she is charitable.

He continues, "Though Anna is younger, she looks forward to spending time with you girls." Stella grimaces at the gentle rebuke but nods her acquiescence and returns to the girls.

Feigning enthusiasm, she says, "It sure would be nice if you could join us tonight, Anna, but you don't have your sleeping clothes."

Anna, always quick, turns to her father flashing her most charming smile, coaxes, "Papa, will you please bring my sleeping costume at the end of the school day and some packets of that new treat?"

Henry smiles and says, "Of course, I will." Glad that that's settled, Henry heads back to the store, hoping that this negotiation will be the toughest one he has to face today.

Miss Glover assigns the senior students a challenging vacation project. They must write down as many words as they can make from the letters in the word, 'conventionalize.' Lucy is quickly bored by the activity after finding just three words—can, live, to—but Stella works diligently. She wants to find the most words. Miss Glover said there were over 300 possibilities, which pushes Stella to keep at it. At first, Stella keeps her list to herself, but as the week goes on, she allows Lucy, Ma, and Mrs. Goldsmith to help—even Da and Daniel join in at times. One day when Belle is over, the three girls sit on the front porch working together. Stella takes a careful count and sees that she has over 200 words. Belle tires of the exercise and says it's making her head hurt, and Lucy wants to go and see if the berries are ripe yet even though they just checked yesterday, but Stella stays with it. Finally, the girls convince her to join them for a walk on the beach. Stella puts her list away before chasing after the girls as they head for the stairs at the top of the bluff.

After spring break, the eldest students prepare for final exams and graduation activities. The students are again going to perform the play *While the Cats Away*. This year, young Frederick Prince, Anna's baby brother, and the youngest student will play the mouse. Anna tries hard not to show her annoyance that her brother will be the star of the play as she sees it, and she is reduced to the role of a bush with no lines, just making whooshing wind sounds when the mouse, 'Freddie' crawls by her.

Each of the graduates has a small speaking part. Bertie, the narrator, reads his lines, but the rest of them must memorize their parts. Stella is not excited about her role in the play, but she is looking forward to reading her 'Declamation Speech.' Stella's speech is of particular significance to her. Since returning to school after spring break, she has been working with Miss Glover, who asked Stella to write an original speech based on the life of Ida Lewis, a lady lighthouse keeper.

Stella is flattered to be singled out by Miss Glover, who showed Stella two articles about Ida Lewis. The July 1869 copy of *Harper's Bazaar* details how Ida Lewis became famous for performing many rescues at Lime Rock Lighthouse in Rhode Island, where she lived with her family. Stella is mesmerized by the story. She returns to her desk in something of a trance and reads it.

When she finishes, Miss Glover asks, "What do you think?"

"I think it's a wonderful story."

"Yes, it is an interesting story. Would you want to present it for your Declamation Speech?"

Stella looks at her teacher with eyes full of wonder and says, "Yes, I would . . . but can I? I thought we were to read from a famous speech written by a real writer?"

"Well," Miss Glover continues, "most students' recitations are taken from well-known authors, but Stella, I think you are a good writer, and since you know so much about this topic . . ." Miss Glover continues, "You demonstrated what an able student you are with the assignment during spring break. You found the most words. Your hard work and dedication should be rewarded. I can't think of anyone better than you to share Ida Lewis's story."

Smiling, Stella says, "I would like to write about her."

"Why don't you work on it and bring it back to me when you've got some ideas on paper, and we'll discuss it further."

Every day Stella takes notes from the magazine's story. In the *New York Tribune*, she reads that "Ida Lewis received a Silver Medal and a check for $100 by a life-saving association." Infused with a new sense of dedication, Stella increases her diligence at Hortons Point. Hoping she might get a reward someday, but her most heartfelt wish is to become the official lighthouse keeper just like Ida.

By late May, Stella finishes writing her speech and presents it to Miss Glover. The teacher reviews it and then sits with Stella to refine it until they are satisfied. Final draft in hand, Stella must practice reciting. She brings it home with her to practice whenever she is alone. When she's feeding the chickens in the morning, Stella practices under the sounds of their clucking.

Lucy noticing, Stella's lips moving, says, "What are you saying, Stella?"

"Oh nothing," Stella says, embarrassed at being caught. Stella wanders off to the top of the bluff to practice. Lucy, curious about her sister's recent interest in being alone, sneaks up and is startled to see Stella standing on the edge, flinging her arms to and fro and reciting. Frightened by Stella's actions, Lu runs over and knocks Stella to the ground.

"What are you doing?" asks Stella as she stands and brushes herself off.

"What are YOU doing?" Lucy retorts, troubled by Stella's odd behavior.

"I thought you'd gone crazy and were preparing to jump off the bluff."

"If you must know, I'm practicing my speech for graduation."

"Will you read it to me?" Lucy asks, stretching out in the grass. Stella stands up tall, squaring her shoulders, raises her head to her full 4' 9" height, and begins . . .

"Ida Lewis, Lighthouse Keeper —American Heroine."

Lucy cuts in, Ida Lewis? Who is Ida Lewis?"

"Just listen, and I'll tell you," Stella says, annoyed by the interruption.

Stella clears her throat and continues: "Ida Lewis was a brave woman. She lived at Lime Rock Light House in Rhode Island with her father, the lighthouse keeper, her mother, two brothers, and a sister. Ida and her mother took over the lighthouse keeper's duties when her father became ill." Ida's father died eight years ago, and her mother was commissioned as the Head Lighthouse Keeper. Stella continues, "Lime Rock is an island in Newport Harbor. Ida was very good at rowing the dory because one of her jobs was to bring her brothers to and from school each day by boat, the only way to get to school!" Even in stormy weather, Ida rowed her brothers. The first year she lived at Lime Rock, she saved four boys whose boat capsized. Ida became a brave sailor and savior to others who might have drowned.

In 1879, Ida officially took over as her Assistant Keeper. Ida's picture was on the cover of Harpers' Weekly, and she received a silver medal. On Independence Day in 1869, there was a parade in her honor in Newport, RI. She met President Grant when he visited the lighthouse, and he gave her a mahogany dory with red velvet cushions. He congratulated her on her strength and courage. Ida Lewis is a woman to be admired. Written by Stella Prince."

Lucy sits up and cheers, "Oh boy, that's good, Stella! Do I have to do a Declamation too? It is my last year of school," she continues with regret. In her excitement, Stella hasn't thought about Lucy's feelings. She wonders if Lucy wants to stay in school.

"Gee, Lu, if you want to keep going to school, maybe you could ask Ma to speak to Da?" Stella suggests.

"No," Lucy continues, "it's ok to stop. Anyway, this way, I'll get to spend more time with baby Martha."

"You sure do love that baby," Stella says in amazement.

"When I grow up, I'm gonna have ten babies!"

"Lucy!" Stella exclaims, scandalized by the thought of her little sister becoming a mother.

"Ma was 18 when she married Da." Lucy continues, "I think 18 is a good age to get married. That's only seven years from now." Stella stares at her sister, mystified at her desire to grow up and be married. As close as these two girls are and as much as they've shared, Stella sees that their desires are quite different.

The night before graduation Stella worries if she's brave enough to read aloud at the assembly. At their evening meal, she asks Ma if she can borrow a black shawl.

Ma asks, "Why do you want my shawl, Stella?" Stella explains that she's written a speech about a lady lighthouse keeper and would like to wear the shawl like a costume.

Ma says, "Fine, but can you share what you wrote?" Stella stands and reads her speech. Lucy giggles, a little nervous for Stella, but soon, she is caught up in the tale. Ma and Da exchange knowing looks as Stella finishes.

"Hmm, says, mom, that's kind of a familiar story, don't you think?"

"Yeah," says Da.

Lucy chimes in, "that's just like you!"

"No, it's not," Stella exclaims, embarrassed by the comparison. "Ida Lewis has two brothers and a sister and rows them to school every day. That's not at all like me. Ida's a hero. I've never saved anyone!"

Ma says, "I think it's a wonderful story, and you've done a good job, both writing and reciting it."

"Thanks, Ma," Stella says, eyes lowered with quiet pride and discomfort at being the center of attention. She continues, "but it's not a story. It's true. I read it in the magazine Miss Glover loaned me."

"Yes, I understand that," says Ma. Lu adds, "I bet you'd like to be Ida."

"Wait a minute," Da says, as he leaves to go up to the tower, "Let's not go killing off the father!"

The girls giggle, and Ma speaking over them, says, "Ok, enough dramatics for one night. Time to clean up in here. Tomorrow's a big day."

Stella and Lucy wake extra early for their last day of school. The girls are both excited to graduate and sad that their school life is ending.

Caroline notices Stella pushing her eggs around on the plate.

"What's wrong, Stella? Are you too excited to eat breakfast?"

Da says, "That's not like Stella."

"It is a big day," Ma continues. Stella and Lucy watch the exchange. They are never sure how Da will be on any given day. He is easily angered, and both girls work hard not to cross him and risk setting off his temper. The girls gather their sacks and run out the back door to meet Belle.

A minute later, Stella comes running back, out of breath, "Ma!" she calls, "I almost forgot—the black shawl."

"Here it is." Caroline gets up and takes the shawl from the hook in the entryway. Stella crushes it with her hands, holding it up to her face, and says, "It smells like sunshine." Giving Ma a quick kiss on the cheek, she dashes out the door.

Belle, Stella, and Lucy link arms as they start their final walk to school. They are excited by the significance of this day in their lives. As they get closer to the schoolhouse, the sounds of happy children rushing inside leave them feeling ambivalent. They spend the morning cleaning and preparing the little schoolroom. Miss Glover directs the older boys to set up chairs in a U-shape under the ancient maple tree for shade. They drag out the heavy wood podium where local dignitaries will make speeches. The graduates will speak from there when it is their turn to recite their Declamations. The children gather in the cloakroom and get into their costumes. While guests arrive and take seats inside the classroom, Lu spots Caroline and George and rushes over to greet them.

When Miss Glover introduces the play, *While the Cat's Away*, the audience quiets. Little Freddie Prince steals the show scurrying from fake bush to fake tree while the more senior students recite their lines. While heavy-handed in tone, the message is that one must make the moral choice even when no one will be the wiser. When the play ends, the audience escapes the hot schoolhouse and gathers in the shade.

Miss Glover takes to the podium and thanks all in attendance. The front row seats fill as local dignitaries arrive. Miss Glover invites the graduates who have prepared a Declamation Speech to come up to the podium. The students line up in alphabetical order by last name. The students line up as follows: Willie Ballard, Elsie Elmer, Frank Hommel, Lydie Horton, Mamie Korn, Daniel McCarthy, Stella Prince, Percy Smith, and Belle Tillinghast. Miss Glover requests the audience to hold their applause till all of the speeches are complete.

Stella is glad she is neither first nor last, like poor Belle. One by one, the graduates approach the podium, and with the support of Miss Glover's gentle presence, they recite their speech. Most of the students have selected a poem or a piece of short literature to recite.

Finally, Stella steps up to the podium. She wraps the black shawl around her shoulders, looks out at the audience, then back at Miss Glover for reassurance. She takes a deep breath and begins:

"*Ida Lewis, Lady Lighthouse Keeper, and American Heroine* - written by Stella Prince" Soft murmurs circulate through the audience, and Uncle Henry seeks out Ma's eye with a nod and a smile. Ma looks down with humility and quiet dignity; Stella is the only student who wrote her own speech. Stella recites Ida's story. Then curtsies as each girl did before her. As she steps away from the podium, spontaneous applause erupts. Stella looks over at Miss Glover, worried at her response to the audience's reaction, but Miss Glover smiles and nods at Stella, then turns to the audience and says, "Yes, well done, Miss Prince. Thank you for that informative talk on the life of a truly heroic woman. By the time poor Belle gives her speech, the audience is restless, and she struggles to get through her reading of Jo's rejection of Laurie's proposal from *Little Women*.

Finally, Principal Van Scoy presents the students' awards. The best map of Long Island 1st place—Willie Billard. 1st place in Arithmetic goes to Frank Glover; 2nd, Percy Smith.

George leans over to Caroline and stage whispers, "The boys are cleaning up!"—there are soft chuckles from those nearby. Principal Van Scoy clears his throat to regain the audience's attention while Miss Glover glowers in the Prince's direction. He continues—Best Speller 1st place, Frank Hommel; 2nd, Lovina Gardiner; Most Pious Award to Lizzie Tuthill; Best Speaking—Elsie Elmer. The most original Declamation Speech goes to Stella Prince.

The Principal turns to Miss Glover, mopping his damp forehead with a handkerchief, and says, "I think that's it for today. Students and families, enjoy your summer." With that, he steps away from the podium, mopping his brow with his handkerchief.

Stella and Lucy rush over to Ma and Da and receive gentle hugs from Ma and a quick pat from Da. Captain and Mrs. Goldsmith pulls them into a shared bear hug from the Captain and kisses on each cheek from Mrs. Goldsmith.

"That was wonderful, girls and Stella," she continues, "you are a marvel." Uncle Henry makes his way through the crowd with Aunt Jennie at his side.

"You two have distinguished yourselves. I'm sure you will be an asset at the lighthouse."

The girls are a jumble of emotions: Lucy rambles about each award and how Stella's speech was the best; while Stella sits and silently contemplates the day, she feels both excitement and apprehension. She wonders if she is ready to assume the job of a wickie—IE, a keeper at the lighthouse.

When the girls get home, there is a small celebration. Martha made a special cake, and baby Martha is so excited by everyone's happy mood she darts around the front yard from one side of the fence to the other. Martha and Caroline settle on the front porch while George retreats to the office to update the *Keepers' Log*. Daniel comes out and smiles at his curly-haired girl. Baby Martha is a little beauty with a broad smile that warms the heart of all she encounters. Even the generally dour

George breaks into a rare smile when he hears her infectious giggle. Lucy and Stella run around the yard pretending to hide so baby Martha can discover them. Then they laugh and begin the game again.

"I don't know how you managed with both the girls so close in age and no fence?" Martha comments to Caroline.

"Mrs. Goldsmith was always a wonderful help though at first, we did have to tie the girls when we both were working outside'" Caroline says, embarrassed at the memory, " I hope the girls and I are a help to you too. It gives me such pleasure to see them enjoying little Martha."

Daniel overhearing the conversation, says, "The Captain often tells the story of how the first time he met the girls, Stella was headed right for the bluff."

"That's right," Caroline replies, smiling, "If it weren't for the Captain's quick thinking, we might have had a tragedy. The Almighty has protected us, and the girls have done well enough despite living so far outside town."

CHAPTER 8

Summer 1881—Spring 1882

Pharologist -
one who studies or is interested in lighthouses.

After chores that summer, Stella and Lucy spend their afternoons swimming and practicing rowing in the dory. Stella is determined to get stronger to help the next time there is a rescue to perform, just like Ida Lewis. Lucy plays at drowning so Stella can practice 'saving' her. One afternoon, Daniel watches the girls practicing and joins them. He demonstrates using one oar to stabilize the boat while the other supports the drowning person and pulls them on board. He even jumps into the water so that Stella can try rescuing him. Grunting and sweating, Stella struggles and, with his assistance, finally pulls Daniel on board.

He falls into the bottom of the boat; laughing says, "Stella, we can only hope that in the moment of danger, you will rally your strength."

Stella, eager to become a full-fledged wickie, practices rowing every day. In late August, Inspector Fanning arrives and observes Stella ably guiding the heavy dory through the jutting rocks and up onto the beach. Stella rushes up the stairs two at a time to warn Da and Daniel of the Inspector's arrival, leaving him gasping as he trails behind her.

While Mr. Fanning reviews the *Keepers' Log* with George, he discusses what he observed of 'the girl' as he calls Stella.

"She looks all grown and is quite an able oarsmen—um, err—oars woman?" he says, stuttering over the awkward term.

George replies, "Both the girls are learning the keeper's job. Now that they're finished with schoolin', they can help year-round."

Mr. Fanning looks down, thoughtfully rubbing his chin, and jots a note on his clipboard.

"Most lighthouse families rely on their children for help. Sometimes the wives and daughters take over the keeper's job, though generally, the officials frown on females assuming too much of the heavy tasks. I have to say, though, that some of them seem well suited to the life." Fanning tells George in an unusually lengthy declaration. "Everything looks in order here. It seems like you have it under control, and with the extra help of both girls, I think you should be able to stay on top of it."

George nods in his direction, wondering at the odd exchange. Caroline calls them to eat on the front porch. Mr. Fanning and George, glad to exit the hot office, head outside where Caroline and the girls have put out a tray of fresh garden vegetables and eggs with homemade bread.

In mid-September, an official letter arrives informing Daniel Goldsmith that his services are no longer needed at the Lighthouse. The same day George receives a letter apprising him of the change and informing him that he will receive a raise of $50.00 per year – making his annual salary $600. George is glad at the increase but realizes that Daniel carries more than his share of the workload that keeps the lighthouse operational. He knows he will need to step up but expects that with the girls' home full-time, they will assume more of the daily chores. Stella has grown quite a bit this summer. She's taller than Caroline and stronger than most women. Each morning, Stella brings the oil up to the lantern room; although, she does it 1/2 a bucket at a time. George reasons; the more she does it, the stronger she'll get.

George doesn't tell Caroline about the letter. He takes off for a fishing trip, figuring to take advantage while Daniel is still working. The following day, Martha tells Caroline about the letter. Caroline tries to hide her surprise, but Martha knows her well enough to realize George hadn't mentioned anything before leaving.

Martha says, "Maybe George wanted to wait till he got back . . . so you wouldn't be upset in his absence." While both women know George lacks any such sensitivity, Caroline hangs her head, heartbroken that Martha and Daniel will have to leave. She sits by the hearth alone to gather her thoughts. Caroline will miss Martha's companionship, but she is more worried about the additional burden their leaving will be on her daughters. Caroline knows that Stella is capable and willing to step up to the role, but even she cannot fill an assistant keeper's job. At only 12, Lucy is more petite and slighter than Stella and not up to many tasks the lighthouse demands. Caroline is pleased that Lucy is more interested in domestic tasks such as cooking, sewing, and caring for little ones. She is sure that Lucy will make someone a comfortable home in time and become a loving mother as long as she can get out from under the daily grind of lighthouse tending. On the other hand, Stella is more interested in the more physically strenuous work traditionally performed by men.

Caroline hears the girls coming back from a walk to collect beach plums with baby Martha. Beach plums have been abundant this year, and Caroline plans to spend the next several days working with the girls putting up the crop for jam. Keeping them busy and productive is not difficult as there is always plenty to do at the lighthouse, and they are willing helpers. Lucy's sunny, pleasant countenance makes her an agreeable companion while Stella resists some of the more domestic tasks, rushing through when it is something she doesn't value. However, Stella's attention to the lantern's daily maintenance is a continuing source of pride for Caroline.

Daniel and Martha pack up for the move back to Cutchogue. Daniel will work at the foundry. He is a hard worker with a family to support and glad to have found suitable work. Baby Martha will grow up in town surrounded by family and friends. Before they leave, Daniel teaches the girls some of the finer points for tending the lantern. How to carefully trim the wicks each morning and the need to precisely measure and record the amount of oil they pour into the bucket each day before they carry it up. They understand that it is essential that the lamp is always ready in case of a sudden change in the weather.

Since George continues to cover the second watch, it should be his responsibility to wipe down and cover the lens to protect it from sun damage and replenish the oil before retiring for the day. But with the girls as his assistants, he leaves these morning tasks for them. One of the girls covers the first watch, and the other tends the morning shut down chores. Although Caroline and the girls understand this is not a fair distribution of the work, they accept George's decision without protest recognizing the futility of disagreeing with him.

The women in the Prince family feel the loss of Daniel, Martha, and the baby. On the other hand, George is glad to work, or not at his own pace. He continues to push the girls to assume more of the daily responsibilities setting up a schedule where they will alternate nights kindling the lantern at dusk then stay up and tend the light. Caroline has to prod him out of bed before he relieves whichever girl has been on the watch that night. The girls return to their bed exhausted but never-the-less are up for breakfast by seven to see to the animals. Caroline worries that their health will suffer on this schedule of reduced sleep, but so far, they seem none the worse for the changes.

Caroline and the girls look forward to Sunday mornings to attend services and enjoy the company of old friends and neighbors. Sometimes they get a ride to Cutchogue and visit with the Goldsmith family. Lucy is always excited about the opportunity to spend time with Martha, who at three is growing and thriving under the care of her extended family.

Martha squeals when Lucy comes in, "Lu–Lu! My Lu-Lu is here!" Lucy is delighted by Martha's welcome, rushing to her and picking her up. She twirls around, both giggling with pleasure. Stella looks up at Caroline and shrugs feigned indifference. Caroline touches Stella on the shoulder to reassure her then they walk inside and greet the Goldsmiths. Daniel is getting wood, and Chary Ann is preparing the Sunday afternoon supper in the kitchen. Chary Ann hears Martha's excited squeals and comes in, hugging Caroline and Stella, laughing at Lucy and Martha's antics.

"I think Lucy has a new name."

"Lu-Lu! My Lu-Lu is here!" Martha calls over and over.

"Hmm, Lu-Lu," Stella repeats, "It does kind of suit her." From that day forward, Lucy is called Lu-Lu or just Lu. She revels in the loving nickname bestowed on her by her first baby. The warmth the Goldsmith family exudes draws Caroline, Stella, and Lu. After dinner, Daniel comments on how early the sun is going down. Stella, ever vigilant, says, "We need to go, Ma," Caroline reassures Stella that her father will pick them up soon.

Daniel says, "Why don't I drive you? It's no trouble."

Caroline responds, "that isn't necessary. Daniel, we don't want to bring you out of your way. George is supposed to pick us up . . ." she pauses.

Daniel says, "It'll give me an excuse to see how the lighthouse is getting by without me. I'll harness the horse, and we'll go."

They exchange sad farewells, bundle up against the cold and head out for the ride back. As they bounce along in the wagon, Stella can't stop looking in the direction of the lighthouse. The sun sinks into the Sound, and still, there's no light from the beacon.

Stella leaning towards her mother and says, "Ma, why doesn't he light it?"

"I'm sure he will in a minute. Maybe there's a problem with the wicks." Daniel shakes the reins speeding up the pace of the horse. They head down the new road, glad that it makes the journey quicker than going through the fields. When they pull up, the tower is still dark. Stella jumps down from the back of the wagon and runs into the house, ignoring the sight of her father passed out at the table next to the cold hearth. She races up the circular stairway and two ladders to the lantern room, makes quick work of removing the curtain and prepping the wicks, then strikes the long match and lights the lantern, adjusting the oil flow to maximize brightness. She surveys the surroundings in each direction, hoping that the delay didn't cause undue danger to any passing ships.

Satisfied that all is well, Stella descends the tower and enters the cottage. Daniel and her mother struggle to get George up the stairs to bed.

Caroline looks over her shoulder and says, "Stella help Lucy tend the fire. Da isn't feeling well." The girls build a fire and stand close, warming their hands. When Daniel comes back down, the chill is just starting to leave the cottage.

He gestures towards the tower. Stella follows behind, saying, "It's ok, Daniel. I got it."

He turns around, bemused, and says, "Is it ok if I just go up and see? For old time's sake?"

"Uh, sure," Stella says, following close behind. When they get to the lantern room, Daniel does a quick check of the lantern then walks around the tower's perimeter. He starts and ends on the northside, grabbing the binoculars; he scans the Sound, searching for sailing vessels in distress.

Returning the binoculars to their hook, he turns to Stella and says, "I guess I miss this more than I realized. I could stay the night."

"Oh, that's not necessary. I'll stay now and take the first watch, and Lucy will relieve me. Err, if Da is still sick."

They avert their eyes, avoiding facing what they both know is a half-truth. George isn't sick. He just drank too much again.

Daniel asks, "Does this happen often?" Stella looks up, weighing her words. While she cannot lie, she fears reporting the truth could have terrible consequences. They might even have to leave the lighthouse. She responds diplomatically, "We all work together here." Daniel accepts the veiled response realizing that her circumstances have made her a premature adult.

"I can do it," Stella says.

"I know you can, but you've had a big day. Go and tend to yourself. I can use some time up here on my own." Stella goes down but returns as quickly as she can, ready to assume the watch. While they both know guests aren't allowed in the tower while the light is in operation; Daniel is a former keeper; not really a guest.

❀

Over dinner in late January, George tells them that a Lampist, a Mr. McCann, is coming next month to take measurements to replace the old lard burning lantern with a new one that burns kerosene. Stella tells them that an article in, *The Keepers Information Sheet* reported that kerosene burns cleaner than lard.

Stella wonders aloud how burning kerosene might change things; "It won't smell like burning pork!"

George says. "And if kerosene burns cleaner, we shouldn't have to clean the lens as often."

Caroline and the girls are excited to have a rare winter guest. They scrub the tower and their living quarters till they gleam. Caroline has venison stew warming on the hearth waiting for George to return from the train station with their guest. Mr. McCann is somewhat rotund and middle-aged. The girls are a bit disappointed, though he is pleasant and complimentary.

Upon entering, he comments on the scent of venison. He sits down and eats with gusto, along with several hunks of homemade bread. He has hot tea with a bit of the honey the girls gathered from the hives. His singular focus is on the meal, but once satiated, he looks around, eager to get up to the lantern room before dark.

George and the lampist go up while Stella, Lu, and Caroline clean up the meal. Stella walks over to the tower's door and tries to listen every few minutes.

Finally, Caroline says, "Stella, why don't you just go up and see for yourself."

"Oh, could I, Ma? I don't think Da would want me there."

"As much as you tend the light, I think you're entitled to be there. If Da says something, just tell him I sent you."

Stella grabs her shawl from its hook and heads out the door as Caroline calls to her, "Stella, please remember your place. Just listen. Don't ask questions or interrupt the men."

"I'll try," Stella calls as she hurries to the tower. Lucy and Caroline exchange knowing smiles. Although ordinarily content to keep her thoughts to herself, Stella will be hard-pressed to refrain from asking questions about the new lantern.

Stella climbs up and enters the lantern room. Da is looking out at the Sound while Mr. McCann goes about his business, carefully measuring the lantern and writing the numbers in his notebook. He repeats each measurement, double-checking the result before moving on to the next.

Stella hangs back by the top of the stairs, and at some point, he looks up and says,

"You look as though you have a question."

"That's Stella always interested in the lantern. She grew up here, you know," Da says.

"I'm happy to explain if you're interested," Mr. McCann says. Stella follows Mr. McCann as he walks around the light. She asks why he measures twice and chooses the specific spots to check. The Lampist explains the need for utmost accuracy. A precise installation is required to ensure effective operation. She is most curious about the new oil they will burn, kerosene. Mr. McCann says he will explain the specifics regarding the oil when it arrives.

"And when will that be?" Stella asks.

"Oh, I expect sometime next month. You'll get a notice from the lighthouse service. But when the new lantern is delivered, I will travel with it and oversee the installation," he continues glancing at George. The latter doesn't appear to be paying attention as the lampist completes his precise work. George says, looking out the windows at the Sound.

"You're lucky you didn't come by ship. The Sound is turning ugly."

"Yes, this is an easy lighthouse, what with it being so close to town," the lampist responds, gathering up his tools, wrapping each in its special cloth, and placing them in the heavy black bag.

"Have you visited many lighthouses?" Stella inquires.

"Yes, that's my job. I travel from one to the other as weather permits."

"Where's home for you?" asks George.

"My family is in Boston. I have to say as much as traveling is hard, it can be nice to get away."

"Hm," George grunts.

Mr. McCann enjoys the dinner they share—salted fish, potatoes, and carrots.

"From our garden," Lucy tells him.

"You folks have it real nice here compared to most of the wickies I see."

George, never comfortable acknowledging the ease in his life, mumbles, and retreats to the outhouse. Caroline responds, "Yes, the Lord does provide. We are blessed, and I thank you, Mr. McCann, for reminding us."

❀

In March, Stella bundles up and heads out in the dory, taking advantage of a clear, calm day. Even though the water is deadly cold, Stella insists on taking the dory out regularly. Caroline and Lu assure Stella that she is more robust than most women, but Stella insists she must practice to stay strong. Bundled up against the chill, she climbs the stairs down to the beach. Once past the break, Stella sees a ship coming. She recognizes the *S.S. Mistletoe*, the steamer that brings their supplies. Stella rows to shore to alert her family that the government workers are here.

"Why are they back?" She wonders. "They just had an inspection last month."

Stella rushes up the 106 steps to the top of the bluff, stops, and scans the Sound with her binoculars to see the ship's cargo. She sees large barrels onboard. The sailors wrap each one in a net then lower it into a dory.

"Oh, the oil," she says to herself. "They must be bringing kerosene for the new lantern." Stella races to the cottage and alerts Lu and Caroline, making bread.

Caroline says, "You two go out to the cold storage and bring in potatoes, cabbage, and salted fish. We'll make a meal for the men. I'll go wake Da."

By the time the first barrels arrive onshore, George is waiting at the top of the bluff with the horse and wagon. He lowers the block and tackle rigging, and the men secure the first barrel to hoist up the 60-foot cliff. It's heavy work, and they need to be careful not to allow the barrels to bang into the side of the sharp rocks and break, spilling the precious oil.

102

They load a barrel into the back of the wagon, and George drives it to the oil house with a couple of the men in back who unload it.

While working with Lu and Caroline in the kitchen, Stella keeps looking out the front window. She longs to be outside, helping the men. She goes outside and paces the front porch, reporting the progress as each of the 50-gallon barrels of oil is hoisted over the bluff, loaded onto the wagon, then unloaded and stored in the oil house.

Caroline sends Stella out to invite the men in for a hot meal. Stella heads to the top of the bluff and sees that all that's left is their usual crate of dry goods. She watches as they hoist the large container up the side of the cliff, grateful for the calm wind. She asks the men to bring the crate to the cottage's front porch, where the family will open it later, but now they were welcome to join them for a mid-day repast.

The Captain and crew come inside. Even the ship's cook joins them and enjoys the meal without the roll of the sea. The men exchange stories of their adventures making deliveries to other lighthouses along the shores of Long Island. Their next stop is Plum Island Lighthouse in the roiling plum gut, where unloading supplies will be far more challenging than at Hortons Point.

As the little group relaxes in the warmth, George and Stella notice a change outside. They go out and see that as calm as the sea was earlier, it's now wild with the wind whipping up 10-foot swells. Stella and the men gather under the porch's shelter and watch as a pounding rain rolls in off the Sound. They unpack the crate on the porch, making a human chain handing each box from one to another and stacking them inside. They discuss their good luck that they finished the delivery before the storm hit. They will not return to the ship tonight.

Caroline wonders how long the men will need to be housed but is glad for the extra space on the other side of their quarters. She asks Lu to start a fire in the hearth on the other side of the house. Stella and George retreat to the tower to kindle the lantern and warn away any ships that might get caught in the storm.

Heavy wind and rain continue for several days preventing the men from returning to their ship. The men take advantage of the quiet time on land, reading books from the lighthouse's library, writing letters to loved ones, and helping with the daily tasks needed to maintain the lantern and assist with meal prep and clean up. The ship's cook proves himself a very able kitchen helper, and Caroline, in particular, appreciates his contributions as he's up each morning before dawn and has hot coffee and porridge waiting for all long before sunrise, as is his custom onboard ship. Though they cannot access any of the ship's stores, the cook, an experienced sailor, is accustomed to making do. He mixes in ample amounts of samp with the oats to extend the porridge. Fortunately, the hens are laying, so they have enough eggs, to which she adds potatoes and onions for hearty meals.

Stella spends most of the time up in the tower, ensuring that the lantern stays lit. She sleeps in short snatches when George comes up to cover. Lu helps out in the kitchen. She enjoys the men's company though some are a little rough; for the most part, they are respectful of Caroline and the girls and grateful for the families' kind generosity.

On the 4th day, Stella spots a ship approaching. She alerts the Captain, who rallies the men and heads out to the beach. The winds have abated somewhat, so they row out to the *Mistletoe* and navigate to deeper water. The new boat comes closer to shore to unload the precious cargo. Stella goes out in the small dory, gets as close as she can safely maneuver, and observes the sailors lower the crate containing the new lantern. She feels like a mother hen, monitoring each step of their progress as they place it into the dory, then rows with some effort into shore. Perhaps, even more, hazardous than lowering it from the rocking ship is hoisting it up the 60-foot bluff. They prove expert at the task—securing it to the block—tackling rig and hoisting it up without mishap. George has the horse and wagon waiting, and he drives the horse to the tower, where the precious cargo is unloaded.

The sailors attend to the job at hand, taking the old lantern out and installing the new one while the weather holds. Two crewmen set up heavy ropes from the tower's outdoor trellis while two others go inside and detach the lantern. It takes all four men to lift the lantern and fasten it to the ropes lowering it to the ground. Then working quickly but with great care, they attach the lines to the new lantern and hoist it up and into the tower. The Prince family looks up in awe as the new lantern is raised.

Once installed, the lampist, Mr. McCann, demonstrates the inner workings of the new lantern. Stella is excited to see how bright the new light burns though the smell it emits is a bit disconcerting. He warns George with a glance at Stella to be sure to log the amount of kerosene they use each night. Meanwhile, the men load the old lantern onto the wagon. They drive the horse to the edge of the bluff, unload, and lower it to the beach, onto the dory, and then back to the boat where it's hoisted on deck for the return voyage.

CHAPTER 9

Spring 1883

Five and Forty More! -
shout out by the crew when the last piece
of blubber is swung onboard.

While Stella works at mastering the new lantern, Lu is far more excited about an invitation they received to celebrate Captain and Mrs. Goldsmith's 50th Wedding Anniversary. Lu is eager to go into town and purchase fabric to make a new dress for this special occasion, but they don't get to the store because of the extra work of housing the sailors. Lu is crestfallen at the thought of going in the same dress she wears to Services on Sunday. Ma reminds her that this is a celebration of the Goldsmiths' long marriage and good health and that they are blessed to have warm serviceable clothing to wear; Lu resigns herself to being a 'plain Jane' once again.

The morning of March 8th is bright with warm sunshine and a hint of spring. Once the morning chores are complete, the girls set about fixing their hair, Lu decides that now that Stella is 15 and she is 14, they are old enough to do away with the girlish braids they wore all their lives, and each assists the other to pull back their hair into a small bun at the nape of their neck. Ma sighs when she sees the full effect with their hair pulled back.

Da assisting Lu and Stella into the back of the wagon remarks, "These two sure are growing up, Mrs. P." Caroline, already seated in the front, looks back and dabs at an unexpected tear. Stella, observing her mother's uncharacteristic display of emotion, pokes Lu. Lu stands and rubs Caroline's shoulder.

"Don't worry, Ma, Stella, and I will be around for a few more years. I'm not going to marry until I'm 18."

"18!" Stella exclaims, "Why ever would you want to get married? And, so young?"

"Don't you want to get married?" Lu asks.

"Hmm, I'm not sure I do, but if I do, it won't be for a long, long time. I want to stay at Hortons Point forever. Don't you?" Stella asks Lu.

Lu shakes her head from side to side, looks up at Stella with kindness, and says, "Maybe the lighthouse is enough for you, but I want a home of my own and a family too." As they ride to the party, the girls wonder how they could be so close and have such different plans for their lives.

At Chary Ann's, they are excited to see friends and family. Captain and Mrs. Goldsmith sit on either side of the hearth and receive guests with warm hospitality. They are surprised at the sheer number of people here to help them celebrate, but a 50th Wedding Anniversary is a rare event, so folks wish to honor the much-loved couple. Stella and Lu find Belle. She escorts them into the dining room, where they behold the most incredible sights. There are delicacies of every type displayed on trays around the table. In the center sits a three-tier-golden wedding cake surrounded by a ring of fifty-lit gold taper candles.

Lu gasps and says, "Look!" Pointing to the large vases of flowers around the perimeter of the room, "even roses! How could there be such a thing? In March!" The girls stare in wonder as they approach and sniff their gentle scent.

The old couple is delighted to welcome their many guests. Their biggest surprise is the arrival of their youngest daughter, Elizabeth, who's traveled from her home out west and brought along her 4-year old daughter Frances, named for her grandmother. Many happy tears flow over this unexpected reunion.

Daniel, the youngest son, stands and calls for quiet. He welcomes everyone, and tears flow as each of the Goldsmiths' children speak lovingly of their parents. Even their grandchildren recite a short poem, and one of the men who served under the Captain at sea tells a story of the Captain's bravery and leadership. Caroline searches the crowd for George thinking he should say something, but she doesn't see him. She suspects he is outside passing a jug of local brew, much to her dismay. Chary Ann invites Caroline, Stella, and Lu to share something about their time together at Hortons Point. Caroline's eyes widen with fear at addressing such a large group.

Caroline hesitates, but Lu steps up, albeit holding onto Stella and Belle's hands, and says, "We loved coming home from school to Mrs. Goldsmith. She is the best baker in the world!" Another round of applause follows the enthusiastic accolade.

Once the speeches are over, the guests line up to partake of the beautiful assortment of delicious food. Belle, Lu, and Stella line up and take a little bit from each dish to sample a taste. Caroline escapes into the kitchen to help replenish as the crowd devours one platter after the next. A hush falls as the Captain and Mrs. Goldsmith stand to cut the cake. The Captain thanks everyone for joining them on this special day and speaks of the good fortune they share and his pleasure that they are so long-lived and surrounded by their children, grandchildren, friends, and neighbors.

Caroline goes outside to find George as it's getting late, and they need to get back to the lighthouse before dusk. She locates him by the barn, talking with the other men, and asks him to get the wagon so they can go. Uncharacteristically, Stella hangs back more eager to taste the golden cake than return to the light. She and Lu share a small piece, hug Belle, the Captain, and Mrs. Goldsmith and make a hasty retreat. Caroline is already on the wagon by the time they get outside, and Da is pacing around waiting for them. Belle follows them out, promising to get together with them soon.

As the Prince family pulls away, they listen to the sounds of the fiddlers' music and guests bidding farewell. The joyful noise follows them, reverberating in their heads long after they can hear it, too soon replaced by the rhythmic clip-clop of Jenny's hooves on the hard-packed mud of the dirt road. They arrive at the lighthouse just as dusk is settling. Stella jumps down as soon as Da stops and goes straight up to light the lantern while Caroline and Lu start the fire. When Stella is sure the lantern's bright light is beaming, she returns to the parlor

Joining her mother and Lu, the three women sit up late, talking about the party by the glow of the fire. They exclaim over each unique item: the beautiful flowers, delicious food, and even a cake with fifty tall gold candles! They never saw such an extravagant display. Ma tells the girls that the Captain's former first mate brought the roses from South America.

They reminisce about the many years they shared at Hortons Point with the pleasant old couple, how stern the Captain could be but also the fun they shared learning to bake with Mrs. Goldsmith. Once again, Caroline tells them the story of how Captain Goldsmith rescued three-year-old Stella from certain peril at the bluff.

CHAPTER 10

Summer 1884

Cooling down-
said of a whaler when her fires are dying.

As the coal fire burns down, a chill settles over the room prompting Caroline and Lu to head up to bed while Stella returns to the tower and checks the lantern. She retreats next to the stove in the watch room, then journals about this special day and their joy in partaking in such a memorable event.

The Prince family grows comfortable in their routine, with Stella and Lu alternating the first shift at the light and Da taking the second shift. When Da goes away on fishing trips, the girls take over. Caroline worries that the girls are not getting proper rest but knows there is no stopping George from his pursuits, and he does bring back what he catches, which supplements their provisions. The 4th of July is its typical festive celebration with family, friends, and neighbors. For the first time, Captain and Mrs. Goldsmith do not attend. Chary Ann reports that the Captain's health has deteriorated since the spring, and he is no longer up to the long wagon ride from Cutchogue to Hortons Point. Alarmed by this news, Caroline promises to visit soon, but the busy summer season leaves her unable to keep that promise.

Whenever she can get away, Stella practices rowing the dory. One day she is startled when tall waves suddenly start rolling into the shore. She beaches the boat securing it to the post as the water pummels the rocky shoreline. She runs to the stairs and starts to climb up but stops as the stairs shake violently under her tightening grip. She fears climbing higher, so she stops and clings to the railing. The shaking lasts a few minutes, though it feels like an eternity to Stella as she struggles to hold on. Her only thought is to get up the bluff and check that the tower is secure.

As suddenly as it started, the shaking stopped though the waves continued crashing behind her.

She races up the stairs and runs to the lighthouse, calling, "Ma, Lu!."

Da calls down from the top of the tower, "We're up here." Stella climbs up the stairs and finds Da, Ma, and Lu examining the lantern for damage. The women embrace.

Tears run down Lu's face, and in a small, shocked voice, she says, "I guess that was an earthquake?"

"Sure was," said Da. "Don't happen much around here, though," he continues.

"I'm just glad we're all safe," Caroline says, hugging each of the girls again and then reaching out and including George in a rare show of affection.

"I don't think I've ever heard of such a thing," Stella says as they check each piece of the glass lens.

"Looks like there's no damage to report. Guess I'd better make a note in the *Keeper's Log*," George says.

"Da, perhaps you should send the lighthouse service a telegram? Or a letter?" Stella asks.

"Let's not go looking for trouble here, Stella. Everything's fine; just be glad for that," Da says.

Finally, Ma, Lu, Stella climbs down the two ladders and the circular staircase. Ma checks the bedrooms upstairs while Lu and Stella sit out on the front porch looking out at the still rough seas.

"Ma was worried about you being out in the boat."

"I was fine," Stella answers, trying to sound calmer than she feels.

"Maybe you shouldn't spend so much time out there by yourself."

"Aw, Lu, I need to stay strong in case we have to rescue someone. People's lives could depend on it."

"People don't expect you to save them, Stella. It's Da's job."

"What's Da's job?" Ma asks as she comes out the door to join them.

"To save people." Stella responds defensively, "that's part of a lighthouse keeper's job, and all of us here are the keepers. Not just Da. If they didn't expect us all to work, the Government wouldn't have let go of Daniel."

"I guess," Lu says, "But there are a lot of other things that we do to help."

"That's true, Lu. Every job at the lighthouse is valuable," Ma adds.

They hear a wagon approaching and see Mr. Tillinghast and Belle seated in the front.

"You folks ok?" he asks as they pull the horse to a stop in front of the porch.

"Why, Mr. Tillinghast, isn't it kind of you to come," Ma greets them. Lu jumps up and helps Belle down, hugging her once she's on the ground. Da comes out of the cottage,

"We're all fine here; you didn't need to check."

"That was something. I can't think of when I felt anything like that around here before. Can you?" Mr. Tillinghast asks.

"Nope," George says, "and hope we don't see another one anytime soon."

Stella nods and reports how she first noticed that the waves got rougher and were splashing over the sides of the dory; she rowed to shore and tied the boat.

"Oh," she says, "I should go check that the boat is still secure." Stella and Belle rush to the side of the bluff and peer over. The little dory is tied but still bouncing in the rough waves.

"Wow," Belle exclaims. "That must have been distressing," Stella says, "Mostly, I was worried about the light."

"Oh, Stella, is that all you ever think about?" Belle asks.

"No, but it is . . . important!" Belle takes Stella's hand and leads her back to the porch.

"I'm just glad you're safe."

❀

An earthquake of a different sort rocks the Prince family a few days after the geological one; Captain Goldsmith died on August 16, 1884. While working in the store that day, the news of Captain Goldsmith's death reaches Uncle Henry.

"I'd better let George and Caroline know."

Jennie says, "Why don't you take the children with you for the ride? I'm sure they'd enjoy an outing."

Twelve-year-old Anna and nine-year-old Frederick are happy to go to the beach. They change into their bathing costumes while Jennie changes two-year-old Edith. Jennie stays back at the store in case she's needed to help out in Henry's absence, but he knows she will retreat to the back porch and spend the afternoon reclining on the lounge.

He settles little Edith securely into the back of the wagon and instructs Frederick and Anna to keep a good hold on her, "The roads are bumpy," he cautions the children. They agree to be careful, but Anna and Frederick soon quarrel, leaving Edith in tears. Henry pulls over and reminds the children that they promised to cooperate. He readjusts everyone's positions, ensuring all are secure, then climbs back into the wagon to begin again.

Caroline and the girls are sitting on the front porch when Henry arrives. Lu is excited when she sees the children are with him. Henry lifts them out of the wagon. The children are all talking at once, excited to go down to the beach. Caroline exchanges a questioning look at Henry, and he asks, "Maybe Stella and Lu can take the children for a walk?"

Frederick asks, "Can we go up in the tower?"

Knowing that Da is in the middle of polishing the brass, Lu says, "This isn't a good time to go up. We can take them to the beach and see what we can collect." Lu, sensing the adults' need to talk, continues, "Come on, Edith, I'll take your hand, and Anna, you take the other, and we'll swing you to the stairs." The girls start running, with Edith giggling between them. Stella and Frederick follow close behind.

Caroline offers Henry a drink, but he says, "Let's just sit for a moment. I've provisions in the basket I'll bring down for them after we speak."

"What is it, Henry? You don't usually come out here in the middle of the day."

"I have sad news, Caroline. Captain Goldsmith died this morning."

"Oh my," Caroline gasps; at a loss for words, she clutches her middle with her arms then reaches for one of the rockers to sit and steady herself. After a moment, she says, "How is Mrs. Goldsmith taking it?"

"As well as can be expected, I guess. He did live a long and productive life."

"He looked well when we last saw them."

"How old was he?" George asks, emerging from the cottage and acknowledging Henry with a nod.

"He was 80."

"Phew," George says with a soft whistle through his teeth. "That is a long life."

"The girls, I need to tell the girls," Caroline says with concern.

"Guess we'll have to go and pay our respects. I have to finish the light." George says, turning to go back into the tower. Caroline turns away from Henry's gaze, embarrassed by George's abruptness.

Henry stands and says, "I'll bring the basket to the children. The beach can be a dangerous place for little ones."

"You don't have to worry about that, Henry. Stella and Lu are quite proficient swimmers and very good with little ones. Lu misses having baby Martha around."

"Hmm, you've given me an idea Caroline. Do you think Lu would want to come back with me tonight? You and Stella are welcome too, of course. I just thought maybe she could lend a hand at Chary Ann's. I'm sure they will have many callers over the next few days."

"I expect Lu will be more than willing to help out." Caroline says, "But, Henry, please don't say anything to the girls until I can speak with them."

"Of course, Caroline." Henry gathers the large picnic basket from the back of the wagon.

At the top of the bluff, Henry sees Frederick in the dory with Stella instructing him on proper rowing technique.

Frederick notices Henry and calls, "Da, can Stella and I go out in the boat?"

Henry looks over the Sound, which is calm today, and says, "If it's alright with cousin Stella."

Lu yells up, laughter ringing in her voice, Not much Stella would rather do."

"Stella, are you ok with taking him out?"

"I'm happy, too!" she calls back. Stella and Frederick push the dory into the shallow water. Then he climbs over the side. Stella gives it a big push and hops in behind him. Henry is more than a little impressed at Stella's strength, maneuvering the little dory through the rocks that jut out along the shoreline and out past the break. She turns the oars over to Frederick, who struggles to pull them through the water.

Lu is entertaining Edith while Anna runs along the beach, picking up shells and rocks then bringing them back for Lu and Edith to admire. Henry is pleased to see all three of his children so well-tended and happy in their separate pursuits. Caroline joins him and sets out the blanket above the high tide line. As Henry walks along the beach with Edith and Anna, Caroline asks, "Lu, could you give me a hand? Lu," Caroline continues, the weight of what she's about to say settling about them. "Uncle Henry didn't bring the children out here on a lark. He wanted to tell us, Captain Goldsmith died." Tears well up in Lu's warm brown eyes, and she reaches for her mother.

"That's so sad, Ma," Lu whispers.

"How are Mrs. Goldsmith and Daniel and Martha? Oh, and baby Martha?"

"I don't think baby Martha understands. And Mrs. Goldsmith? I expect she knew the Captain's time was coming. But still, it's going to be hard on her. Uncle Henry suggested he take you to the Goldsmiths to help out?"

"Me?" Lu asks, "What could I do?"

"There will be people stopping in to pay their respects, and Chary Ann might need some help around the house and in the kitchen. Not to mention baby Martha could use some looking after with her parents caught up in the loss."

"Of course, I'll go if I can help."

"I'll speak with Stella," Caroline continues, "but I expect she'll want to stay here tonight. We'll go tomorrow and pay our respects."

Stella rows back, with an exhausted Frederick sitting at the bottom of the boat, looking on in awe of her strength and skill. Once the dory is tied, he climbs out and throws himself down on the blanket next to his father.

Henry looks over at Caroline and the girls and says, by way of explanation, "He's a bit dramatic. Takes after his Ma, I expect," he continues in an unguarded moment. They drink thirstily then quiet down while they eat. Caroline takes advantage of the children's distraction to take Stella aside and tell her about the death. Stella is surprised and saddened at the news. She agrees to help Caroline prepare a dish to bring tomorrow as long as they're back to tend the light.

Lu packs and loads her satchel into the back of the wagon. She climbs up, and Henry passes each of the children to her waiting arms. Henry feels far more secure on the trip home with Lu riding in the back, keeping the children entertained and safe. As the wagon pulls away, George turns to Caroline and snarls,

"Weren't you the cozy little group down on the beach."

"George, don't be ridiculous," Caroline responds to the implied criticism. He follows her into the kitchen, where he continues to rant. Stella retreats to the tower to prepare the lantern and escape her fathers' tirade.

George is not happy that Lu went with Henry.

"What if we need her here?"

"You already have Stella," Caroline says, "Why would you need Lu too?"

"If I get sick tonight, then Stella will have to stay up with the light all night." Frustrated by George's impertinence and the sad news. Caroline says, "Maybe you better not get sick." She rushes outside and plops down in the rocker, hoping the breeze off the sound will help settle her thoughts on this sad day.

Once she lights the lantern, Stella joins her mother on the porch.

"Did Da go up to sleep?" she asks.

"He better!" Stella stares at her mother in the growing darkness, wondering where she's found this new fierceness. Stella rests her hand on Caroline's arm, recalling the day's news, "We had many good times."

"Yes, they were like family. We will include them in our prayers."

"I always do, Ma." The two women sit and rock, drawing comfort in their shared silence as the moon casts a soft glow across the calm waters of the Sound.

Captain Goldsmith is laid out in Chary Ann's parlor. Folks come from all over to pay their respects to the widow and their children. Lu is a tremendous help to the Goldsmiths throughout the difficult time, and Henry notices how wonderful she is with children. After the burial, Henry approaches Caroline and George with a new request. He asks if Lu would stay with him and his family for the last two weeks of the summer. His children are bored and cross with each other, and he thinks Lu might help out while the Nanny is away.

George shakes his head no and mutters, annoyed by the request until Henry continues, "Of course, I will pay her for her time."

Caroline, embarrassed, says, "No, Henry, that won't be necessary. I'm sure Lu would love to help out."

George scowling at Caroline, barks, "It's up to the girl, but no reason she shouldn't get paid. Stella will have to pick up her load at the lighthouse; if she's gonna work, she should have something to show for it."

George stalks off, and Henry turns to Caroline and says, "Is it alright if I ask her?"

"Of course."

Henry approaches Lu, entertaining a small group of children, and takes her aside.

"Aunt Jennie and I were wondering if you'd like to come and help with the children. Just till Edith's nanny gets back. Of course, I will pay you for your work." Lu gasps with surprise and looks up, wide-eyed.

Frederick comes over, grabs Lu's hand, and says, "Come on . . . we're waiting for you."

Lu laughs and says, "You go start. I'll be right there."

Then turning to Henry, she continues, "I'd love to, but I'd have to ask Ma and Da."

"I did," Henry replies, "They're fine with it."

"Really?" Lu asks.

"Your Da is ok with it as long as Stella fills in for you. Maybe you should speak to her?"

Lu smiles and responds, "Oh, she'll be fine."

Stella noticing what appears to be a serious discussion comes over to investigate.

"Fine? About what?"

Lu pulls Stella aside and says, "Uncle Henry asked me to stay and help with the children."

Stella replies, "You said no, of course."

"Stella, it's just until Edith's nanny returns. Just for a few weeks, and he's going to pay me!"

"So you want to do this?" Stella asks incredulously.

"Yes, Stella, I do. I know you're worried about the light, but you can do it yourself, and I'll make it up to you when I come back. I promise."

"Ok, if you want to, but what about Ma and Da?"

"Uncle Henry already asked them both, and they're fine." Lu returns to the impatient children and quiets them. Stella stands rooted to the spot wondering, "How is it that Lu will have a real job and Stella, the older sister won't!" She struggles to fight off the unusual feeling of jealousy at her sister's good fortune.

Stella finds Ma in the kitchen and whispers, "Da is fine?"

"What are you talking about, Stella?"

"Lu staying at Uncle Henry's?" Caroline replies,

"I wouldn't say fine, but since Henry is going to pay her, he couldn't very well say no. But Stella, perhaps we should have discussed this with you? You'll have to do her work at the lighthouse."

"I guess it's alright," Stella says.

After cleaning up, Caroline and Stella look for George to get back. As they work their way through the crowd, they make heartfelt goodbyes to each of the Goldsmith children and, of course, a special hug for Mrs. Goldsmith. They go outside and spot George behind the barn imbibing with a group of men.

"George," Caroline calls from the corner, just out of sight.

"Uh-oh," one of the men yells and taunts in a childlike sing-song voice, "Somebody's in trouble." Caroline shakes her head in disgust, no better than a group of children. Worse! She thinks at least children will learn proper behavior. This group is beyond learning. With a sheepish smile, George comes around. Slurring his words, he asks, "What is it, Mrs. P?"

"It's time we get back."

"Already?"

"Yes, it'll be dark before we get there if we don't leave now."

"But Stella can take care of the light," George answers.

"Stella is with us. We need to get back," Caroline scolds. George raises his shoulders in a careless shrug and heads inside the barn. Caroline joins Stella and Lu, hugging like they're parting for life rather than a few days.

"Is Da getting Jenny?" asks Lu.

"Yes. Now Lu, please let us know if you need anything during your stay." She gestures for the girls to follow her off the porch, and out of carshot, she continues, "I think the children are used to being catered to, so you may have your hands full and don't let Aunt Jennie take advantage," this last part whispered into Lu's ear.

Lu hugs Ma and says, "I'll miss you all, and I will take care."

Stella trying to hide her feeling of abandonment says, "Now we can write. You haven't kept up with your journal. You must send us a letter every day."

"I'll try," Lu says evasively, "I don't know how much time I'll have."

Stella looks towards the barn. Since there is no sign of George, she says, "I'll check on Da."

Entering the dark barn, she sees her father struggling to tighten the harness. One of the other men offers to help, but he gruffly responds, "I can harness my own damn horse. Why would I need your help?" Stella steps forward with purpose but cautiously approaches her father, who is still struggling.

"Oh, Da, is that buckle caught again? Sometimes it sticks. Let me see if I can do it. Smaller hands can work the leather through easier." George steps away, and Stella tightens the harness on the horse. George climbs into the front, and Stella rushes off to get out of the way as he whips the horse into motion.

"You alright?" asks the man who tried to assist George.

"Yeah, I'm fine."

"I hope you don't have far to go. I'm not sure he'll make it."

"No, it's not far," Stella responds, head down with embarrassment as she rushes out.

Da pulls up, and Caroline climbs into the front of the carriage with Lu's assistance. While Stella gets into the back, Da takes off without so much as a wave to anyone. Jenny takes off at a quick clip, but as they approach the North Road, the wagon slows to a standstill. Stella turns and kneels, holding onto the back of the seat to see what's wrong. Just as she positions herself against the wagon's backboard, George slumps over towards Caroline. It takes both women to keep him from falling off, but eventually, they wrestle a half-awake George to the back of the carriage, where he passes out.

"Now, what are we going to do?" asks Caroline.

"I can drive, Ma. Don't worry." Assures Stella. Caroline and Stella climb back into the front of the wagon, gathering their cumbersome skirts.

"I sure do wish women could wear trousers," Stella says when she's settled behind the horse. Stella shakes the reins as Caroline calls out, "Go, girl!" The horse hesitates as if questioning the change of driver. It takes a click of their tongues and a hard shake on the reins before the horse begins to move down the North Road.

Smiling, Stella looks over at Caroline and says, "Boy, you got that 'go girl' thing down, Ma."

"I've been riding in wagons my whole life. I expect I could drive one if there were a need."

"I expect you could," she responds, nodding her head.

Feeling confident, Stella says, "Isn't it odd that Da named the horse Jenny just like Aunt Jennie?"

"I'm not sure odd explains that. Your father has a long history of resentment towards Henry. His family always seemed to have more and do better, and I don't know? Maybe that's why? Kind of your father's idea of a joke? Best we don't make anything of it."

As they approach the lighthouse, dusk is settling, and Stella looks to her mother, unsure whether to get the horse in the barn or see to the light?

"Stella, you go on up to kindle the beacon. I'll see to the horse and Da."

"Are you sure?" Stella can't remember Caroline ever tending to the horse and doubts Da will be of any use. But the light needs to be kindled now. Caroline nods her assent.

Stella handles the light for the night, fighting off sleep in the watch room. Before dawn, she hears George come in and go up to bed. She wonders if he'll come back to relieve her, but he falls into bed next to Caroline and goes back to sleep. His heavy footfall on the stairs wakes Caroline. He reeks of alcohol. When he starts to snore, Caroline goes to the girls' room and climbs into Lu's bed, hoping to sleep till first light as she expects Stella will be exhausted, having taken the watch all night. She will have to tend to the animals as well as the household responsibilities as experience tells her George will not be of any use as he recovers from his overindulgence.

After the night watch, Stella sleeps most of the next day. She finally comes down, roused by the heat. She sits out on the front porch with Caroline enjoying the view and the soft breeze off the Sound while they husk the corn Caroline picked that morning. Stella loves corn on the cob, and they will have several ears tonight. Caroline picked all that was ripe to make and store samp. After husking, she'll remove the kernels and place them in baskets in the sun to dry. Then crack them. Caroline knows samp stores well and will come in handy during the long winter months to extend their food supply.

The two women discuss their sadness over the loss of the Captain and their concerns for Mrs. Goldsmith.

"Poor Chary Ann, what with this heat and a houseful of people to feed." George comes round the side of the cottage.

"It's about time you showed your face," he says to Stella. Stella has all she can do to keep from snapping back, but she holds her tongue.

Good as her word, Lu writes each day telling of the antics of the Prince cousins. She is a bit perplexed at the abundance of toys and clothes the children have, unimaginable compared to the simple manner in which she and Stella grew up. The children ask Uncle Henry to visit Hortons Point on Sunday after church. Henry thinks it's a capital idea, and even Aunt Jennie, who has perked up a bit with Lu seeing to the children, agrees to a beach outing at the lighthouse. Frederick can't stop talking about rowing with Cousin Stella. Tired of Frederick's boasting, Anna insists she wants to learn to row. Henry attempts to dissuade the girl, but Jennie puts a stop to it, declaring,

"Rowing is not ladylike, and no daughter of mine will partake in such a pursuit." Anna collapses in tears, and Lu is upset to learn how others may perceive her sister's pursuit. Loyalty pulls her to want to defend her sister, but she holds her tongue and turns her focus to comforting the girl as she settles the excited children down for the night.

When Lu and Stella first see each other on the way into Sunday service, they lock into a tight embrace and only let go when they overhear Aunt Jennie, in a stage whisper, say to Caroline,

"Is that quite usual? She's only been away a few days?"

"The girls are very close, and it's the first time they've been apart," Caroline answers straining to contain her annoyance.

"They better get used to it. They're growing up. They can't live at the lighthouse for the rest of their lives." Stella turns wide-eyed at Aunt Jennie but holds her tongue while Lu pulls her away, saving them from further censure.

After Sunday services, they join Henry's family on the ride back to the lighthouse. Thoughts of the future weigh on Stella. No Lu? No lighthouse? Why can't they live here for their whole lives? Stella has no wish to marry and can think of no higher calling than to serve as a lighthouse keeper like her hero Ida Lewis. However, Aunt Jennie's comments have sent Lu's thoughts on a whole other track. Of course, she loves her mother and sister, but Lu does not wish to live at the lighthouse all her life. She longs to meet other young people, have fun, fall in love, marry, and have her own family. Of course, she will always love Stella and Ma, but she does not wish to spend her life in the cold and damp keeper's quarters tied to the unrelenting demands of the beacon.

CHAPTER II

Autumn 1885—Summer 1887

Plum-Pudding Voyage -
a short leisurely tour, a mere picnic

Belle comes by to tell Stella and Lu there's going to be a dance. Lu is thrilled at the chance to have fun with people their age. She uses the money she earned looking after her Prince cousins and buys deep green fabric to make a new dress for the event. While she and Caroline are not seamstresses, she knows that Chary Ann and Mrs. Goldsmith will help her.

On the other hand, Stella is not excited at the prospect of attending a dance. She is always apprehensive about being away from the light at night and leaving its operation to Da. Ma assures Stella they can manage for one night. Ma is happy to have the girls attend the event, but she checks with the Reverend the following Sunday to ensure it will be properly supervised. She learns that the Reverend and his wife will chaperone, so she teaches the girls a few dance steps that she remembers from her own youthful days in Greenport.

Lu asks Chary Ann for help sewing a new frock. She is glad to see that although Mrs. Goldsmith has slowed down in her advanced age, she is still quite lively of the mind and happy to explain how to measure and cut the fabric. Chary Ann's expert sewing skills help Lu assemble and fit the dress in time for the big night. Stella is content to wear one of Ma's old church dresses that they fix up with a bow at the neck, but when Lu comes down in her new dress, the family stops and inhales in unison.

"Why Lu," Ma begins, "You look lovely." The deep green fabric highlights Lu's dark eyes and accents her light brown hair.

Sighing, Stella says, "You look so grown up." Sixteen-year-old Lu smiles and twirls around the parlor, happy to be the center of attention.

Mr. Tillinghast picks up the girls. Burt and Henry jump down from the back of the wagon and help them climb up. The young people huddle together against the growing chill but feel awkward - no longer children but not quite adults. When they arrive, they are drawn inside by the music and greet old friends. They walk around the perimeter, watching the few couples already dancing. The girls gather together with some of their friends from school. Dan asks Lu to dance. She smiles bravely and heads out into the center of the room to join him in a gentle waltz.

Belle is approached by an older boy who bows and asks her to dance. She nods in assent and looks back at Stella, a mix of fear and excitement flashing across her face. Stella hangs back until Henry, one of the last two people left from their group, turns to Stella, bows, and offers his hand. Stella gasps, but looking over at the dancing couples, she nods, and they set off hand in hand to join the fun. When the music stops, Stella joins Belle, and they gossip with a few other girls from school.

One of the main topics is 15-year old Anna, who Belle agrees is far too young to even be at a dance, let alone dancing and flirting! The evening passes pleasantly for most though Stella is never able to relax. She goes outside several times and is reassured to see the lighthouse's beacon shining in the distance.

Lu enjoys dancing with several young men, but Edward Scott steals her heart. At just 18, Eddie is short and slightly built with flaming red hair. After several dances, Lu brings him over to meet Stella and Belle. He is quite talkative and regales the girls with stories of his experiences since coming to America.

He is the youngest of 13 from Ireland and arrived in New York last spring to stay with his mother's brother, who lives in Brooklyn. His uncle works for a jeweler and thought he would have work for the quick-witted boy to learn. While the jeweler appreciated the young man's work ethic, eagerness to learn, and polite manners, there wasn't enough work, but the jeweler suggested he head out east to establish himself. He even provided him with a small cache of jewelry to sell on commission.

Eddie took the Long Island Railroad east for parts unknown. Just three hours after leaving the bustle of Brooklyn, he arrived in sleepy Greenport with nothing but his small beat-up valise and some spare change. The familiar scent of saltwater propels him forward to the ticket booth to ask the agent for assistance. Eddie introduces himself and asks if he would be so kind as to direct him to a place where he could find lodging and work.

The ticket agent, who grew up in Greenport, sizing up the rather dapper young man, says, "You don't look like you know much about physical labor."

"I can't say I've done much work with my hands, but I'm not too proud to learn, and I'm a quick study."

"Hmm," the clerk looks him up and down, "How old are you? If I may ask?"

"I turned 18 in November. Me Mum and Dad sent me from Ireland to stay with my aunt and uncle in Brooklyn, but I couldn't find work, so my uncle's employer suggested I seek work at one of the tourist houses. I can cook, wait tables, and wash dishes. I'll give my employer an honest day's work for a fair wage and a place to sleep."

"Oh, I see," says the clerk. "I believe the Conways are looking for help. I think the wagon with supplies should be heading out. Ask at the dry goods store across the road."

"Thank you," Eddie says, tipping his cap as he walks out of the station.

He talks his way into a ride out to the Conway's Boarding House next to Hortons Point, promising to help unload when they arrive. Eddie whistles when he catches sight of the Long Island Sound from the bluff where the Inn is situated. The Conways, an older couple who just completed renovations take a chance and hire this newcomer, who comes with a letter of reference from a jeweler in Brooklyn. Eddie proves himself a hard worker and functions as a jack-of-all-trades throughout the summer season. The Conways rely on the energetic young man, and guests are charmed by his bright smile, flawless manners, and lilting Irish accent.

By the end of the dance, Eddie is smitten with young Lu and her with him. Stella and Belle are dismayed, and later at Belle's, they pummel Lu with questions:

"What can you be thinking? He's so small . . ." says Stella.

"And even worse," Belle joins in, "He's Irish! With red hair!"

"Isn't it lovely?" says Lu breathlessly, "Maybe we'll have red-haired babies." Both the girls gasp at her immodesty! Stella shakes her sister and admonishes, "Now Lu, be sensible. You just met him."

"I know," she exclaims, "but, but he's SO handsome." Stella and Belle exchange startled looks and burst out laughing. Lu looks over at them, hurt. "He is!" she gushes.

The next day Lu, lost in her private thoughts, lags behind Stella as they walk back to the lighthouse.

Stella turns around and addresses her, "Come on. We've got to get back. I'm sure there will be extra work with both of us away all night." But there's no hurrying Lu, so Stella walks on at her usual rapid pace leaving Lu behind.

When Lu gets to the cottage, Caroline asks, "So? Did you have fun?"

"Oh, Ma! I did!" Caroline turns from the dough she's kneading, surprised at Lu's tone.

Lu plops down onto the rocker by the fire and says, "Ma, I met a boy . . .

No! A man!" she exclaims.

"You did? Who is he? Do we know his family?"

"No," Lu answers, looking down as she continues, "He's Irish."

"Irish!" says Caroline. "How did he get here?"

"He told me he's the youngest of thirteen children back in Ireland. His Ma and Da sent him here to stay with his aunt and uncle in Brooklyn."

"Brooklyn?" Caroline repeats. "Why is he here? Why was he at the dance?"

"He works at the Conways."

"The Conways? Right next door?"

"Isn't that amazing? I think that just shows it's meant to be."

"What's meant to be?"

"Me and Eddie."

"So, his name is Eddie?"

"Yes, Edward Scott. And he's so handsome!" Lu exclaims as Stella comes into the room and says, "No, he isn't. He has red hair! And he's little!" She continues. "Not much taller than Lu."

"He is so taller than me. And why does that matter? He's so nice and polite. I love to listen to him talk."

Caroline says, "I guess that was a special dance, alright. Are we going to meet this young man?"

"I hope so," Lu says, and at the same time,

Stella exclaims, "I sure hope not!"

The girls, surprised by their contradictory statements, burst into laughter.

Later that day, Stella cleans the windows outside the tower and spots Eddie walking towards the lighthouse. There's no missing that red hair of his, she thinks.

When he gets close enough, he calls out to her, "Hi, be careful up there." Stella glances down at him and resumes her window washing.

Eddie calls up, "Mornin'. Is Lu around?" Stella points with her free hand toward the back of the cottage. Eddie shrugs and walks back towards the barn. Lu is mucking the stalls when Eddie comes in and, peering through the darkened space, says, "Hi!"

Startled by the unexpected visitor, Lu touches her hair only to spread dirt on her face.

Embarrassed, she whispers, "Hi."

"I hope it's alright; I just thought I'd come over and check out the lighthouse. I've never seen one up close before."

"I guess lots of people haven't. When I finish, I'll take you up to the top."

"Not sure your sister would approve that." He says with some trepidation.

"Oh Stella, she's just a grump sometimes," Lu answers, then feels a pang of guilt for being disloyal to her sister.

Chuckling, Eddie says, "I guess we all are sometimes."

The two young people fall into a routine of spending spare moments together. Eddie wins over Stella with his genuine interest in the lighthouse. He always pitches in when he comes and proves himself a willing student and a capable worker. When he leaves the North Fork to return to Brooklyn for November and December, Lu is crestfallen. During this time, they exchange daily letters nurturing their newfound love.

Eddie returns in January and endears himself to Caroline and Stella with his amiable personage. The toughest nut to crack is George, who has spent little time with the young man and appears unaware of his impact on the women in the family. Caroline finally speaks to George about Lu's fondness for Eddie. He is surprised that things have progressed so fast. George invites him on his early spring fishing trip, much to Caroline and Lu's consternation. Eddie, ever eager to please, agrees to go.

They set sail from Southold Town Beach east to Montauk Point.

Eddie can't help but admire the tall tower of Montauk Lighthouse as they pass. He assists as best he can, but seasickness prevents him from being much help. When night falls, the men's excessive drinking leaves him wondering about their very safety. He has seen enough of the troubles drinking can cause back home in Ireland as his own Da was one to knock back a few too many, but Eddie never took to the drink himself.

The next day they sail around Orient Point. They come across a large school of codfish and spend hours reeling them in - as fast as they cast, they catch. Finally exhausted by the sheer number of fish they catch, they continue onto Hortons Point to drop off their bounty. Eddie is relieved to be back on dry land and politely declines to continue on the voyage. Lu is happy that Eddie is back safely, but after a quick greeting, she and Caroline start salting the fish while Stella prepares the outdoor pit for smoking; George and his cousin sail off to continue fishing.

❖

By the spring of 1887, the young couple is well-established, and though Lu is only 18, she eagerly waits for Eddie to propose. They have discussed Eddie's many plans for the future. He wishes to open a jewelry store one day. On a delightful May evening, they walk into town with Caroline, who will stay with them at the cottage in Southold overnight. Lu and Eddie attend a play, *The Loan of a Lover*, put on by the Universalist Sewing Society. On their walk home, Eddie takes Lu's hand, pulls her over to stand under a gas streetlight, gets down on one knee, and says, "Lucy Prince, I wish for you to be my bride." Lu gasps as Eddie slips onto her finger a delicate, gold ring with a small forest green emerald flanked by two tiny diamonds. He says:

"It's the color of my native land, but from now on, my home will always be with you if you accept?"

Tears roll down Lu's cheek as she utters an enthusiastic, "Yes!"

The young couple embraces, then rushes home to share the news with Ma. Caroline is not surprised as Eddie, ever proper, had already asked her and George for Lu's hand in marriage. Caroline worries about how young Lu is though she is not much younger than when she married George. Caroline hopes her daughter will have a more comfortable and happier life than the one she has known with George and his 'sickness' as she thinks of his excessive reliance on alcohol.

Lu is apprehensive about telling Stella. She isn't sure how her sister will respond, but she expects Stella will come around in time. That night Lu finds Stella reading by firelight. Stella gestures with her chin at Lu's hand, noticing the shiny speck of light from her finger.

"What does this mean?" Stella asks.

"Eddie and I are betrothed."

"When are you going to marry?"

"In August."

"August? So soon?" Stella exclaims in horror.

Lu kneels at Stella's feet and implores, "Please be happy for me. You know I've loved Eddie since the first night we met, but we haven't rushed into anything. Eddie's been saving money to set himself up in business."

"What sort of business?" Stella asks.

"Jewelry, of course," Lu says. "You know what a good salesman he is. He sells out his jewelry every summer."

"So he'll still work out of Conways?" Stella asks.

"We don't think so; we're hoping Uncle Henry will provide him space at his store. We could live in Da's cottage on Prince Lane and be close to Eddie's work. Of course, Eddie will visit his clients to show them precious jewels in the privacy of their homes, but the Prince Dry Goods will serve as a spot for people to peruse some of his more casual wares and get to know Eddie." Lu explains their plan to Stella. Unfamiliar with the jewelry business, Stella eyes her warily, "Does Ma know about this plan?"

"Yes."

Stella looks up excited for the first time, "Why doesn't Eddie get the job as the assistant keeper? Here at Hortons Point!"

Lu frowns, "There is no assistant keeper position first of all, and he isn't well suited to that kind of work."

Disappointed, Stella responds, "I see."

Lu continues, knowing she is breaking her sister's heart, "I don't want to live here my whole life. We want to have our own home."

Lu stands and retreats out the front door. She's hurt by Stella's unenthusiastic response to her news. She believes in the correctness of their decision and assures herself that Stella will come around in time.

During the next several months, wedding planning is on Lu's mind. They speak with the Reverend and select August 11 as the date for the wedding. Eddie continues to work for the Conways and is excited about the successful summer he had—selling out of all of the jewelry his uncle's boss let him have on memorandum.

After church, Eddie approaches Henry to discuss renting space for a jewelry display in the store. Henry suggests they speak during the week rather than discuss business on the Lord's day. Eddie realizing his mistake makes such an eloquent apology to Henry that he is already won over. During the week, they meet and order a locked glass case and pick a spot near the front window to display the jewelry.

Lu ordered pale cream silk fabric for her wedding dress. Caroline gave her her wedding gown, and Charry Ann removed the lace from it and sewed it around the high neckline of Lu's dress. With Mrs. Goldsmith's exacting instructions, the Charry Ann fashions a fitted garment with fabric gathered down the front that balloons below the waist with a modest bussell in the back. The leg-o-mutton sleeves puff at the shoulder and tighten at the elbow. Lu's fittings require her to wear a whalebone corset. Although not accustomed to wearing one, she smiles despite the pinching of the garment, recalling the stories the Captain told them about whaling.

Caroline is pleased that the new couple agreed to move into the cottage on Prince Lane. Although it has fallen into disrepair over the years, Caroline is quite sure with George and Eddie's help; it will be habitable again before the wedding. George uncharacteristically jumps right in, putting his carpentry skills to good use, and repairs the front porch and roof. Eddie adds home repair to his already over-packed work schedule, replacing rotting floorboards, loose handrails, and sanding the wood doors that swelled in the dampness.

Once the carpentry work is finished, Caroline and Lu scrub the cottage with carbolic acid and water, wiping every nook and cranny. Eddie dragged the old furniture out onto the front lawn to beat out years of dust. He leaves it in the sunshine for a few hours while Caroline and Lu scrub the empty room. Caroline shares with Lu some memories of good times in this home when she and George were first married and where her daughters were born.

Next, they remove years of grime from the windows. The smell of vinegar reminds Lu of the many hours she and Stella spent cleaning the windows in the tower. She smiles with pride and surveys how the once ramshackle house now shines. The cottage is tiny with a one-room parlor/kitchen, a small nook next to the hearth that serves as a laundry/bathing/birthing room, and two loft bedrooms up the stationary ladder; Lu and Eddie will share the bigger bedroom in the front. Both women discuss the possibility of little ones someday sharing the smaller bedroom just as she and Stella did when they were babies before moving to the lighthouse.

With the heavy cleaning complete, the two women set up the bedroom with fresh linens and a colorful new wedding quilt contributed by Grandmother Merrill and her quilting bee. Lu looks forward to living in town next to the church where they worship. Many Prince family relatives and neighbors stop in and welcome the young couple.

❈

The heatwave of 1887 continues, and on Thursday, August 11, there is no reprieve. Lu is unaware of the heat as Caroline assists her dressing that morning. Caroline's eyes fill with tears when she sees her baby in her bridal gown. She helps Stella place a few wildflowers in her hair from those Lu herself had gathered that morning for the small bouquet she carries.

They set off for church by foot, the Tillinghasts joining the procession with Belle and Stella walking proudly on each side of Lu. A large crowd has gathered for the 10 a.m. service, with both the Prince and Merrill families represented. Eddie's aunt and uncle traveled from Brooklyn with his two brothers, who stand up for him. The Conways and a few of Eddie's friends fill his side of the church.

After the service, Lu and Eddie lead a procession of guests from the church to the lighthouse. Walking arm-in-arm, they greet everyone they encounter along the way. Friends and neighbors bring their special dishes to contribute to the feast. Eddie and Lu are overwhelmed by the outpouring of love and generosity shown by all who attend. Eddie's aunt and uncle even brought a three-tiered wedding cake from a bakery in Brooklyn, though how they'd managed to carry it all that way is the source of much speculation.

A few local musicians who Eddie met working at the Conways provide the entertainment. When they play an Irish jig Eddie, and his brothers get up and dance, much to the enjoyment of the crowd and the embarrassment of Lu. The festivities continue into the evening, and as the sun begins to set, Stella, ever aware of her responsibilities, excuses herself and goes up the tower to light the lantern. The crowd cheers as the light castes its brilliant white glow north across Long Island Sound, east to Orient, south to Peconic Bay, and west towards New York City. Eddie postulates that on this bright and beautiful night of celebration, the light might be seen all the way to Brooklyn and maybe even across the Atlantic to his birthplace in Ireland.

A lively discussion ensues regarding how far away the light can be seen on land and sea. Some have seen it from the train that runs along the Connecticut shoreline, while others say they've spotted it as far away as the eastern point of Fire Island. Stella knows that the light reaches Shinnecock Lighthouse to the south on a clear night. The beams from the two towers intermingle across the center of the Eastern end of Long Island.

As the guests begin to gather their children and prepare to head home, Eddie and Lu offer thanks for sharing in their special day. Lu hugs Stella then turns and folds into her mother's arms; steading herself, she turns to Eddie and takes his hand as thoughts of the evening ahead distract her from the well-wishers who crowd around to wave them off. They ride to their new home for the first time as man and wife in the back of Uncle Henry's carriage surrounded by the sleeping children.

Arriving at the cottage on Prince Lane, the young couple hops off and waves as the carriage pulls away. They walk inside hand in hand, and Lu's unease increases as she and Eddie are alone for the first time. Lu looks up into his eyes and draws courage from the kindness she sees there. She takes his hand, leading him towards the stairs to their bedroom to begin their new lives.

Eddie pulls back; surprising Lu, he says, "I, um, just need to go to the outhouse first?"

Lu laughs, "Of course, I should do that too."

Returning, Lu goes into the small bedroom, too self-conscious to undress in Eddie's presence. She puts on the new nightgown that Caroline had laid out for her. Chary Ann and Mrs. Goldsmith made Lu a soft cotton nightgown with white embroidery around the modest neckline and tiny buttons down the front. She is thankful for this surprise, made by loving hands; she tiptoes back into the bedroom where Eddie is already in bed under the covers, eyes closed. She approaches the bed and sits on the edge. He takes her hand into his warm one and strokes her arm, hoping to relax her but having the opposite effect.

She leans over to kiss him and is startled by loud singing coming up the street. Eddie jumps out of bed, hurries to the front window, and opens it. Smiling, he gestures to Lu to join him. She walks over, quite sure she recognizes the sound of at least one of the disorder singers gathered below. They see the shadows of a group of men who sound none too harmonious, attempting to serenade the young couple but clearly the worse for having imbibed on their way. Eddie laughs at the jokesters, but Lu is less than pleased by the loud intrusion. Despite Lu's discomfort, Eddie joins in singing the old Irish lullaby, "A Sailor Lad Wooed a Farmer's Daughter"—changing farmer to lighthouse keeper, much to the amusement of all.

"Ok, fellas, that's enough for tonight." The men laugh raucously then begin a rendition of "Goodnight Ladies" while retreating towards town.

"Ah, Lu," Eddie says with gentle affection, "they mean no harm. They're just wishin' us well on our weddin' night." Lu, reassured by Eddie's tender tone, heads back to their marriage bed and climbs in on her side, pulling up the quilt. Eddie feels her smiling in the dark as he joins her, and they explore each other in new and exciting ways learning the joys of a loving relationship.

CHAPTER 12

Autumn 1887—1888

High and Dry - a beached ship

S tella takes on Lu's role at the lighthouse. In reality, Lu hadn't done much of the lighthouse work during the past several months; and Stella doesn't mind being extra busy as it helps keep her mind off of how much she misses her sister. Ma, Stella, and Lu alternate sending letters each day, as promised, and every Sunday, they meet at church. After services, Lu and Eddie come back to the lighthouse and stay as late as they dare. George drives them home, allowing him time in town to be with his buddies. He doesn't return on Sunday nights, much to Caroline's embarrassment and dismay.

"On the Lord's day," she mutters, "does that man have no shame?" Stella does not comment on Da's behavior. She's just glad for a hot breakfast before she heads to bed, having tended the light all night and completed the morning set up.

A few weeks later, Stella sees the *S. S. Mistletoe* anchored offshore flying the flag of the inspector.

"Oh no!" bemoan Stella, the inspector is here, and George has not yet returned from his night out. Stella hurries down the stairs and alerts her mother. There was a quick tap at the front door and in walks, not Mr. Fanning as they expected, but the new inspector, Fred Rogers. He introduces himself to the two women. They offer him lemonade and biscuits and invite him to sit out on the porch to enjoy the cool breeze, but he insists on heading up to the tower to begin his inspection. Stella accompanies him and explains that George is in town getting supplies. Stretching the truth makes Stella uncomfortable, but if she were to admit that she has no idea where George is or when he might return, the consequences could be enormous. She provides Mr. Rogers with a detailed report on the daily upkeep at Hortons Point.

When they come down from the tower, Mr. Rogers asks to review the *Keepers' Log* in George's office. Stella and Caroline exchange quick frantic looks. Noting the sweat rolling down Mr. Rogers' face, Caroline suggests that since it's so warm inside, wouldn't he prefer to sit out on the front porch and have a refreshing drink of lemonade. She also mentions Lu's new husband is an Irishman, as she notices Mr. Roger's brogue.

Persuaded by the heat inside the cottage and the lure of a cooling drink, the inspector goes out on the front porch, and Caroline brings out the refreshments. The three sit together while Caroline distracts Mr. Rogers with questions about himself: where he's from and how long he's been working for the government.

They hear George pull up behind the cottage; Stella excuses herself, rushing around to the barn and informing George that there is a new inspector. Mr. Fanning retired, and the new inspector, Mr. Rogers, is waiting to review the *Keepers' Log*. George goes into his office through the back door to update the records. Stella settles Jenny down in the barn and returns to the front porch, where Ma tells Mr. Rogers about Lu's wedding.

George comes out and says, " I didn't realize anyone was here."

"I thought your daughter told you?" Mr. Rogers says dryly.

"Come into the office. Unless you'd rather sit out here in the breeze."

"No, that's quite alright. I just need to review the *Keepers' Log* and get back." The men go inside while Stella and Caroline sit and rock on the porch, hoping George has recovered from his night out.

George reviews the *Log* with Mr. Rogers answering his questions regarding recent occurrences, and surprisingly, Lu's wedding then walks him to the bluff and watches with a sigh of relief as he rows back to the ship. George mentions to Caroline his surprise that the new inspector asked about Lu's wedding.

"That is rather odd," Caroline responds. "Maybe his daughter is marrying soon?" she speculates.

The mystery is solved when a letter arrives from the Lighthouse Service informing George that his pay has been cut back from $650 per/year to $550, which he made before eliminating the Assistant Lighthouse Keeper position. George is incensed. After reading the letter, he comes out of his office and rages at a confused Caroline.

"What is it? What's happened?" she queries. He rushes outside to find the hidden jug he keeps for just such emergencies. After a few swigs, it dawns on him, "Lu's wedding. That's why 'the mick' was so interested in Lu's wedding. Now that there's one less mouth to feed, they can justify paying me less."

George storms back into the parlor, jug in hand, ignoring Caroline's prohibition about drinking.

"Caroline," he bellows as if she's not right in the room, "Look at this!"

Caroline takes the letter from George, reads it, and gasps, "Oh my!"

"That dirty son-of-Ireland," George roars.

Caroline gasps, "George! Why your own son-in-law is an Irishman, and you'll not find a harder-working lad."

"I'm not talking about Eddie. I'm talking about Fred Rogers!"

"I know but calling him names won't make it better."

"George," Caroline implores, "Don't go off in anger." Caroline worries about George's reaction. She frets over George's welfare if he allows himself to succumb to the lure of the drink but feels her anger rise at his inability to cope with life. Caroline goes down the stairs to the beach, hoping to calm herself with a brisk walk. She is confused to hear George calling. Caroline expected him to head off to town, but his actions are often unpredictable. She shields her eyes against the sun's glare, looks up, and sees him peering over the top of the bluff.

"What are you doin'?" George asks in a conciliatory tone.

"Just trying to cool off." He waits as she climbs up the steep stairs, gathering her long skirt and working her way up, gripping the handrail.

At the top, George helps her step off, and Caroline, a little out of breath, says, "I don't know how Stella does it?"

"Our Stella's not like other girls. Sometimes, I think she's more like a man."

"George! Don't say such things."

"Just think about it. She doesn't have any interest in boys or dresses like Lucy."

"I know, but she's just herself."

"Yeah, what's that?" he asks lewdly.

Caroline blushes and looks up at him. "Don't be talking sin about your daughter."

"Oh, Caroline. Do you have to bring God into everything? I'm just saying."

"I know what you're saying, and I don't want to hear it. You of all people should be grateful to Stella for all she does and how she takes over when you're not . . . not here."

"What's that supposed to mean? Are you saying I don't do my job?" Caroline looks him straight in the eye, and mustering her courage, says,

"You do when you're not sick. Without Stella, you wouldn't get to go off on your jaunts with your buddies."

"I feed this family when I hunt and fish."

"That's true, George, but what about Sunday nights when you drive Lu and Eddie home? You don't bring food back then."

Caroline steps up onto the porch and into the cottage. George shakes his head in disgust and storms around back, escaping from his wife's criticism.

❁

On Sunday, March 12, 1888, the Prince's enjoy an early spring day attending services at the Methodist Church. Lu is beginning to show, and Ma is uncomfortable with her being out in public. Lu can't bear the idea of being shut in already, so she and Eddie wait for George, Caroline, and Stella to arrive then walk to church together, hoping to be less conspicuous surrounded by her family. After the services, they walk back to Lu and Eddie's rather than ride out to Hortons Point. Caroline packed a hamper full of Lu's favorites, and Stella baked Mrs. Goldsmith's Stollen, a special treat that the whole family enjoys.

Following the afternoon meal, Da announces that they need to leave.

"A storm's brewing, and we'd best not get caught in it." Caroline and Stella make hasty goodbyes to Eddie and Lu. Then they walk out to the wagon George readied. He helps Caroline up on the seat at the front while Eddie assists Stella up onto the back. She sits on the small bench with hay bales propped high on both sides for her to lean on during the ride home. They arrive at the cottage just as the skies open up. The women rush inside. Stella heads up to the tower to kindle the beacon early as the darkened skies require an intense light for any mariners passing by.

When George comes in, Caroline says with a wistful sigh, "She's becoming quite the little homemaker, our Lu."

"Yup," George replies, preoccupied, "Mrs. P., don't forget to tend the fire. No telling what this weather will bring. Spring storms can be the worst, and I don't like the looks of this one. I'm going up; I am not feeling well," he says, heading to bed.

As darkness closes in, Caroline climbs up to the watch room, bringing coal for the stove and her heavy shawl. Stella is in the lantern room, watching the pounding surf below. Caroline pokes her head through the opening at the top of the ladder. Stella is startled by her mother's presence as the noise of the driving rain and wind drown out the sound of her ascending the stairs.

"Come on down and sit with me by the fire for a while," Caroline urges. Reluctantly, Stella climbs down the ladder and joins her mother.

Caroline says, "Da went to bed." Looking out, she adds, "At least it's rain and not snow. Though it is getting colder, I fear."

"I'm hoping it'll end by morning. It always seems worse in the dark." They both look up as a ferocious gust of wind rattles the windows.

Caroline is knitting a sweater for the new arrival.

"When will the baby come?" Stella asks.

Caroline looks up from her knitting says, "Surely, you can see Lu's changed appearance."

"I don't know," Stella says, embarrassed at her ignorance.

"I believe it should arrive late in the summer."

Stella nods and says wistfully, "This is what Lu always wanted."

"Yes, it is; she seems quite happy in her new life. Though I know you miss her."

"Don't you?" Stella asks.

"I do, but it's not a mother's place to keep her children with her all her life. I don't mean to offend. I am grateful that you are here and would not wish for Lu to leave, but it was always her dream, and at least she is only a short distance away. I do look forward to staying with her when her time comes."

Stella looks at her mother with surprise. She hadn't thought about what would happen once the baby arrived. Stella would like to stop time and have things stay the way they were, but of course, that isn't possible. Eddie is a trustworthy fellow even though he's an immigrant. He is hardworking, and he hasn't fallen victim to the drink like so many of his fellow Irishmen.

Yawning, Caroline says, "I'm sorry, dear, but I must go to bed."

"Of course, Ma. I'm quite accustomed to the solitude up here in the tower. I feel quite safe despite the storm. I'm glad that I can do my job keeping the light burning."

"This might be a good time for you to say a prayer for anyone out at sea; they will be in for a rough night," Caroline reminds her as she climbs down the ladder to the circular stairway below. As soon as Caroline leaves, Stella heads back up to the lantern room to make sure it is burning effi-ciently and searches for signs of ships on the Sound. Resigning herself that she cannot see through the driving rain, she returns to the watch room and prays as Ma suggested but soon dozes off in the warmth of the stove.

When George comes up to relieve Stella, the wind has picked up, assaulting the windows with icy bullets. Though glad for the relief, Stella is reluctant to leave her father in such severe weather. He urges her to sleep now in case she is needed later. She heads to bed, stopping to scoop up a hot brick for the bottom of her bed. She is grateful for the warmth it generates and falls into a deep sleep despite the roar of the wind outside.

At dawn, George wakes Caroline and asks her to get Stella up as they are in for a long day. The rain has turned to snow - a lot of snow! Caroline suggests that Stella be allowed to sleep late as she may be needed during the night, but their conversation wakes her, and she calls, "I'm up."

George goes downstairs, saying, "I'm going to tend the animals. 'Could use some hot coffee and porridge. Wouldn't expect any eggs with all the upset of the wind." Caroline layers on her woolen dress and heavy shawl.

She taps on the door to Stella's room and says, "Alright, if I come in?"

"Of course, Ma," Stella replies, still under the quilt.

"I'm going to leave this door open, so you'll get the last of the heat from our fire. I'm heading down now, but you take your time. Da says the rain has turned to snow, and the wind hasn't let up at all." Stella pulls up the warm quilt, dreading the day ahead.

Stella dozes on and off, but the morning chores are waiting: carrying fresh oil up to the lantern and wiping down the lens. Draping the quilt across her shoulders, she walks over to the front window and is surprised to find she can't see through the falling snow. Looking down at the porch roof, she is struck at how fast it accumulates. She guesses there are 12 inches already. Stella says a silent prayer that no ships are out at sea, for even with the beacon glowing at the top of the tower, the snow may be too thick for it to penetrate.

Downstairs, Stella spoons porridge into a bowl and pulls her chair close to the hearth. Ma sets a couple of loaves of bread to rise while George curls up in the corner on the small cot. Stella bundles up and heads out to fill the oil can and brings it up to the tower to keep the light burning throughout the day.

The Princes stoically make do with the small comfort of a hot fire as the storm rages on for three days. George tries to keep a path cleared from the cottage to the barn and the outhouse, but after the first day, he abandons the outhouse and reverts to using the chamber pot. Stella remains in the lantern room, searching in vain for any vessels that may run aground. Visibility is diminished even in the middle of the day due to the blinding snow. Distressed, Stella and George debate whether to go outside on the little wrought iron walkway to clear the windows. They decide it would be foolhardy in the icy conditions. Besides, any improvement would be short-lived as the driving snow continues to mount up.

They extinguish the lantern in the middle of each day, trim the wicks, and wipe off the soot that accumulates on the lenses. Then rekindle it hoping what small illumination might be visible will serve as a navigational aid to any ships out on the Sound. George thinks it futile as no vessel will survive in these winds. Nevertheless, Stella keeps the light burning.

Caroline worries how Lu and Eddie are faring in the storm. As the days drag on with no communication, her concerns grow. After three days, the snow and wind stop. George attempts to walk into town. He takes off late in the morning, bundled in his warmest clothes, but he returns a short time later, much to Caroline and Stella's surprise. Caroline helps him remove his wet clothing and drapes it over the fire while Stella runs upstairs and gets him dry ones. He sits by the fire, wrapped up for warmth, and reports that he couldn't make it even as far as the North Road as there are drifts as high as 15 feet. George feared climbing over them if they gave way, and he might fall in and suffocate. No matter what direction he tried to go, it was impassable, so he returned home to wait it out.

On Friday, Stella, wiping the tower windows, is surprised to spot Eddie's compact yet unmistakable form. His bright red hair peeks out of his cap as he trudges towards the lighthouse. Eddie walked up from the North Road, leaving behind the crew he'd joined the day before to help clear the railroad tracks. Wishing to reassure Lu, he walked up here to check on the family.

They welcome him like a returned warrior. Eddie removes his wet clothes and wraps up in a blanket. Stella hangs his clothes to dry while Caroline gets him bread and stew. He tells them that the trains have not run since Monday afternoon between mouthfuls. There has been no mail or newspapers all week. There are reports that passengers were stuck on the train to the west but have since dug themselves out. The Long Island railroad hired a crew from Southold to dig east and meet up with Greenport workers working their way west to get the train running again.

Laughing, Eddie reports that "the crew from Greenport dug west for

12 cents an hour, and the workers from Southold dug east for 20 cents an hour. When the two groups met, they cleared an 18-foot drift resulting in 30-foot tall walls on each side of the tracks. The men discovered the pay discrepancy, and a strike ensued. Railroad officials conceded, and all the men received 20 cents an hour to get the job done early this morning. Today, Friday is the first day they expect the train to make it to Greenport."

Caroline is relieved to learn that Lu was safe and comfortable when Eddie left her on Thursday morning. She longs to see her but writes a brief letter sending her love and prayers for Eddie's safe return home. The family continues in their routine glad to be getting back to normal. Since the sun is out, they don't need to keep the light burning during the day. On Tuesday, March 21, just one week after the massive snowstorm, a 36-hour rainstorm struck, melting most of the snow. The effects of the rain immediately following the heavy snowfall caused massive flooding. The streets are again impassable, and many in town take to using rowboats to get around to check on neighbors' well-being and attend to necessary chores after such a long period of being shut-in.

The road isn't passable until the 25th, but as soon as it's cleared, George takes Stella and Caroline into Southold to stay with Lu and Eddie overnight with the expectation that he will pick them up the next day. George is pleased to have time to himself after the prolonged period of being shut in with family. He takes care of personal business and heads back to Hortons Point to get the lantern-lit knowing full well that Stella will keep watch from Lu's back porch. His sense of duty to complete his job is no greater than his fear of the scolding he would receive from his wife and daughter should he not attend to the lantern by sundown.

As soon as he gets the lantern squared away, George uses the time alone to hide the jugs of local brew he'd obtained while in town trying samples out as he goes. Predictably, he overdoes it and doesn't wake up until the early afternoon when he makes his way back to Lu and Eddie's in time for a good home-cooked meal. He is relieved that Caroline's good humor at spending time with Lu saves him from the severe redressing he'd expected.

CHAPTER 13

Summer 1888

Watch Room-
a room in the tower located immediately beneath the lantern room,
with windows so the keeper can observe weather conditions.

Caroline and Stella spend the early mornings tending to the garden. Stella enjoys the feel of the warm sun on her back as well as the quiet companionship she shares with her mother. Before the sun gets too hot, they walk into Southold to join Lu for the noon meal. After eating, Stella walks back to Hortons Point to sleep before starting her shift at the lighthouse.

In mid-July, George drives Stella and Caroline to services with Caroline's belongings for a prolonged stay. Stella reluctantly walks back to the lighthouse right after services as rain is threatening, and she may need to kindle the lantern early. Although she wishes to see her sister and partake of the family's Sunday dinner, she realizes that her responsibilities as a keeper are even more important than time with family.

By three in the afternoon, Stella lights the lantern, then sits on the front porch peering through the dark as the increasing wind whips up white caps on the Sound. Periodically, Stella checks on the lantern to ensure the strong winds haven't blown out the beacon, then returns to the parlor and makes a small supper of eggs and samp mixed with a few early greens from the garden. She is glad they can grow their own vegetables and wonders how other keepers on rocky island outposts manage.

George doesn't return that night. Stella is not surprised by this and doesn't give it much thought as she makes herself comfortable up in the tower. She brings up her warm shawl and settles in the watch room, alternating between reading and checking the lantern to ensure it is still burning brightly. Dozing off and on till the first hint of light wakes her. Pleased to see the sunrise, she stands, stretches, and heads back up to the lantern room to extinguish the light and wipe the lens and windows down. She walks around the lantern, taking in the 360-degree views and pausing to watch the familiar scene of the Tillinghasts cows heading out into the field to the South. She looks towards Lu and Eddie's and says a silent prayer that they are safely asleep in their cozy home. Stella extinguishes the wicks, trims them, and wipes the lens but seeing rain clouds blowing in across the Sound; she prepares to re-kindle. The mist off the water enlarges into clouds of fog as it hits the bluff, reminding her of Lu's expanding belly. The rain soon surrounds the lighthouse and continues south, eventually overtaking the farms and fields as it extends to the Bay.

Finished with the lantern, Stella goes down to make breakfast. Da has Jenny with him; Stella hopes he found a protected spot for the old horse to keep dry during the night. She's surprised to realize that she doesn't care whether her father is warm and dry but pushes the uncharitable thought out of her mind. Even though Da is unreliable, he isn't bad; he just has a weakness for the local brew. Somehow she is more suited to the daily rigor of maintaining the lighthouse than her father and not for the first time feels blessed to have this respected work to perform.

Stella expects she is in for a long quiet day of keeping the lantern burning and staving off the chill that the rain brought. She cooks a couple of eggs she collected, adding them to the porridge and samp mixture she warmed next to the pot of coffee.

Although Stella hasn't had much sleep, once breakfast takes the chill off, she goes back up to check that all is well with the lantern. She brings up a fresh supply of kerosene, then wraps up in her warm shawl and attempts to update her journal. As the warmth grows and with an adequate meal in her, she dozes.

When awakened, Stella is pleased to see that the sun is out. She climbs up the ladder and finds Da has extinguished the flame.

"I tried not to wake you," he says sheepishly.

"I didn't realize you were here."

"I'll take the night shift if you want to sleep," Da says, guilty for leaving her on her own.

"No, that's ok. I'll be fine." Stella responds, not wishing to give her father the satisfaction of knowing she was affected by his irresponsibility.

❦

They settle into an uneasy give and take without Caroline to smooth the way. Stella sorely misses her companionship, not to mention her attention to the household chores and hot meals. Stella attempts to cook, though she has no genuine interest or talent for it. George starts to throw together meals of his own, and over time, he proves himself a more able cook than Stella. They get by with the additional meals from Caroline when Stella visits during the week and large family dinners after Sunday services. George often joins them at these Sunday mid-day meals. Sometimes he offers to drive Stella back to Hortons Point in the wagon. If it's not unbearably hot, she walks home, freeing him up to visit with his buddies around town, even though she knows he will more than likely not get back to the lighthouse that night, requiring her to tend the lantern on her own.

Stella notes the weather conditions on scraps of paper that she leaves in the *Keepers' Log* in Da's office so he can copy them when he sits down to catch up with his paperwork. She knows they are supposed to log the weather each day, but Da is erratic in his record-keeping. Stella is proud to help though it worries her when she notices Da is not making daily notations. Stella longs to log in to the book herself, but since she is not an official keeper, she isn't permitted to make notations in the official government document.

As Lu's time grows close, the unrelenting heat contributes to her discomfort. In the afternoon, Lu sits outside under the shade of the old buttonwood tree. Caroline does what she can to keep her comfortable with cooling drinks and damp cloths for her head and neck.

Lu is grateful to have her mother nearby during this worrisome time. While Lu longs for the baby to come, she is apprehensive about being a mother. She worries that at just 19, she's not ready for the responsibilities of motherhood. Caroline reassures her that she was 19 when Stella was born, and Lu had the advantage of living with Martha Goldsmith at the lighthouse and learned much when she helped out with baby Martha.

One evening she raises her concern to Eddie, who responds, "Too late now, Sweetie." She laughs at his matter-a-fact approach to life. Eddie sees the world through the eyes of an immigrant; grateful for all of the opportunities this new country provides and ready to tackle any obstacles.

Lu welcomes the distraction of Stella's frequent visits. Chary Anne comes by with news of Mrs. Goldsmith and freshly laundered baby clothes—cherished hand-me-downs from her now-grown children. Aunt Jennie makes an obligatory visit on Sunday, full of neighborhood gossip; she reports that Caroline is missed at services and brings a new white baby sweater set. Lu is entranced by the present even as Caroline thinks about its impracticality but catching herself, she gets up to refill Jennie's glass of lemonade. Uncle Henry dropped Aunt Jennie off and took their children for a cooling ride along the Bay. He returns with the three little ones dozing in the back of the wagon. Aunt Jennie stands, criticizing Henry for tiring the children out and worrying that they won't sleep tonight now that they've napped. He ignores her, fussing as he assists her into the carriage, gives Caroline a tender embrace, then waves to Lu, maintaining his distance out of respect for her fragile condition.

Lu feels mild pain that comes and goes over the next week. The midwife assures them all is as expected. When Stella visits that Friday, Lu is experiencing increasing discomfort. Caroline asks Stella to stay. Stella wants to help but feels her first duty is always to the beacon. Caroline, well aware of Stella's dilemma, assures her that Da is more than capable of tending to the light but that her sister needs her here. Stella acquiesces to her mother's request and sits at Lu's side, reading aloud, to distract Lu. Caroline sends Eddie to get the midwife. While the women try to comfort Lu, Eddie retreats outside, distressed by his wife's moans.

Finally, in the middle of the night, the baby enters the world with a robust cry. While the midwife tends to Lu, Caroline cleans the newborn. Then calls Eddie and presents his daughter. He holds her up under the glow of the lantern on the parlor table, beaming with pride and smiling over at a radiant if bedraggled Lu. Lu reaches out, eager to hold the baby for the first time. He hands her the tiny bundle for her to examine. Caroline beams at the new family. Stella stands back, sweating profusely.

Not sure what to do, she escapes out the front door, "I'll be on the porch if you need me." Caroline joins Stella on the porch.

The two women sit in companionable silence until Eddie comes out carrying the baby and says, "Lu is sleeping. Do you think I can put this wee one down?"

Caroline rises with some difficulty, and Stella noticing her mother's exhaustion, stands and says, "I'll take her. I'll watch over Lu and the baby. Ma, why don't you sleep? I'm used to being up at night anyway."

Caroline is both surprised and pleased by Stella's offer, "Thank you, dear; I could use some rest. Call me if you need anything." Stella places the baby in the small cradle, the same one she and Lu slept in when they were born. An exhausted Caroline smiles down on her first grandchild and goes upstairs for some much-needed sleep.

The newborn sleeps for several hours while Stella rocks watching over her sister and the little one. When the baby begins to make soft mewing sounds that remind Stella of the Tillinghasts baby lambs, she rocks the cradle with her foot, and that settles the babe back into a deeper sleep. After another hour, the baby emits a soulful whimper followed by a series of cries surprisingly loud for such a tiny creature. Stella startles awake, gently picks up the baby, crooning to her softly, says, "Your Ma is asleep little one, and you should be too."

Lu says, "I'm awake. Let me see her." Stella brings the baby over to Lu as Lu awkwardly pulls herself up to a sitting position and exposes her breast for nursing. Stella waits for Lu to settle then hands over the now whimpering baby. Stella looks on in awe as Lu places the newborn to her breast. The baby latches on with a soft smack of her lips.

"Sit down, Stella, we're fine now," Lu whispers as if her voice might disrupt the nursing baby.

Stella returns to the rocker and looks on with wonder saying, "How do you know how to do that?"

"Hmm, I don't know. I guess from watching Martha when little Martha was born."

"I don't remember that," Stella says.

"You were probably off cleaning the lenses or something," Lu teases.

"I'm surprised you lasted the night here."

"Ma wouldn't let me leave," Stella admits.

"I am glad you're here, and I'm sure Da kindled the light."

"Yes, he did. I can see it from your back porch."

"I know." Lu replies, "I look out for it when I'm feeling lonely. But when I see the beacon, I know that you all are safe and taking care of business."

The baby starts wiggling in Lu's arms, "Here, Stella, take her and burp her while I switch to the other side." Stella takes the baby and places her up on her shoulder, "Ok. How do I burp . . ." as Stella says the word burp, the baby expels a soft grunt. Again, Stella is amazed by the similarity between the baby sounds and a baby lamb, but she keeps these thoughts to herself, sure Lu wouldn't like the comparison.

Stella hands her back to Lu and returns to the rocker.

"Have you thought about what to name her?"

"Eddie and I spoke about naming her for both our families, but he said there are more 'wee ones' over in Ireland than his 'Mam' can count, so we are naming her for Ma, Caroline Merrill Scott."

"Oh, Lu! Ma will be so pleased." The sisters smile as the now satiated baby burps again. Stella takes her and starts to place her back in the cradle.

"Um, Stella . . . did you check her diaper?"

"I hadn't thought of that." Stella is surprised again by Lu's understanding of what to do.

Stella changes the baby, wrapping her in a fresh diaper and copying how Ma swaddled her in the blanket last night. She places her in the cradle, and when the baby lets out a soft cry, she rocks it, and baby Caroline falls back into a deep sleep.

Stella wakes to see the baby is once again at her sister's breast, and Ma standing at her side, says, "Thank you, Stella, for being such a good aunt. Why don't you try to get some sleep before the heat of the day builds up?" Happy to comply and accustomed to sleeping during the day, Stella goes up to the loft and falls into a deep, restful sleep.

Stella wakes to the scent of Ma's fresh bread.

She is surprised to hear Da cooing at the baby, and when she comes down, he looks up with a big smile on his face and says, "So, I guess you've met little Caroline?" Stella nods, brushing the crown of the little one's head.

Da continues, "I came over to pick you up if you're ready to come back to work." Ma glances over her shoulder as she tends to the cooking.

Stella turns to her and asks, "Ma, do you think you can manage here without me?"

"I guess we can though we do, so appreciate all you did last night."

"I'm glad I could be here, but I wouldn't mind getting back."

"Let's eat first and let Lu sleep as long as she can."

At that, they hear rustling from the other room, "I'm awake! Doesn't anyone want to see me?" Da looks confused then gestures for Stella to take the baby.

He gets up and walks to the tiny makeshift birthing nook and looks in at his younger daughter, "You okay? You did good."

"I'm glad you approve," Lu says. Ma comes into the room and asks Lu if she feels up to getting out of bed.

"Yes!" Lu exclaims, "I'd love to get out of this room. Maybe use the outhouse?"

"I don't know about that. Stella . . ." Ma calls, "Can you bring in the chamber pot?" Da makes a hasty retreat leaving the women to attend to Lu.

Ma rushes back to the fire to keep the chicken from burning.

"We can't have this good meal wasted." She exclaims and is surprised to see that George is turning the chicken.

"Isn't that a sight?" she remarks.

George, embarrassed as if caught in the wrong, hands the long fork to Caroline and steps back from the flame. Stella places the baby back in her cradle and assists Lu into the parlor. Lu attempts to sit on the wooden chair but realizes she's too uncomfortable to sit at the table. She allows Stella to lead her back to bed, where the freshly stuffed mattress is gentler on her tender bottom.

Stella makes up a plate for Lu and brings it into her, sitting on the side of her bed and looking down at the sleeping baby. Lu enjoys her mother's fresh-cooked meal but wonders how long it will be until she

THE LADY LIGHTHOUSE KEEPER

can be up and about again. Caroline reminds her there is no rush, that her only job is to tend to the baby. Reassured, Lu dozes off. Stella and Caroline retreat to the parlor. Stella gathers her belongings and goes out to see if Da is ready to go. George is glad to be on his way though he would prefer Caroline join them. After quick hugs, Stella promises to come back later in the week.

Over the next month, Stella and George struggle to manage the lighthouse and the house. George proves himself a better cook than Stella, but neither are attentive to the household chores. Stella is relieved of the burden of cooking and eats whatever he prepares. She looks forward to the frequent visits with her mother, Lu, and her niece. George often accompanies her, happy to have a hearty mid-day meal prepared by Caroline.

Lu is back on her feet by the middle of September, and the baby is thriving. Caroline's sad to leave. However, she is eager to get back to her garden. George and Stella bring her home, promising to return on Sunday after services. Lu, keen to be out and about, wonders aloud how soon she can join them.

Caroline admonishes, "The good Lord understands a new mother's need to recover before subjecting herself and a newborn to eager folks at services."

Stella and George are happy to have Caroline back. She attempts to put their quarters back in order but loses interest and instead writes to her mother and sisters about the wonders of baby Caroline. Mid-week, George drives Caroline back to Lu's. Stella often accompanies them and spends the night, though she always worries until she sees George has the beacon lit.

CHAPTER 14

Winter 1889

Eye to Eye, from -
the scope of a Right Whale's flukes when 'sweeping.'

Following an inspection, George receives a letter criticizing conditions at Hortons Point. Angry, George writes a response and reads it to Caroline and Stella. He complains that the lighthouse was a two-man operation until the last few years, but now he handles it on his own. Stella rushes out of the room, fighting tears of anger.

Oblivious to causing hurt, George says, "Where'd she go in such a hurry?"

In Stella's defense, Caroline says, "George! Stella does a lot!"

George, genuinely confused, says, "But she's just a girl. She can't do what a man can."

"That may be true, George, but she does more than her share."

"Are you saying Stella does more around here than me?"

Caroline knows that if she provokes George, she'll have two angry family members, so she backs down and murmurs, "I'll speak with her."

Caroline finds Stella in the lantern room, gazing out at the view. Stella looks up, still angry, but recognizing her mother's soft step on the ladder, she sighs, knowing her mother will try to smooth things over.

"How are you, dear?"

Stella looks at her mother and says, "Why doesn't he see all I do?"

"Maybe he can't? If he acknowledged all you do, he'd have to look at himself." She pauses, taking in the view, then continues, "He does have a point. There were two keepers here in the past."

"But, now I'm the assistant. I ensure that the lantern is operational at all times."

"I know you do, but there is much that needs tending that you can't do."

"Would you want me to do whitewashing and masonry?" Stella asks with uncharacteristic sarcasm.

"Of course not; no one expects you to. I know all you do. But, he has his demons."

Stella looks up, surprised that Caroline mentions George's weakness.

Caroline wishing to change the subject, says, "You received a letter from Belle? How are she and her new husband?"

"Belle asked me to come and visit. I think I should go."

Descending the ladder, Caroline warns, "Please don't decide in the heat of anger." Stella turns as her mother descends the ladder, "Maybe I need a break. You and Da both get away; he has his fishing trips, and you Lu's. Maybe it's my turn."

"You could spend a few nights at Lu's and see how that goes?"

"I have spent time at Lu's, but I still feel responsible for the beacon when I'm there. I think I want to go where I can't see it; maybe then I will be free from the hold it has on me."

That night, Stella writes to Belle. She shares the news of baby Caroline's arrival and asks if she could visit in the spring? Belle is newly married and lives up-island in Huntington. Belle is delighted to receive Stella's letter and senses more behind it.

She posts a quick note that says, in essence, "When can you come?"

When Stella tells her parents of her plans, Da says, "Stella, this may not be the best time. What with Lu and the baby."

Ma says, "I think they're getting along fine now the baby's over six months old, and Lu is back to her old self."

"Yes, but" George continues, "I need to get out fishing in March. I don't want to miss the winter flounder."

"Ok, I'll tell her I can come in April."

"That sounds fine," Caroline says, turning to stare down George.

Jumping up from the table, George says, "I'm going to bed. You better check the lantern." Shocked by his commanding tone, Stella gets up and goes to the tower. Caroline sighs, completes the evening chores, then climbs up the stairs to speak with Stella. Stella is sitting by the fire in the watch room, writing Lu, and pouring out her grievances at their father's selfishness. Caroline goes up to the lantern room to calm herself. After a short while, she goes back down to Stella, and they discuss plans for Stella's trip in the spring.

"Belle said her husband sails into Greenport a few times a year; I might be able to travel with him by ship." Now it's Caroline's turn to look surprised.

"Is that what you want to do?"

"Oh, Ma, that would be a dream come true. You know I am an able sailor in my dory. I would love to have the chance to sail around Orient Point and up Long Island Sound to Huntington Harbor."

"Sounds like your mind is made up, but please be careful."

"Of course, Ma, you know I wouldn't take any unnecessary risks."

"That's true, Stella. You are a steady girl."

"Thank you, Ma. If you don't mind, I'd like to finish my letter to Lu. I think it will take a rather different tone now than when I started."

Later that week, George receives a letter from the Lighthouse Service. He tells the women, "In April, they're sending a mason to work on the tower. But nothing about my request for help." Caroline gives George a warning look.

Stella remarks, "Good. I'll be with Belle then. I don't need to be here while they're working."

"Aren't you something," George says in surprise. "In that case, I'd better make plans for fishing. Long as we don't get one of those late storms like last year."

"They don't usually come two years in a row," Caroline says, eager to have George away for a while.

❈

March passes faster than usual as Stella's plans take shape. Belle's husband and crew will be delivering supplies to Greenport around March 30th, and she can travel back to Huntington on the return trip. Belle wrote that the ship her husband is an officer on is an old whaler, and it has a Captain's wife's quarters in the center of the main deck. Belle traveled on it last summer when she moved to Huntington. She assures Stella she will be comfortable and safe in the little room.

Stella takes her mother's advice and purchases fabric at Henry's store, sharing her plans for visiting Belle with him and Aunt Jennie. Henry asks how she will be returning, and Stella admits she didn't make plans for her return.

He suggests, "Write when you are ready to return. I often have deliveries coming out east. We may be able to include you in one of my wagons."

"From Huntington?" Stella asks.

"Sure, though you'd have to make a stop at a roadside Inn along the way.

"Thank you, uncle. I will give you notice as to my plans before my welcome wears thin."

"I'm quite sure you and Belle will find much to chat about. You were always so close." Aunt Jennie continues.

"It must be hard for you to remain at the lighthouse with Lu gone." Henry frowns at Jennie, who looks up from her perch in the back of the counter, feigning innocence at poking salt in the wound.

Ignoring his stare, she continues, "Have you heard the news of our Anna? She is so busy with her wedding arrangements. It's going to be quite the affair."

"I'm sure it will," Stella responds indifferently. "I should go. I wish to take this fabric over to Chary Ann so she can get started on a traveling costume."

"Yes," Chary Ann is quite busy with the spring season coming up. Anna has three new frocks she's asked her to work on for her upcoming engagements." Jennie is showing no signs of stopping; her incessant chatter. Leaves Stella wondering how to get away. Henry recognizes her distress and says, "I'll drive you over to Charry Ann's, Stella." Relieved, she excuses herself and heads out.

Stella shares her plans with Chary Ann, who commits to making her a complete travel ensemble with a long skirt and fitted jacket from the dark brown wool fabric, an ivory blouse with a fitted bodice, and a sash to tie at the neck. This new style is unlike anything Stella has worn before, but Chary Ann assures her it will be both modest and in keeping with the fashion of the day. They set up an appointment for Stella to return in two weeks for a fitting.

Stella walks to her sister's and spends a pleasant afternoon cooing at her niece and chatting. Eddie comes in.

Having overheard the conversation earlier between Jennie and Stella at the Prince's Dry Goods Store, he is glad to see her in high spirits; and queries, "Now, what shall we call this fair, babe?" His Irish brogue is never more pronounced than when he's holding little Caroline. Lifting her high overhead, the baby squeals, and he continues, "I believe Caroline is rather a serious name for one so smiley as she. Let's ask Aunt Stella what she thinks."

Flattered Stella replies, "It may get confusing with Ma ...," she continues, "Ma's cousins call her Caddie. So, we wouldn't want to use that, but how about Carrie?"

"Carrie," Eddie repeats, "Hmm, that is a fine name for this little beauty. That is if your Ma agrees?" he continues handing the baby to Lu as she begins to whimper.

"I think Carrie is perfect; she murmurs," preparing to nurse the baby.

"I'll be on my way," Stella calls, heading out the door.

Stella chats with passers-by in town then heads north back to the lighthouse. She arrives in time to admire the sun setting over the Sound as she kindles the lantern. With George away, Stella and Caroline fall into a comfortable routine of daily lighthouse maintenance and household chores. Eddie and Lu visit with baby Carrie, as she is now known. Aunt Stella carries her up to the lantern room, explaining how the lantern works to the silent child who appears to be contemplating the information. A sudden heavy rainstorm forces them to spend the night. Caroline and Stella are happy to have Lu, Eddie, and the baby with them even longer. The next day being the Lord's day, they attend services together, relishing the smell that rises from the damp earth, with its promise of a return to the warmth of spring. Stella spots the first of the crocuses springing up. She gathers a flower for each of them, and they put it in their hair though Caroline is quick to remove them as they approach the church.

That afternoon, while Caroline rocks her namesake in the cradle, Stella tells Lu her plans for visiting Belle by ship. Eddie, the only one of them who has ever spent any real-time sailing, having traveled from Ireland just a few short years before in steerage, warns Stella that being on board a ship takes some getting used to. Many folks are laid low by the continuous rocking though others seem to take it in stride.

"And which group did you fall into?" Lu asks.

"It took me the better part of the journey to get my sea legs,' as they say."

Lu and Stella laugh, but Caroline says, "Now, girls, we don't know how Stella will manage."

Stella, quite surprised at this warning, says, "But Ma, I spend so much time out in the dory."

"Yes, that's true, but this may be a different experience."

Eddie asks, "Where on board will you be staying?"

"That's the best part," Stella says. "It's an old whaling ship, and I will stay in a cabin on the main deck. It was for the captain's wives."

"Whoah!" Eddie says. "That could be quite nice, I expect."

Lu smiling at Stella, says, "I am so happy for you having such an adventure. And will you come back that way too?"

"No, Uncle Henry offered me a ride on one of his delivery wagons."

Caroline shakes her head and says, "What would we do without Henry?"

"Yes, he is a good man," Eddie concurs of his boss, who has been more than generous in assisting Eddie to get his jewelry business established.

Stella and Caroline walk back to Hortons Point before dark. On the way, they discuss how Lu and Eddie have made the cottage into a comfortable home.

Stella notices a longing in Ma's tone and asks, "Do you still miss living in town?"

"Sometimes, but our experiences at Hortons Point, raising you girls here . . . I wouldn't trade that."

"If Da could have found steady work, would we have stayed on Prince Lane?"

"Perhaps, but it's not for us to question the Lord's plan." Stella sighs as the two women continue their walk.

CHAPTER 15

March 1889

Breach, a Half -
A whale's leap, partly clear of the water.

Before first light, Mother and daughter exchange loving embraces as George loads Stella's trunk onto the back of the wagon.

Stella reassures Caroline, "Don't worry, Ma; I'll be fine." But her tentative voice reveals her apprehension about taking her first big trip on her own.

Releasing Stella from her grasp, Caroline says, "The Almighty will protect and keep you safe."

"Let's go," George barks, "The ship's not gonna wait for the likes of you." Caroline frowns at George. He ignores the look and commands, "See to the lantern." Stella climbs on for the early morning ride to Greenport.

They drive into the darkness; Stella glances back at the beacon drawing comfort from its steady beam. She is wearing her new travel suit of warm brown wool with her heaviest shawl that she tucks around her to ward off the pre-dawn chill. As they pull away, Caroline waves, hoping this trip will provide Stella with a much-needed break and a renewed appreciation for the many blessings in her life. She returns to the tower and prepares to extinguish the light. Though not her usual routine, Caroline expects she will need to assume many of Stella's duties while she is away.

Despite the early hour, the docks in Greenport are already a hub of activity. George pulls up alongside the old whaling vessel. Stella is mesmerized by the organized chaos of workers loading the ship as she waits at the bottom of the gangplank for Belle's husband, Neely. She is grateful when he comes down and greets her, shaking hands with George. They unload her trunk, and George makes a hasty retreat.

Belle's husband guides Stella up the gangplank. Stella begins to feel a bit dizzy but attributes it to the excitement, and of course, she's had no morning meal. The dizziness grows as Neely shows her to her tiny room at the center of the deck, then excuses himself to get back to the preparations needed for the ship to set sail.

Stella inspects the tiny cabin that will be her temporary home. There's a cozy bed along one wall, an upholstered chair, and a ladies writing table on the other. A window on each wall allows her to view the men preparing to sail east out of Greenport harbor towards Orient Point. Standing in the center, she can almost touch the sides with outstretched arms. She is glad for Belle's precise instructions to carry a small carpetbag on board with her sleeping costume and a change for the next day.

Her queasiness increases, but she remains in the cabin as Neely requests for her safety. The closed-in space and the peculiar ship smells contribute to her growing discomfort. Stella notes that everyone is busy doing a job except her and wonders if her inactivity adds to her ill feelings. She is unaccustomed to being idle, and as the rocking of the ship continues, she lies down on her bunk and falls into a light sleep.

Sometime later, she's startled awake by a crisp knock on the cabin door.

She hastily rises from the bunk, at first unsure of where she is, then remembering answers, "Yes, just a moment."

Attempting to push her hair back into its severe bun, she opens the door at the same time the ship rocks forward. The man is holding a tray of boiled herring and tea. The combination of the smell of the fish and the rolling deck proves too much for Stella. Unable to contain herself, she vomits violently. Stella grabs a cloth to hold in front of her face as she continues to heave. She is grateful she hasn't eaten anything since last night, so only stomach bile comes up.

The sailor, accustomed to landlubbers, places the tray on the deck beside him and offers his arm, saying, "Why don't you come out and get some fresh air."

Stella, besieged by a furor of emotion, feels both physically shaky and embarrassed by her lack of control. The need to hold onto something overrides her embarrassment, so she takes his arm and walks out of the cabin. He escorts her to the nearest railing, and Stella grips it, looking down at the rolling seas. Though her head is pounding, she perceives a drop of relief once she is out in the breeze.

The sailor says, "I'm Jon, the ship's cook." Stella makes brief eye contact, unable to sustain even the slightest conventional greeting as she continues to hold on to the rail, trying to counter the ship's continuous rocking. Jon suggests she look towards the horizon to get her sea legs. With great effort, Stella raises her eyes; while the pounding in her head continues, she starts to feel a bit of relief as the wind blows across her face, and the clean ocean breeze clears away the pungent smells.

"You stay here. I'll get Neely." Stella nods, unable to speak, and tries to gather her wits about her. She remembers Eddie's conversation about his journey across the ocean and is grateful that her journey is only overnight. Stella continues to hang onto the rail, struggling to keep her eyes open and look out at the horizon; it feels like hours pass before Neely approaches.

"Oh, my." he says, bemused, "Looks like our lighthouse keeper is not much of a sailor." Stella turns and gives him an irritated look, then turns her head back to track the shoreline, realizing her mistake. Any sudden movement provokes the urge to vomit.

"The good thing for you is we will be in sight of land the whole way. Maybe you should have some tea, though; it might help settle you down. Should I have cook bring you up some, or could you come below with me to the galley?" Stella takes Neely's arm wishing to avoid the cook, hoping not to set eyes on him again for the rest of the voyage. Stella takes a few steps, then pulls away and lurches for the railing.

"Ok," Neely says. "I guess you better stay here, and I'll bring it to you."

Stella turns to him and whispers, "Thank you, I'd just like to return to my cabin, but I, um . . ." she stops, not wanting to explain to him that she left a mess in the cabin.

Neely says, "It was seen to; a chamber pot and rags are there should you need them." He extends his arm as they make their way back to the little room at the center of the deck.

"Maybe if we open the windows, the breeze will help, and we can leave the door open if you'd like." Stella gives a slight nod and sits down on the comfortable chair. Holding her head steady and keeping her eyes focused straight ahead, she releases her grip on Neely's arm.

Stella remains in the chair, sleeping fitfully, the breeze keeping down her urge to vomit. Occasionally, Stella stands and takes in the beauty of the shoreline as they sail past. She is filled with awe when she spots the white beacon at Hortons Point, reflecting on all that goes into keeping the light operating and grateful for its guidance as travelers have been for more than 30 years.

The winds are in their favor, and they make good time. Neely and Jon check on her as their busy schedules allow, which gives her the time to adjust her appearance and maintain a little dignity. Just before sunset, Stella hears before she sees the hubbub of the busy harbor. Stella stands and gazes out the windows at ships with flags from countries around the world. Then, taking hesitant steps outside, she grabs onto the railing as the boat jolts into the dock. Neely escorts her down the gangplank, handing her off to an ecstatic and bemused Belle.

The two women hug, and Belle looking over a disheveled Stella, who is still wearing her now stained traveling suit, remarks, "Methinks you are a landlubber, Miss Lighthouse Keeper!"

Neely laughs and says, "You are correct, my dear." He hugs his wife and continues, "I'll be home late; you'd better get this one something warm to eat. Start with something light," he warns, heading back up the gangplank.

Belle wraps her arms around Stella's waist and says, "I hope the rest of your visit will be pleasant."

"I'm sure it will," Stella says with growing enthusiasm. Although her head is still throbbing, she notices that the nausea has begun to subside.

"How far is it to your home?" she asks, eager to get comfortable.

"Just a few blocks. Can you walk?" Belle asks with concern.

"Of course," Stella assures her, "I'm starting to feel more myself already."

Stella and Belle walk through Huntington's busy streets, then turn onto a quiet lane. Belle opens the door to the little cottage that she and Neely share with his elderly parents. Belle escorts her to a back bedroom that will be hers during her visit and brings a cup of tea and biscuits.

Stella sits up, thanking Belle; she says, "I'm so embarrassed."

Belle replies, "I want to hear all about it, but drink this while it's warm and then get some sleep. Would you like me to run you a bath first?"

"No, yes . . . I don't know," Stella shrugs. "I just, I just felt so awful . . . the whole time!" she exclaims.

"Why don't you finish the tea," Belle urges, "I'll come back and check on you in a bit." Grateful for her friend's understanding, Stella drinks the warm tea, takes a few bites of the biscuit, and then stretches out on top of the bed. Belle returns; seeing that Stella is asleep, she places the afghan over her and closes the door.

The dear friends spend hours reminiscing about growing up together and news of neighbors. It's surprising to Stella that Belle knows more about folks back home than she does. They laugh together over fond memories and teeter on the edge of impropriety when discussing Anna and her upcoming wedding. Feeling guilty, Stella reminds Belle of how good Uncle Henry always is to her family.

Belle shows Stella's Huntington's many unique shops. Stella enjoys window shopping admiring the variety of items for sale. They go inside a store that only sells items for children. Belle is drawn to the tiny baby items with detailed embroidery and smocking around the neck, touching each with reverence. Stella selects a warm sweater set for baby Carrie made of soft ivory yarn with pants, a top, and a matching bonnet with a silky ribbon to tie around her chubby cheeks. She feels a genuine fondness for the child and wonders what it might be like to have a baby of her own someday. She pushes this thought out of her head as quite impossible as she knows herself to be too single-minded in her dedication to the lighthouse to take on the all-encompassing responsibilities of a child, not to mention marriage.

She searches for something to purchase for Ma, wishing to give her something pretty and impractical, but knowing Ma will most appreciate a practical gift. She settles on a beautiful Robin's egg blue shawl. Though she'd love one for herself, she dismisses the idea of making such an extravagant purchase. Instead, she enjoys browsing through a bookstore and selects a new journal for herself as well as a few postcards that she'll mail to friends and relatives during her stay.

Back at the house, Stella is comfortable in the cozy room off of the kitchen. Neely's parents are the most aged people; Stella has ever met. Stella is proud to witness the loving way Belle cares for them. Stella and Belle fall into a companionable routine, with Stella assuming much of the heavier work accustomed to her job at the lighthouse. At the same time, Belle enjoys showing off her culinary expertise.

Neely returns from his voyage with tales of New York City. He teases Stella regarding her misadventures on board, telling them that the cook hasn't stopped talking about the lady lighthouse keeper who couldn't find her sea legs. Stella smiles and averts her eyes. Belle sensing her friend's discomfort, gives him a threatening look.

After two weeks, Stella writes to Ma and Uncle Henry, informing them of her wish to return. Henry responds with a note saying he is sending a wagon to Huntington to pick up supplies, and there will be room for Stella to ride along. They will leave at dawn on the morning of Thursday, the 25th of April. Stella is relieved to have this plan in place, and though reluctant to leave her good friend, she is grateful for the time they spent together but also eager to return to her beloved lighthouse.

While packing, Stella wonders about the next leg of her adventure; a two-day carriage ride.

Neely teases, "I hope land travel is more to your liking." Belle taps him on the shoulder with reproof, but Stella, now more accustomed to his gentle teasing, gives him a quick hug.

Belle and Stella enjoying a quiet day at home, are surprised by a knock on the door. Stella opens it and is pleased to see it is Lu's Eddie. Eddie explains that he has just arrived and must see to Henry's orders, but he came to let Stella know he'll return at dawn to start their journey home. She is relieved and grateful to Uncle Henry for sending her familiar brother-in-law as her travel companion for her return trip.

Stella lays out her travel clothes. Having had such a difficult time on the boat, she's doesn't wear the new travel suit but rather one of her older frocks with a shawl for warmth.

Stella lies awake that last night at Belle's. Before first light, she is dressed and waiting for Eddie. A sleepy Belle comes down when she hears the wagon outside. She gives her dear friend a long embrace and wishes her a safe journey. Eddie helps Stella up onto the front of the wagon, and they take off through the still quiet streets of Huntington, then turn east into the rising sun along Middle Country Road.

Stella dozes as the carriage's gentle rocking lulls her to sleep, and the noise of the wheels along the packed dirt road makes conversation difficult. They stop and have a quick dinner at a roadside inn and then head south to Yaphank, where Eddie will pick up sacks of milled wheat.

Late in the afternoon, they arrive in the large industrial town of Yaphank. Yaphank has two stagecoach lines, a stop on the Long Island Rail Road, and a center for travelers, with modest places for women to see to their needs. Stella recalls that this town was known as Millville because of the many grist mills powered by the flowing Carmans River. Stella observes the power of the river when she and Eddie go around back in search of the outhouse. When she returns, they walk inside a noisy, smoke-filled establishment; the stench of beer stops Stella at the door, but Eddie's firm grasp propels her forward to a table in a corner. They enjoy a hearty meal. Looking around, Stella notes that the other patrons are almost all men. Some are engaged in animated discussion, while others sit and eat a simple meal. A few looked at Stella disapprovingly.

Eddie apologizes for the rough conditions, but they are about half-way home and will spend the night. The Innkeeper's wife shows them to their rooms. Stella has a private room with a window that looks out onto the bustling street below. She fears the boisterous exchanges from the restaurant will keep her awake, but much to her surprise, she falls into a dreamless sleep under the warm quilt. Stella is startled awake by loud tapping on her door. She gets up and walks over but hesitates to open it.

"Yes," she says through the door.

"Mornin', Stella, it's Eddie." Stella opens the door a crack, happy to see his familiar smile.

He says, "Time to get going."

She throws her outer clothing on and heads out, relieved to find Eddie waiting in the hallway. Grateful for his consideration, Stella proceeds down the stairs to the now quiet restaurant. They eat a substantial breakfast of fried ham and eggs. Eddie looks up after clearing his plate and grins,

"It's a man's breakfast, but you did well," as Stella finishes the last of her plate. They wait in line at the mill as the workers load up the 100-pound sacks of cornmeal and wheat flour that Henry ordered, then head north the way they came last night, turning east onto the Main Road for the final leg of their journey.

Stella takes in the sites.

The pounding of the horse's hooves on the dirt road covers them in a dusty haze each time a wagon passes from the opposite direction. Though uncomfortable, she is grateful to be on land shuddering at the thought of her journey by sea. As the sun moves overhead, Stella begins to recognize familiar landmarks. They stop in Riverhead, alongside the Peconic, then continue east as the river enlarges into the open Bay. She is on the edge of her seat as they pull up to Uncle Henry's store in Southold.

Ma and Aunt Jennie are sitting on the front porch. Stella jumps off the wagon and throws herself into Ma's arms as if she's a toddler returning from a trip to grandma's. Caroline is grateful for her safe return though she is taken aback at Stella's uncharacteristically exuberant greeting.

Uncle Henry comes out to check the wagon's cargo and greets Stella. Stella thanks him for his thoughtfulness in sending Eddie to be her escort. His familiarity was a comfort to her throughout the journey. Henry says how happy they are that she is home safe and promises to have Stella's trunk delivered in a day or two, then drives her and Caroline home in the small wagon.

Stella strains forward to catch the first glimpse of the tower and the

Sound. She is grounded by the sight and scent of the crisp salty air.

When they pull up alongside the majestic view of the water, Stella sighs, saying, "I never want to leave."

Caroline, somewhat taken aback at Stella's enthusiasm, says, "We have missed you."

Stella replies, "It was wonderful to visit Belle, but I did so miss the lighthouse." As they draw near the tower, Stella gasps, Oh, I see they've completed the new masonry. It looks quite substantial."

"I believe the workmen were skilled though Da may have a different opinion.

"That's Da," Stella says. Caroline smiles, taking this as a sign that her time away has softened Stella's anger at her father.

Once inside, Stella heads up the tower's stairs and climbs the ladders to check out the lantern. She notes that it needs a thorough cleaning and begins wiping each pane of glass with care. Da calls, "supper," and Stella stops and turns, taking in the 360-degree view. Humming with pleasure, she descends and joins Caroline and George in the parlor. Stella digs in with relish. She gets up, takes a third helping of stew, and accepts the last biscuit Ma offers.

George says, "She hasn't lost her appetite."

Ma asks, "Is Belle a good cook?"

"Oh, I guess she is good enough, but I think I missed the way you prepare things."

"And, if she ever wants to be invited back," George adds, "she probably needed to hold back." Caroline glares at George, but Stella smiles as she scrapes her spoon against the now-empty bowl of stew.

"That was delicious," she says with pleasure, "Now I'll go back up to the lantern. I see it could use a little extra attention before I light it. I'll take the full shift tonight, Da, if you'd like."

"Sounds fine to . . . " George trails off as Caroline cuts in,

"I don't think that's a good idea. You've been traveling all day. You need your rest."

George nods and says, "Ma's right, I'll relieve you." Stella hovers by the door, eager to get back to the lantern.

Caroline continues, "I'll come up and keep you company after I clean up."

Stella is eager to return to the tasks at hand, wiping down every surface and preparing the light for the night's work. Da comes up with oil and returns with coal for the keeper's room, banking the little black potbelly stove and calling up to Stella.

"Bout time you got that lit, don't you think?"

Stella, intent on her cleaning, hadn't noticed that the sun was setting, says, "Yes, Da."

Stella trims the wicks and kindles the lantern, then turns to watch the setting sun. She draws a deep breath at the glowing pink and gold light as the sun descends below the horizon.

She hears Ma coming up the stairs and calls to her, "I'm in the lantern room. It was a beautiful sunset." Ma climbs up the ladder and joins Stella facing west as the last glints of sun collapses into the Sound.

Shivering, Ma says, "Why don't we go down and sit by the stove?" Stella turns to her mother, who notes a glistening of tears in her eyes.

She touches her arm and murmurs, "I'm glad you're home, dear."

Stella asks about Lu and the baby. Caroline is at a loss to answer, and Stella wonders when Ma last saw Lu. With Stella away, she had to stay at the lighthouse. Stella feels guilty when it dawns on her that her little adventure may have caused her mother some distress.

Caroline says, "They came a few Sundays ago. The baby is growing so fast. Maybe we could visit tomorrow?"

"I'd like that," Stella replies with more enthusiasm than she feels. She would prefer to stay home and finish polishing the lens and brass fittings;

she agrees to go to relieve her guilt for keeping her mother from one of her few pleasures, time with her granddaughter.

"I hope my trunk gets here before we go. I have gifts."

Caroline responds, "Our best gift is to be together. We can invite them to come out after the Sunday service. I expect your trunk will be here before that."

"Knowing Uncle Henry's efficiency, I expect it'll be here quick enough," Stella replies. Stella notices that her mother looks older and worn out even in the soft glow of the lantern light.

"Why don't you go on to the bed, Ma. I'm content to write in my journal and catch up with some reading. I picked up a fascinating new book in Huntington, *Work*, by Louisa May Alcott. The store had the complete collection of her books to honor her death last year. She was only 55 when she died."

"Hmm," Caroline says, "that is not so young a passing but perhaps surprising for such a prolific writer."

They hug, and Caroline says, "I'm so glad you're home." Then she retreats down the ladder and the circular stairs where she banks the coals for the night before heading to bed.

The familiar sounds of the intermittent hissing of the wicks in the lantern and her mother's soft steps on the stairs soothe Stella as the lighthouse settles down for its night's work, lighting a path across the Sound warning ships to stay away from the dangers close to shore.

CHAPTER 16

1889–1894

Eclipse -
an interval of darkness between appearances of a light.

The summer of 1889 is eventful at the lighthouse. Government carpenters finished the new barn and built a roof over the cistern. These improvements are most welcome as the freshwater well in the Tillinghasts field is a long walk, especially when carrying back the full buckets of water. Stella enjoys the workmen's pleasant company. An added plus is that workers staying on-site keep George in line.

Once the workers finish up, the influx of summer visitors makes leaving the property even just for Sunday services impossible for Stella. Caroline walks to services, but Stella enjoys sleeping a little later in the morning then having a quick breakfast in relative quiet before the first of the visitors arrive for tours of the tower. While she is brief in her explanations, she is always polite and enjoys guests' reactions to the impressive 360-degree views from the lantern room.

George takes umbrage with a recent inspector's report that criticizes the condition of the lighthouse. George does less in response to the criticism, which leaves more for Stella. Then he takes off on an extended fishing trip, showing no regard for the increased summer workload. Caroline, ever the buffer, assures Stella that she'll help out while George is away. The two women throw themselves into the busiest season of the year, helping to bury their resentment at George. A familiar pattern with no apparent resolution.

❊

Around midnight on March 30, 1891, Stella returns to the lantern room and sees an unusual phenomenon. The northern sky lights up in scrolling shades of green, like a sail luffing in a gentle wind. She never saw this glorious sight before, but from her extensive reading, she realizes this is an aurora borealis, a rare phenomenon in these parts.

Unable to contain her excitement, she rushes down from the tower, then runs to the bottom of the stairs at the back of the cottage and calls, "Ma, Da, Come quick!" They awaken and join Stella in the tower, watching in awe as green lights swirl across the horizon.

"The northern lights. Aren't they beautiful?" asks Caroline.

"Yes, and so unusual to see from here," Stella says, as the dark overtakes a final swath of brightness.

Breaking the spell, Da says, "Goin back to bed." Ma shivers slightly and leans into Stella. Stella drapes her cape over Ma's shoulder, realizing she is just in her bedclothes. The two women remain in the tower arm-in-arm and enjoy the peace of the moment.

As the chill takes over, Stella says, "I guess we better go down by the fire."

Reluctantly, Ma moves away from the view of the navy blue sky awash in stars.

❊

Over the next few years, Lu and Eddie are blessed with two more daughters Eliza, born July 1890, and then in June of 1893, Agnes Scott arrives. Lu responds to each addition with the instincts of a natural-born mother. Caroline assists her with each new birth but is relieved to see Lu back on her feet and running her small household after each baby. Stella enjoys visiting her sister and her nieces though she is not comfortable with the commotion they create and worries about her sister's health with three children, and Lu is not yet 25 years old. At the same time, Eddie proves himself to be an enterprising and industrious businessman.

In October 1893, with Ma and Da's blessing, Lu and Eddie purchased from Seth Tuthill the old Prince Homestead and have it moved to the Prince property on the southside of the blacksmith shop just past her parents' cottage. Moving the old house is a community undertaking. Many townspeople gather with George directing the men who remove the old home from its foundation, then transfer it onto an extra-large flatbed wagon pulled by a team of oxen. The old farmhouse needs repairs, but during the fall, George dedicates himself to fixing it up to his daughter's specifications, proving that he is a capable carpenter when he wishes.

In December, they move into the grand old farmhouse and are excited to host their first family Christmas in their new home. Lu decorates the house with greens, and a large spruce tree is brought in and placed in the center of the parlor.

Every morning little Eliza comes down the stairs and announces, "There's a tree in our house!" After services, Stella, Caroline, and George arrive for a mid-day meal and gift exchange, after which most of the extended Prince clan stop in, including Uncle Henry, Aunt Jennie, Anna with her Beau, Fredrick, and Edith. This gathering is the first of what Lu and Eddie hope will become a family tradition of get-togethers in their new home.

Stella is quite puzzled and none too pleased when cousin Edith attaches herself to Stella, asking seemingly endless questions about her work at the lighthouse. While Edith is a bright little thing of 11, Stella is unsure what to make of her and spends much of the afternoon avoiding her. Stella throws herself the kitchen clean-up and even changes baby

Agnes as yet another excuse to escape Edith's attention.

Caroline often stays in Southold with Lu. With three girls under the age of 5, Lu is grateful for her mother's help. George uses the little Prince Lane cottage as a refuge of his own under the guise of returning to carpentry. He often takes meals at Lu's, which leaves Stella in full charge at Hortons Point. While she misses her mother, she is glad for time alone, as winters' quiet descends.

Caroline feels pulled between her eldest daughter's isolation at the lighthouse and Lu's young family's needs, but the grandchildren always win. Caroline continues to pray that George will finally turn away from the drink. She takes an active role in the Temperance Society led by Reverend Howell. She hopes that George will be forced to stop and become the man Caroline believes he can be when alcohol is banned.

Unfortunately, the Scott family's pleasure in their new home is short-lived. On May 25, 1894, only five short months after moving in, a heavy spring storm with loud cracks of thunder and streaks of lightning woke Eddie. The biting acrid smell of fire assaults him, and he shakes Lu. They rush to the girls, wrap them in blankets and race out of the house. Once they are safe, he storms back inside to remove the valuable cache of jewelry from the basement. The 'Eagle Hook and Ladder Company' dedicated volunteer firemen arrive, and with help from their neighbors, the fire is put out but not before the house has burned to the ground. Uncle Henry assists Lu and the girls to her parent's cottage. Lu collapses in a chair with her three babies in her arms while Henry makes a small fire to take off the chill.

Lu yells—"No—No, fire!"

Henry puts it out and says, "I'll drive to the lighthouse. You'll want your mother." Lu nods almost imperceptibly.

From the tower at Hortons Point, Stella is alarmed to see flames light up the southern sky and worries about the source. In the quiet of the night, Stella hears the carriage and rushes outside to learn of the tragedy. She wakes Ma and Da; Caroline dresses, and Stella gathers blankets. Henry drives them back to Prince Lane, where they find the girls still huddled in Lu's arms. Her soot-covered face shows the stain of her tears that are flowing freely. Caroline instructs Stella to take the babies and attend to them. She sits with her daughter allowing her to relay the horror of the night, reminding her how fortunate they are that no one was harmed.

At dawn, baby Agnes wakes for a feeding, and Stella brings her to Lu. They hear the carriage outside, and Eddie carries in the rocking chair that George made before their first baby was born. Lu breaks down when she sees the chair, one of the few items they salvaged from the ruins of the fire.

Eddie holds his wife and the crying baby and says, "'tis only a house. We'll get another." falling into his Irish brogue.

Suddenly Lu says, "Oh, Eddie, don't we have insurance?"

"Yes, and I've got the papers. They were in the box in the basement by the inventory, so yes, we will be fine. And aren't we fortunate," Eddie continues gesturing with his free arm, "We've your Ma and sister here already and this cozy cottage to keep our little ones safe and warm while we re-build."

Lu reaches out and takes the baby, holding her close, says, "This is a sad day, but Eddie is right; all that is important is here."

Little Eliza begins to cry, having woken in a strange place. Caroline gathers her onto her lap. A knock on the door brings the first neighbors offering support. Lu cries startling baby Agnes who bawls. Stella takes Agnes and puts her on her shoulder, where she burps loudly, prompting soft embarrassed laughter among the adults. Eliza, never one to be left out, imitates the loud burp.

Caroline holding back a smile turns the child to face her and says, "Now, Miss Eliza, that isn't very ladylike."

Eliza, never at a loss for words, says, "But baby Aggie did it." The adults exchange softly at the little one's bold retort.

As word of the devastating loss spreads, an outpouring of love and support bolsters Eddie and Lu. It seems not a day passes without a neighbor dropping off some outgrown clothes from their children and baskets with covered dishes. Lu is exhausted all the time, caring for the three little ones and the emotional toll of sorting through the debris of their former home. She often naps in the afternoon when baby Agnes sleeps and is grateful for Caroline's assistance with the older girls.

Caroline and Stella are concerned about how often Lu cries. Caroline offers to take the two older girls back to the lighthouse with them for a while. Lu tears up and begs her not to go, as she feels unable to manage on her own Alarmed by the changes in Lu, Caroline agrees to stay.

When Stella leaves to get back to the lighthouse, the smell from the fire permeates the spring air. She walks over to the ruin to find Eddie covered in soot, sorting through the ashes. He looks up as she draws near, and she sees the tear stains down his soot-covered face.

"Oh, Eddie. Why do this?"

"I don't know, Stella; I just can't seem to stop."

"This is a difficult time. But life is full of hardship. You must carry on." Stella hesitates to bring up her concerns about Lu. The once energetic and youthful man appears to have aged ten years in the last week.

She doesn't wish to add to his burden but is always one to tackle a problem head-on; she continues, "Ma and I are worried about Lu."

Eddie listlessly responds, "Yes, she is heartbroken."

Stella recognizing she can't help, leaves the morose man to his search and trudges back to the lighthouse. She is not surprised that Da is not at Hortons Point and takes a short nap; then, preparing for the possibility that he will not return in time, Stella sets up the lantern and lights the wicks. She returns to the parlor and prepares a simple meal before returning to the tower with her journal and a heavy shawl ready to tend to her night's work once more on her own.

❈

With an immigrant's resilience, Eddie rallies and persuades Lu that they need a fresh start. Staying in Southold is a constant reminder of their loss, so he convinces her to make a change. He contacts business associates in Sag Harbor, where many of Eddie's best customers reside, and formulates a plan to open a jewelry store on the South Fork with the insurance money from the fire.

Lu is reluctant to move to the South Fork, "So far from her family," but Eddie presses his case, feeling that he is fighting for their future. Lu and Eddie go out to the lighthouse in late June to discuss their idea. Lu decides that telling practical Stella first and getting her on their side will help win over Caroline and George. She invites Stella for a walk on the beach and relays their plans. Stella is shocked as Sag Harbor, while not so far away as Brooklyn, where Eddie's brothers live, is a boat ride across Peconic Bay or a long day's wagon ride west to Riverhead then back east on the South Fork. Lu explains to Stella that Eddie sees this as a way to rebuild their lives. Stella agrees as they both seem rejuvenated and supports them as they tell Caroline and George over a strained mid-day meal.

After they leave, Caroline sits on the front porch watching the glow of the sunset over the water. Once she kindles the lantern, Stella joins her mother. She raises the question of Lu and Eddie's plans.

Caroline speaking as much to herself as to Stella, says, "I guess it's what they need to do, but I don't see why they have to go all the way to Sag Harbor."

"I know it is hard, but they'll only be a short boat ride away. We can still stay with them."

"But they're just getting back on their feet."

"Now, Ma, I think Eddie is right that seeing and even smelling the ruin of their home only makes them sadder. Starting fresh in Sag Harbor could be just what they need. And they have the insurance money to get them set up."

"Yes, Eddie is a good businessman. Uncle Henry is going to miss him too."

Eddie finds a promising location for the storefront in the middle of town and an old whaling captain's home a few short blocks away to provide them with plenty of space for the family. There's even a main floor bedroom where Caroline and Stella can stay. After services the next week, Lu invites Stella and Caroline to see the new place. Caroline agrees, but Stella suggests that George go while she returns to Hortons Point.

Cousin Waitley's boat is docked at the end of Prince Lane. When the family gets on board, he navigates around Shelter Island and docks at Sag Harbor. They walk through the quiet village with many shops shuttered on the Lord's day.

Caroline comments, "Even more than in Greenport." Lu sensing her improving mood assures her that they will explore the shops soon. Eddie stops and shows them the storefront he rented.

They turn away from the wharf and walk down a tree-lined street with elegant homes. They stop in the middle of the second block, and Lu points with pride at the grand three-story white structure. "Look, Ma, it even has a widow's walk at the top."

"I can't quite see it from down here, but I'm sure it will do."

Eddie says, "Come on; I have the key. It's the first the girls will see their new rooms. They can each have their own though I doubt they'll need that for some time."

As the little group enters the large foyer, a grand stairway leads to a gallery.

George exhales a soft whistle and asks, "How many bedrooms does it have?"

"There are six bedrooms on the second floor and even a small room for tending to nighttime abolitions," Lu says with a slight blush.

Eddie adds, "And the outhouse is a two-seater."

"Eddie," Lu gasps in embarrassment.

"Aint that somethin'," George mutters.

"Come see the kitchen, and there's even a library." The adults walk through the grand home while the three little girls run from room to room.

Little Carrie stops and approaches her father solemnly, "but what if there's a fire?" she asks.

Eddie squats to eye level and says, "No fires here, wee one. We're having a lightning rod installed."

"Like at the lighthouse?" George asks in disbelief, "do you really think that's . . ." his voice trails off as the three adults stare at him.

"I guess if it makes you feel better," Caroline says.

The little group heads back to the boat, where Waitley waits for their return.

"Uncle Waitley, you should have joined us."

"That's ok; I got some things done. Always plenty of maintenance on a boat."

"Like a lighthouse," George says.

"Yeah, but at least you got Stella," Waitley replies.

CHAPTER 17

June 1895—Winter 1896

Give Leeway -
to allow extra room for sideways drift of a ship off the desired course.

In early June, Stella is surprised to receive a thick envelope from Aunt Jennie.

Curious, she opens it then groans, "No! Why?" she exclaims.

"What is it, dear?" Caroline asks. "Aunt Jennie, or rather Cousin Edith, has invited me to attend her graduation."

"Hmm," Caroline responds, taking the envelope with the letter and a printed invitation.

She reviews it and says, "Isn't that sweet."

"Sweet?" Stella exclaims, "Why would I want to attend Edith's graduation?"

"I believe she admires you."

"Why?"

"She is interested in the lighthouse. On several occasions, Henry has said how she enjoys coming out here, and he so appreciates the time you spend with them. There is no question in my mind that you should go."

"I guess so," Stella says, remembering how kind Uncle Henry is. "Ma, you have got to come. I can't possibly go on my own."

"The invitation is to you, but I think it will be alright for me to go."

On the 28th, Stella and Ma walk over to the schoolhouse. As they climb the steps and enter the front door, Stella is flooded with memories of her own graduation some 17 years earlier. They spot Uncle Henry and Aunt Jennie sitting in the front row with two empty chairs that they've saved for them. Stella and Caroline join them as the ceremony is about to begin. They sit and listen to the students' speeches—Stella, tired from her nightshift battles dozing off. Finally, the teacher calls Edith Prince.

Edith marches up to the center of the room and proclaims, "Patriotism!"

Stella jerks awake at Edith's loud voice but struggles to pay attention to the young girl's speech until she realizes she is speaking about her, Stella, and her work at Hortons Point. Edith equates tending the lighthouse to a patriotic duty that ensures the safe passage of cargo and passenger vessels. She describes the routine and diligence necessary to maintain the lantern as a symbolic beacon of patriotism to our country.

Spontaneous applause follows the speech, as the audience is moved by the well-written and dramatically recited declamation.

At the end of the program, Edith comes over to Stella and presents her with a copy. Stella awkwardly embraces the child, flattered but uncomfortable with the attention. Caroline hugs Edith and thanks her on behalf of the family while she gives Stella a stern look over the child's shoulder.

❈

Lu is finding it hard to settle into their new home. She hasn't recovered from the horror of the fire and is still irritable with the children. When Lu's malaise lingers, Caroline insists that she see a doctor. Lu returns and confirms what she suspected; she is with child. Caroline is worried that another baby may be too much for her beloved daughter. But she holds her tongue and prays for Lu's strength to return.

Having sailed through her previous pregnancies, this one takes her by surprise. She delays rising in the morning and naps in the afternoons. A local woman comes in to help. Caroline insists on taking the three girls home to Hortons Point to give Lu a proper rest, and Lu agrees. Lu and Eddie spend the weekend at the lighthouse with the family, making the long drive by horse and wagon from Sag Harbor west through the Hamptons and Riverhead and then back east on the North Fork to Southold. The trip proves exhausting for Lu. Though she is thrilled to see the girls, she doesn't participate in the family picnic on the beach.

George arranges for Waitley to take them back to Sag Harbor on his boat late Sunday afternoon. Unlike Stella, Lu enjoys the boat's gentle rocking and watches the sunset and the moon rise as they dock in Sag Harbor. The visit so revives Lu that she leaves the men to wrestle with getting the horse and wagon off the boat and walks home on her own in the glow of early evening. Hoping these good feelings will stay with her

The following week Waitley picks them up in Sag Harbor, and they make the much quicker and more pleasant journey across Peconic Bay late Friday afternoon. The girls relay their adventures, helping Aunt Stella wipe the windows and their discoveries on the beach and working with Grandma in the garden. Lu is grateful for her family's continued support but feels it is time to resume her responsibilities, and the girls are excited to go home. Caroline is worried, so Stella agrees to stay with them for the week.

Stella struggles to follow Lu's directives for cooking and tending to the family and is grateful when Friday afternoon rolls around, and she sails back to Southold. One week away from the lighthouse caring for three little ones is quite enough of domestic life for Stella.

Caroline returns to Sag Harbor, accompanying Lu to the doctor, who assures them that all is fine, but she needs to rest. George and Stella manage at the lighthouse. Winter takes hold, with longer nights and the increased vigilance required to keep the light burning. Stella notices George struggling to stay on top of it all and suggests he spend time at Lu's with Caroline over Thanksgiving. George leaves early Sunday to go scalloping.

Stella attends services on Thanksgiving morning and is surprised to see Belle and Neely. Neely's parents died earlier that fall, and Belle plans an extended stay with her parents. Stella is uncharacteristically talkative, telling them that she hasn't gotten seasick when sailing with her Uncle across Peconic Bay from Southold to Sag Harbor.

Neely jokes, "Sounds like the lady lighthouse keeper is getting her sea legs."

Belle invites Stella to join them for dinner, and she spends an unexpectedly sociable Thanksgiving day with the Tillinghasts but, of course, leaves promptly to ensure she is back at the lighthouse before the sun goes down.

Da returns from his visit to Sag Harbor alone.

Stella hoped Ma would return with him, but he says, "Lu is feelin' poorly and needs Ma to take care of the little ones."

Stella and Da fall into their familiar routine, but she is lonely without her mother's company and visits from Lu, Eddie, and the girls. Da tells her to take time off for Christmas and go to Sag Harbor. Despite her loneliness, Stella is reluctant to leave Da in charge, but she agrees after letters from Lu and Ma urge her to come. Sensing her distrust, Da is annoyed and steps up his efforts to tend the tower.

A few days before Christmas, Da brings Stella to Southold, and she sails to Sag Harbor. Ma is walking baby Aggie in her pram along the docks when Stella's boat arrives. The two women hug. Stella shares her pleasure in having Belle back home, and Ma fills her in on the latest antics of her nieces as they stroll along the pleasant streets, enjoying the winter sun. Before going into the house, Caroline pauses and warns Stella of Lu's decline.

"She has lost quite a bit of weight though her condition appears to be flourishing despite her difficulties."

Once inside, Stella admires the many homey touches Ma has made, turning the austere mansion into a warm home. Lu rises from the sofa and greets Stella. Stella is surprised by the change in her sister's appearance, for, despite her drawn face, her abdomen is quite large. As they hug, Stella can't help but notice a bump from her sister's protuberance and pulls away, embarrassed.

Lu laughs and says, "Don't be alarmed; that's just the new little one greeting you. He's quite active."

When the big girls arrive home from school, they are excited to see Aunt Stella and take her by hand to show her the new rabbit hutch and chicken coop. Although Stella is happy to visit, she feels like an outsider, and as darkness falls, she wonders if all is well at the lighthouse.

Ma, sensing Stella's mood, says, "Leaving Da alone at the tower is good for him." Stella looks up and grimaces in silent protest.

Caroline rebukes, "It is his responsibility, after all."

At bedtime, the girls ask Aunt Stella to tell them a story. Stella is pulled out of her reverie by her nieces and rises to the occasion to help meet the demands of Lu and Eddie's busy life. Stella and Caroline spend the days leading up to Christmas decorating the stately home. Lu directs from her perch on the sofa, only getting up when necessary. Stella observes that Lu often absences herself during meals and heads to the outhouse.

She mentions her observation of this rather odd behavior to Ma, who explains, "The smells of the meal preparations often start Lu's vomiting. Though, it happens less often now. When I first arrived, she was sick most of the day." They enjoy a quiet and uneventful Christmas. Ma is pleased to attend the Old Whalers Church in Sag Harbor though she misses worshiping with family and friends back in Southold.

On New Year's Day, they welcome Belle, Neely, and her parents. Belle is awed by the majesty of the mansion. It gleams under the twinkling of the oversized candlelit tree Eddie set up on Christmas Eve. They enjoy a delicious mid-day meal of roasted goose with all the trimmings. For dessert, Stella serves the stollen she baked from Mrs. Goldsmith's recipe. She and Lu share memories of their years at Hortons Point. Eddie entertains Neely and the older guests with yarns about his childhood in Ireland while the children scamper around, searching for a comfortable lap on which to settle. Liza and baby Aggie climb on their father's legs while Carrie snuggles close to her grandma and namesake. Belle invites Stella to join her in the parlor, where Lu retreated to during the meal.

Belle says, "Isn't this grand! The three of us together again."

Lu smiles as Belle squeezes in at the far end of the sofa. She pats the spot next to her, and Lu pulls up her feet to make room for Stella, who joins them.

Belle exclaims, "I have news that I want to share with both of you. I'm in the family way!"

"That's wonderful! I thought you were looking, hmm, a bit well-fed?" Lu says.

"That might have something to do with Ma's home cooking," Belle replies, patting her middle.

Stella says, "I'm glad for you both. I better go and clean up," then jumps up from the sofa and hurries out of the room.

Lu and Belle exchange looks of concern. Belle whispers, "It must be hard for her to see us so happy with our lives."

"I don't think she wants this." Lu continues, "She's happiest on her own at the lighthouse."

"That's such a lonely life, though," Belle responds with concern.

"It's the only life she's ever known," Lu replies.

"Yes, but we both were able to—to grow up?" Belle reluctantly admits then feels ashamed for being critical.

"I think Stella was always grown up. She's more responsible than both of us put together." Lu says loyally.

"I guess," Belle continues, "But I wonder if she wouldn't be happier, ...

married? . . . with children? On Thanksgiving, she was at the house and asked Burt all about Henry."

"Henry Boisseau?" Lu exclaims.

"Maybe she's interested? Even Da commented on it after she left," Belle explains.

"I think she was just being polite. I can't imagine her with Henry Bousseau," Lu says in disbelief. "Maybe someday she will marry, but for now, I think she's content."

Neely comes in and says, "Sorry to interrupt, but it'll be dark soon, and we need to head out." He continues, "Stella has decided to join us."

"I'm ready," Stella calls.

"Stella! Lu asks, "Where are you going?"

"I need to get back to the lighthouse."

"But I thought you were going to stay and help Ma at least through the ..." Lu, ever mindful of decorum, hesitates.

"You and Ma will be fine for a couple of weeks. I'll come back later in January. Da's been on his own long enough," she says with typical bluntness.

Ma joins them and says, "I guess you're all set to go?" She hugs Stella while the adults exchange farewells. Neely takes Stella's satchel, and the little group walks down to the dock where Neely's crew is waiting to bring them back to Southold and their carriage.

Stella is grateful for the ride back to the lighthouse. Neely assists her out of the carriage and leaves her bag at the cottage door. She waves to her friends as they pull away. Stella stares out at the water, transfixed by the vibrant orange and yellow hues of the winter sunset as it dips into the Long Island Sound. She turns just as the light from the tower begins its night's work, warning ships away from the rocks and shallows of Hortons Point.

❀

Despite Da's good intentions to see to the lighthouse, Stella finds much is needed to get it in order. She spends the first few days thoroughly cleaning the tower and the cottage while Da looks on, not daring to comment. One night, Stella is awed by the rare display of the northern lights dancing across the sky over Long Island Sound. In all her years on watch, this is only the second time she has seen this stunning demonstration of nature's beauty. She wonders if the keepers at Montauk and Shinnecock Lighthouses are also witnessing this unique event and feels camaraderie with them.

Stella writes to Ma and Lu about the beauty of the northern lights and assures them she will return by mid-January to await the new baby's arrival. On the 15th, a tired Stella returns to Sag Harbor and is startled at how large and swollen Lu has become. Ma reassures Stella that everything is alright as the baby will come soon.

Early in the evening, Lu cries out from the sofa where she's been sleeping. Stella, asleep in the room off the kitchen, wakes.

She goes to her sister, who says, "I think the baby is coming. Please wake Eddie to get the midwife but try to let Ma sleep a bit longer and don't wake the girls!"

On January 19, 1896, John Francis Scott, a healthy baby boy, was born. He is by far the largest baby the midwife has ever delivered, and he enters the world with a robust set of lungs breathing on his own from the first. All are relieved. Lu is exhausted but grateful for a healthy son. Ma cleans, wraps, and brings him into the parlor, where Eddie is pacing in front of the fire. Caroline places the new babe into the proud Papa's arms and looks over at her granddaughters, who crept downstairs during the excitement and are now asleep on the sofa like a pile of puppies. They wake at the commotion and insist on seeing their new brother.

"He's big!" asserts Carrie, ever the unflappable eldest.

"He's tiny!" Liza says, patting the baby's hand.

"Baby," declares little Aggie, not to be left out.

Ma says, "Now that you've all seen him, I think you'd better get back to bed. You big girls have school tomorrow."

"I'll see to them," Eddie says, nodding at the girls.

He hands over his son to Caroline, smoothing the swatch of dark hair on his head, and remarks, "He is a bonnie boy." He scoops up Aggie and herds the two older girls towards the stairs.

"Oh, Daddy," Carrie and Liza scold, "That's what you always say about babies." sounding like two little old ladies.

"What can I tell ya, my little lasses? All babies are beautiful to me. Though none so much as my little Aggie here." he continues curling her close to his chest, "No, wait, it's Liza who's the bonnie girl, no it's Carrie . . . !"

Giggling, they tramp up the stairs. A loud groan escapes from the birthing room, and they freeze.

Turning to Eddie wide-eyed. Liza asks, "W-what's that?"

"I think it's Ma," says Carrie.

"I want to see, Ma," Liza exclaims with concern and starts to head back down the stairs.

"No, no, my little ones. Your Ma needs to rest. You will see her when the sun comes up and not a minute sooner." The girls recognize their father's firm tone and climb up to bed, exhausted now that the initial excitement has passed. Caroline smiles at the proud papa, and cuddling little John, goes back into the warmth of the birthing room to present him to his Ma for his first feeding.

Lu doesn't bounce back after the birth of John, so Ma takes charge. She is 28, and this is her 4th child in 8 years. At Ma's suggestion, Eddie has the doctor stop by to check on Lu and the baby. He declares both are fine and suggests that Lu may need more time due to the difficulty of the pregnancy and the delivery. Stella, always eager to get back to work, takes the doctor's declaration as a sign she can return to the lighthouse.

Ma is disappointed that Stella is so anxious to leave, but Lucy chides her, saying, "Don't you see Ma, the Lighthouse is Stella's baby? Just like I'm your baby, and John and the girls are mine."

CHAPTER 18

February 1896

A New Slant -
reducing sails to achieve an optimal 'angle of heel' to
prevent the boat from pulling over.

Upon returning to Hortons Point, Stella is surprised to receive a letter from Aunt Jennie with an enclosure from Cousin Edith. Now 14, she is planning an ice skating party at Great Pond and requests Stella be a chaperone. There will, of course, be a male chaperone for the boys. A dismayed Stella writes to Ma and Lu about this strange request, but they both urge her to go. Stella requests specifics, and by return post, a letter from Aunt Jennie again includes a note from Edith, who writes:

> *Dear Cousin Stella,*
>
> *Thank you. Thank you. Thank you.*
> *We will have so much fun! You too!*
>
> *Best regards,*
> *Your Cousin Edith*

Aunt Jennie's letter is a bit more informative and reads:

Dearest Stella:

Thank you for agreeing to chaperone Edith's skating party. A gentleman, a former seaman from Orient, has agreed to pick you up on his way to the event. His name is George Herbert Terry, and he is known to be of sober habits and upstanding morals. We have every reason to believe you will be safe in his charge as he is the uncle of one of Edith's guests and will chaperone the young gentlemen. After skating, all are invited back to our home for refreshments by the fire. Your assistance is most appreciated.

Warmest Regards,
Aunt Jennie

When she finishes reading, Stella purses her lips and huffs, "What have I agreed to?"

Da comes in, and seeing the letter in her hand, asks, "What's that?"

"I'm to chaperone Cousin Edith's skating party and am to be picked up by the male chaperone."

Da, smirking, asks, "And who might that be?"

"George Herbert Terry? From Orient!" she spits out the words as if it's a distant and disreputable locality.

"Can't say I know the man, but I'm sure if Henry and Jennie think he's up to chaperoning, he should be capable of driving the likes of you."

Stella shares this unexpected news with Belle, who is now in her confinement. Belle is excited for Stella to meet a young man.

"Wait, Belle, you're getting the wrong idea. I don't know anything about him."

"You know that he's not married, or he wouldn't be chaperoning, and he's from Orient, and someone's uncle and Aunt Jennie declares him fit, so he must be!"

The women giggle like schoolgirls as they often do at their continued disdain of Jennie's high and mighty ways.

Mrs. Tillinghast comes in and says, "It feels like no time has passed hearing you two in here thick as thieves. What's all the laughing about anyway?" Much to Stella's embarrassment, Belle tells her mother the story of Stella's upcoming chaperoning with an unknown gentleman.

Mrs. Tillinghast responds helpfully, "I have a cousin in Orient. I could write to her and ask about him if you'd like?"

"Please don't go to any trouble," responds Stella.

"It's no trouble, dear." Mrs. Tillinghast continues as she walks out of the room. Stella looks at Belle, eyebrows raised in horror.

"Belle, please stop her."

"Listen, my friend; there's no stopping her now, and what's the harm anyway?"

"I don't know. I just feel uncomfortable having people talking about me."

"They're not talking about you. They're talking about George Herbert Terry!"

At the end of the week, Stella receives a letter from Belle and learns that George was a ship's cook for most of his life but now works at the Orient General Store. He resides in his family home on Navy Street, is 41, and has never married. '41? Really? That's almost old as Ma!' she exclaims. The information about Mr. Terry only adds to her apprehension, but seeing no way out of her commitment, she puts it out of her mind and tends to business as usual.

❋

The night before the skating party, Stella works the early shift. Da uncharacteristically considerate comes up at 1 AM and says, "Why don't you get some sleep. You've got a big day tomorrow."

Stella climbs down the ladder but stops on the stairs reminding him, "Don't forget to check the . . ."

"Hey," he cuts her off. "Don't you be telling me my job."

Stella hurries down and picks up a brick from the hearth to warm the cold bed. She lies awake and misses Ma. Though she knows Lu needs Ma right now, she wishes she was here to help her prepare for the outing tomorrow.

Stella's up before the sun kindles the hearth and makes breakfast for herself and Da. When Da comes down, Stella heads up with the kerosene and goes about the morning routine, wiping the residue off the windows and lenses, then pulling the dark curtains around the windows to block the sun. Stella loses herself in her work. When she notices Da heading to the outhouse, she realizes she'd better wash up and get dressed.

Spending so many long winter nights in the tower, Stella has grown to hate the cold, so she doesn't relish the idea of spending the afternoon at an ice skating pond. She's never done anything like this before, chaperoning a group of young girls. She wonders once again as she dresses for the ordeal. What could Aunt Jennie be thinking?

Stella hears the noisy wagon full of boisterous boys pull up and steels herself for what she expects to be a trying day. Da comes down from the bedroom.

"I thought you'd be asleep by now," Stella says.

"It wouldn't be proper if I didn't meet the 'er . . . (he coughs into his hand), young man." Stella realizes da knows that George Terry is not young and wonders where he came by this information.

Stella and George go outside. While George Prince introduces. While George Prince introduces himself to George Terry, the driver, one of the youths, leaps down and assists Stella up onto the front seat. They pull away before George Terry looks over and acknowledges her with a quick nod.

She mumbles a brisk, "Good morning," but her words are lost over the sounds of his "Huh" and quick lash at the horses as they take off at a brisk pace; her awkwardness increases as they jostle along the dirt roads arriving all too quickly for Stella's liking at Great Pond.

Stella is relieved to see Henry walking over. He tips his hat to George and walks around to assist Stella.

They exchange warm hugs, and he says, "I guess you two are acquainted?"

"Not really," George says. Henry looks confused.

Stella explains, "It was noisy, and we didn't get the chance."

"Oh, my," Henry says, eyes twinkling.

Then let me do the honors, "This is my niece, Miss Prince." Turning to George, who lifts his hat politely. "I'd like you to make the acquaintance of Mr. George Terry." Blushing, Stella looks up into George's eyes and observes his steady gaze that lingers. He is thin yet broad-shouldered and quite a bit taller than her. She senses genuine kindness and maybe even longing.

Tilting his hat, George responds, "Nice to make your acquaintance even if under these unusual circumstances."

Henry continues, "I hope we're not imposing on you. Edith was quite insistent. Of course, for proprieties sake . . ." he falters and waves an arm to the crowd of young people who are gathered just out of earshot. "If you could just keep a headcount and make sure they are all safe, I will be back in 2 hours. You can follow me back to the house for dinner."

"That's not necessary . . . " George says.

"We think it is."

"That is most kind of you, sir," George says.

Stella smiles and notices Edith dancing around at her side says, "I think our young charges await." Edith takes Stella's hand, and they walk over to the young people putting on their skates.

She calls out, "Everyone . . . this is my cousin Miss Prince. She's the lighthouse keeper at Hortons Point." Edith turns to his nephew and says, "Well?"

The youth says, "Um, this is my Uncle George, um . . . Mr. Terry. He's just a cook."

George, chuckling, turns to Stella as the young people resume talking among themselves.

"Clearly, a cook is not held in such high regard as a lighthouse keeper."

Stella, relieved to see he does not appear offended, says, "Cooking is a valuable skill. One I've yet to master, I'm afraid."

"A lady lighthouse keeper is of far more interest."

"To be honest, it's my father, who is the official keeper, though I am his able assistant," Stella adds.

George smiles, "Able? Is it?"

Stella blushes and says, "I don't mean to boast."

"No, but I see the Prince women are cut from the same mold."

"Excuse me?" Stella asks.

"Your cousin Edith has a solid sense of herself, shall we say . . . organizing this event we find ourselves attending."

"You would be correct there. Edith knows her own mind."

"With all due respect, I venture to suggest the same could be said of you, Miss Prince." Stella smiles, pleased with this assessment of herself as a woman of substance. George strolls over to assist the boys while Stella moves closer to the fire and searches the skaters. She would be hard-pressed to say which of them she is responsible for other than Edith, of course, who does seem to have the group well in hand.

By the time Henry returns, the girls are happy to climb up into the back of his wagon. He assists Stella to sit up front with him while George gathers the boys to follow. A short raucous drive ensues, and when they arrive at the Prince's home, Jennie has a bountiful spread ready with soup, sweetbreads, and hot chocolate. The hungry skaters are most appreciative and enthusiastically partake. As the afternoon light is fading, Stella's apprehension grows. Parents start arriving to pick up the young ladies, but Edith insists that all must stay and finish a game of charades.

Henry notices Stella's frequent glances out of the window and says, "Shall I take you home?"

"I hate to pull you away, but it doesn't appear that George and the boys are ready to leave."

"It's no bother. I know you have responsibilities, and we do so appreciate your help today. I'll just let Jennie know, and we'll slip out." Relieved to get away, Stella heads outside and climbs up into the wagon. Henry makes quick work of guiding the horses back to the lighthouse.

The sun has set when they get to the lighthouse, and the beacon is not lit. Stella jumps down from the wagon and races into the tower. She takes the steps two at a time, quickly igniting the wicks. She goes down to the parlor and finds Henry struggling to get Da up to bed. Judging from the jug on the table, he has once again over-imbibed. Stella assists Henry with Da, then walks downstairs in uncomfortable silence.

Henry looks at Stella and asks, "Should I stay and help with the night watch? I don't know that he'll wake and relieve you."

"No, that's not necessary."

"I think this isn't the first time," he says, gesturing towards the stairs.

"Well ... " Stella hesitates, embarrassed and reluctant to say too much.

"I know you do more than is proper around here."

"No, no ... Uncle Henry. It's not like that." Stella says. "I love working at the lighthouse, and Ma says, Ma says ... Da is sick. He can't stop himself."

"This is why we need the Temperance Law to pass; spirits ruin folks' lives." Henry retorts.

"Ma says, Da might have been different? . . . before the war?" Stella mumbles.

"Yes, that might be so. But many fought and even were wounded but still didn't give in to this weakness. Please forgive me, Stella, for speaking so directly. I don't mean to upset you. If you are sure you will be fine, I do need to get back."

Stella banks the fire and then heads up to the watch room carrying a can of kerosene to refuel during the night. Stella writes to Ma and Lu to tell them about her day while it's still fresh. She acknowledges that while she hasn't made up her mind about Mr. Terry, she has to admit he made a favorable impression.

Several days later, Stella is just finishing up the morning routine when she sees a wagon approaching. It's too cold to be a casual visitor. Curious, Stella goes down as Da comes in from seeing to the animals.

"Did I hear a wagon?" he asks.

"Yes. I wonder who it is?"

Da goes out, and Stella hears him issue an uncharacteristic chuckle and a warm greeting, "Hello there. Nice to see you again." Stella burning with curiosity pulls on her shawl and heads out to join Da. She is surprised to see Mr. George Terry.

"Hello," she says with more enthusiasm than she feels. Mr. Terry gets down, shakes Da's hand, and tips his hat to Stella.

"I didn't know you left the other day. I hope everything was all right?" he asks.

"Oh, I just needed to get back to the tower," she says, blushing as she recalls how they found Da.

"Would you like to come in?" Stella asks.

"I don't want to impose. I was just going to Henry's and thought I'd stop."

Da says, "Come on in. It's too cold to stand out here. Stella, give the man a cup of coffee. If you've got the stomach for it, you can try some of her porridge." he says with a snicker. Mr. Terry steps up onto the porch, and they go inside. Stella pokes the embers back to life in the coal fire and pours a cup of coffee. Next, she stirs the porridge they'd had for breakfast.

Da asks, "Have you been in the tower?"

"No."

"Stella can give you a tour. She knows all about it. Been doing it all her life."

"So I've heard," Mr. Terry says. Stella blushes and busies herself, pouring coffee.

Da says, "No, thanks, Stella. If you don't mind excusing me," he says, turning to Mr. Terry, "I need to get to bed. Been up most of the night."

Mr. Terry says, "I didn't mean to disrupt your schedule."

"No, that's fine. I work first shift; then, Da covers during the night when I sleep."

Stella sits across from George and sips her coffee.

"Would you like porridge?"

"I wouldn't mind a little something warm if you're sure it's no trouble." Stella jumps up from the chair and gets the bowl spooning in porridge.

"If Ma were here, she'd have some of her tasty biscuits, but I never learned to make them."

"I thought you were a baker?" Mr. Terry says. Stella is curious as to who has been talking to him about her. "Aren't you known for your Stollen?"

"It's Mrs. Goldsmith's family recipe. She taught Lu, my sister, and me when we were just girls right here at this table. Captain Goldsmith was the head keeper when we were little. So his wife was like a grandma to us."

Mr. Terry takes a spoon of the porridge and grimaces.

"I hope it's ok?" Stella says, noting his expression.

"Guess I'm used to my own cooking."

"Yes, you're a cook. Let me take that." Stella says, reaching for the bowl mid spoonful.

"No, it's fine," he says gallantly.

"You know, when you live alone, you get set in your ways."

"I, um, wouldn't know though Da and I are pretty set in our ways."

"Sometimes, I think it might be nice to have someone else around. Even if it did mean, things might have to change some."

Rising, Mr. Terry says, "I better go." Stella, startled by his quick exit, follows behind.

"Thanks for stopping by," she murmurs, looking away. Stella realizes she never showed him the tower. He tips his hat and climbs up onto the carriage.

"Oh, did you want to see . . . " she says, gesturing to the tower.

"No, that's fine. Maybe another time."

CHAPTER 19

Spring–Summer 1896

Keel over - to capsize, exposing the ship's keel.

I n early March, Da and Ma attend the wedding of their neighbor's son. Stella goes to the church service then walks back to Hortons Point while Ma and Da go onto the reception. Ma plans on spending the night at the Prince Lane cottage.

She's been dividing her time between Prince Lane and Sag Harbor as she says, "I've spent too many cold winters at Hortons Point."

Stella doesn't expect that Da will return to cover his shift. His unreliability has increased this spring, so Stella often does the entire night watch on her own. She naps in the afternoon in anticipation of being up all night and prepares herself a simple meal of potatoes and eggs before she begins her night's work tending the lantern.

Da imbibes heavily at the wedding then joins some buddies to serenade the newlyweds at their home. When the rowdy me arrive, they realize the young couple is not home. In alcohol-induced high spirits, they play a prank, bringing some farm animals into the cottage. Laughing uproariously, they tie the cow to a chair in the kitchen, put the pig in the parlor, and release chickens in the bedroom. They close the front door and head out back to hide behind the barn. The couple comes home, having been waylaid at the bride's parents' house, both of them worn out from the long day, and notice the barn door is open.

The groom heads to the barn and yells, "The cow is missing."

"What?" the exhausted bride exclaims. "What bad luck we are having."

"I don't understand," the groom continues scratching his head.

"You go inside, and I'll look around."

The bride pushes open the cottage door and screams. The groom runs into the cottage and sees what has alarmed her.

"At least we know where the cow is." he states with surprise, "I just don't understand . . . "

The bride yells and bursts into tears.

"The mess! What's happened here!"

"Don't worry, my sweet. I'll get it out," the groom says, attempting to calm her as he leads the cow out the door. Walking into the parlor, the bride slips and falls, calling out to the groom, who ties the cow to the porch railing and rushes inside. He sees the pig sprawled under the table and the bride lying next to him, having slipped on the pig's waste.

They hear the loud guffaws of the three jokers who poke their heads in the door and say, "Sorry, didn't expect such a mess." One man takes the cow and leads it back to the barn while the other two gather the chickens' —feathers flying. The groom takes her into the now empty bedroom, where she collapses on the bed in tears.

He tries to calm her, but she is inconsolable and bellows, "Get those animals and your friends out of here." He stands, leaving her in tears, and pushes the pig outside, picking up what mess he sees along the way. The pranksters, still laughing, having been well-fueled with the local brew, offer him a swig from the jug and attempt feeble apologies. As the bride's crying grows louder, they pat him on the back and rush away, somewhat sobered.

The bride cries herself to sleep in the groom's arms, and in the morning, she demands, "I want them arrested."

"Oh, sweetheart, they didn't mean any harm."

"I don't care. They shouldn't get away with that."

"They were so drunk they might not even remember what they did."

"I remember, and they ruined our wedding night."

"It doesn't have to ruin our day, too, you know. You stay in bed and rest. I'll tend the animals, then come back and join you."

The bride lays back down, trying to get comfortable, and hears a loud crash from the other room and a howl from the groom. She rushes into the parlor and sees that he slipped on more animal waste and is lying on the floor.

"That's it. We're going to the sheriff. They need to pay for what they've done." she exclaims angrily.

"I don't think we should. They didn't mean anything by it," he says, rising   from the dirty floor.

"I disagree. We're going to the sheriff," she demands.

The angry bride and reluctant groom follow-through, and the sheriff questions the three perpetrators.

Their only defense is that "They meant no harm and will make reparations to the couple for any damage they may have caused." While this satisfies the groom, the bride insists they press charges.

The Lighthouse Service is notified of the pending legal charges against Keeper Prince. In early May, the Inspector comes to Hortons Point with his supervisor. After a quick inspection, the men gather in George's small office. Stella hears the raised voices. After the heated exchange, the supervisors file out and return to the waiting ship. Stella doesn't know what to think and wishes her mother was present. She heats the evening meal and waits for George.

When he finally emerges, he says, "You do the watch alone tonight. I'm going to town." She nods, then goes up to the tower and prepares for the night ahead.

Stella falls into a light sleep, waking intermittently to check that all is well. As the sun rises, she extinguishes the wicks, wipes the glass windows down, removes any remaining sooty residue, and then drapes the black cloth around the windows to protect the precious Fresnel lens from the glare of the sun. While on watch, Stella writes to Ma, telling her what happened.

Satisfied that the tower is squared away, Stella climbs down and pokes the fire in the parlor back to life. As there's no sign of Da, Stella goes out to tend to the animals, comes in, eats a quick breakfast, then heads up for some much-needed rest. Falling into her bed, she pulls the covers over her head to block out the light of day and descends into a deep sleep.

Stella continues to hold down the fort at the lighthouse. George stays at Prince Lane with Caroline though he does come out infrequently to give Stella a break.

Stella's loneliness and fatigue grow as the warmer weather brings daytime visitors. She is required to show them the tower and explain how the lantern works. Without Ma or Lu close by, it all falls to Stella. After services on Sunday, the three women gather at the house on Prince Lane, and Ma discusses the repercussions of George's arrest.

She says, "Da expects the Lighthouse Service will discipline him. He fears he will be transferred to an isolated outpost or, even worse, discharged." Stella and Lu are both dismayed to learn of the severe nature of the legal problems George has brought on himself.

Caroline pleads, "Stella, under the circumstances, you must give serious consideration as to how you wish to proceed. You are not officially the keeper, and as such, you will have to leave if Da is transferred or worse, let go."

Stella, alarmed at her mother's warning, rises, saying, "I need to get back."

She trudges off, carrying the weight of the world on her shoulders. Stella retreats further into her isolation at the lighthouse and, for a time,

even stops attending Sunday services claiming that the strain of showing guests around on top of working most nights alone requires her to
sleep when she can. Lu and Eddie come out on Sunday and urge her to
consider how her behavior affects Ma. Stella writes Ma a letter apolo-
gizing and assuring her she will attend services next week.

Caroline responds by return post:

Hortons Point
June 13, 1896
My Darling Stella,

*These are difficult times we are facing. I am glad to receive your
letter and know in my heart that the good Lord is watching over us.
I hope you are coming to accept what will be.*

*Belle and I spoke of you last week. She is worried about you
and our current situation.*

*I hope you will write to your cousins on Block Island and make
plans for the 4th. I know you have enjoyed spending time with them
in the past, and this year more than ever, getting away will do you
good. I am pigging along as usual and trying to keep Da on course.
Even though he has brought this disgrace down on us all, he still
struggles to conduct himself with decorum.*

*Da has gone to the lighthouse most afternoons. I hope he is
meeting his responsibilities, and you are not taking it all on yourself.*

Your loving,
Ma

Prince Lane,
Southold NY
June 18, 1896

Dearest Mother,

I am grateful for your love and support during this difficult time.
I wonder if the Reverend Marshall was thinking of us in his sermon,
"the Lord doesn't give more than we can bear." I pray that's true, for,
at this moment, I cannot picture my life away from Hortons Point.

Though I worry about the lighthouse's consistent operation in
my absence, at your urging, I have posted a letter to my cousins on
Block Island and will visit over the weekend of the 4th.

Since you asked, Da has not spent much time here. I walked over
to Belle's and spent the afternoon enjoying the antics of her little
ones. Belle is a true friend, but there isn't anything anyone can do.
We must wait for the court and the Government's decision.
Your Loving Daughter,
Stella

Hortons Point
Southold, NY
June 17, 1896

Good Morning Dearie,

I welcomed your letter of last evening and am glad you will visit
Block Island. Do not despair over operations at Hortons Point. Da

must see to his responsibilities. I fear you take too much on yourself. I do so appreciate your dedication to carry on even in the face of our current shame.

Glad you survived the storm. Da was stuck in all day with nothing to do. He checked on the boat but got wet, returned cursing everything black and blue, then slept the afternoon away.

Wish you attended the church meeting Thursday night. Though we did have good attendance, several brought pies, a delicious ending to an awkward gathering. Letter writing to our representatives seems to be the way to move the Temperance Law forward.

The Rosary Society prepared the sanctuary Saturday afternoon for the monthly baptisms. We trimmed with greens and pink roses from Misses Cartiers' gardens. So kind of them to make such generous contributions when they have so little themselves. I hope they know what pleasure—need to add the word, know.

Have you found time to weed? I will come up there this week to help. Our garden is blossoming with pink geraniums, primroses, peonies, and pansies, all coming to flower. It is a joy to see the fruits of one's labor.

Be kind to yourself and rest when you can.

Your loving,

Ma

Rhode Island
July 6, 1896

Dearest Stella,

Hope you are enjoying your stay on Block Island. How is every-body after the 4th? Living, I hope, as we are here. I arrived safe Friday. While Da was tending the tower, I went into the office and searched for mail from the Government to no avail. So either he hasn't received word, or he destroyed it. He has not said anything about the future.

On to more pleasant subjects, we had a crowd of local folks, summer returnees, and new visitors who came out to picnic at Hortons Point the day of the 4th. Most lasted into the night to see the fireworks displays. They were quite spectacular. Of course, Da and I had the best view from the tower, there was quite a spectacle over Shelter Island, and all-around to the east was ablaze.

However, I must tell you about my mishap. I weeded the gardens earlier in the day and picked blackberries to bake a pie. When I removed the pie from the oven and went to put it on the hearth, somehow it hit and went bottom up on the floor. I saved part of the crust though the inside was all over the oilcloth. Needless to say, we were not able to share the pie with the guests, but Da still enjoyed the salvaged bits during the night, none the wiser for the mishap.

Many were asking for you on the 4th. Belle and Neely came with their family. Belle sends her good wishes and is glad you have gotten away. Lu and Eddie came too. Their little ones grow like weeds and keep Lu hopping though I can't say when I've seen her more content.

I will stay on at Hortons Point, at least until your return next week.

Your loving,
Ma

When Stella returns, she is glad for time with Ma. They fall into their easy companionable ways, with Stella assuming responsibility for the lantern and George spending most of his time on Prince Lane. After dinner one evening, Caroline and Stella sit on the porch enjoying the cooling breeze off the Sound. As the sun starts to go down, Stella gets up from the rocker to light the lantern.

Caroline says, "I've wanted to mention something to you."

"Can it wait?" Stella asks, impatient, to go up to the tower and prepare the lantern for the night.

Reaching out, Caroline catches Stella's arm and says, "I want to say this now as I've been putting it off. I expect it will give you something to consider while you tend the light."

"Okay," Stella responds, guessing that her mother will ask her to reconsider returning to Southold. Instead, Caroline brings up an unexpected though related matter.

With a quick inhale, Caroline says, "George Terry has been inquiring about you."

"What?" Stella exclaims.

"Yes, Aunt Jennie spoke to me on the 4th."

"Aunt Jennie! Since when do you give credence to anything Aunt Jennie has to say." Stella responds impertinently.

"Stella! " Ma exclaims, "Please don't speak ill of your elders."

"I'm sorry, Ma, but you know Aunt Jennie loves to gossip."

"I believe she is looking out for your best interests. She just wanted you to know that Mr. Terry seems interested in you."

"That's ridiculous!" Stella says as she stands and rushes inside, running up the stairs as fast as her long skirt allows. She stops to catch her breath before continuing up the ladders and loses herself in her night's work. Caroline continues rocking on the porch, recognizing that Stella is uncomfortable with the thought of others discussing her plight, but she hopes she can get through to her. Caroline fears George's run-in with the law will, in all likelihood, mean the end of their living at Hortons Point.

❊

Stella's dependence on the weather and the tides provides a familiar rhythm supporting her through this challenging summer. This busy time of year allows her to avoid the haunting thoughts of having to leave. On August 27, 1896, George is remanded to criminal court in Riverhead. Caroline accompanies him, but Stella stays at Hortons Point, unwilling to give the appearance of supporting him and fearing she will be unable to contain her anger at the public humiliation he has brought down on them all. At the end of the long day, George and Caroline return, while George attends to the animals; Caroline takes Stella out on the front porch to review the day's events.

Shamefully Caroline says, "He is charged with Public Drunkenness and Disorderly Conduct." Caroline continues, holding back tears that have been building all day. "He received a suspended sentence due to his war record, good standing in the community, and responsibility to perform the essential duties of maintaining the light." She continues with difficulty, "He is required to perform community service and will be on probation for one year." Tears of shame flow down her face as she stammers, "The barrister says he was let off easy."

"Really!". . . Stella explodes. "He's an upstanding community member? I hate to think what this place would be like if there were more like him."

"Now, Stella, please don't be cruel. It does not flatter you to take that tone. He is still your father. And . . . " Caroline says, walking over to her daughter's side and touching her shoulder.

Stella pulls away, backing up and speaking over her mother with growing force and volume, "I must calm down? This is why I didn't go. He's protected, but we endure public humiliation because of his behavior!" Caroline, struck dumb by the ferocity of her daughter's words, gasps as she sees George standing at the edge of the porch. He approaches Stella, and Caroline steps in front of him, fearing he will harm her.

He looks over Caroline and sneers at his daughter, "At last, we hear the truth! If that's how you feel, then you can just go ahead and do it all. I'm done!" he shouts and stalks off. Stella is shocked. Shaking, she rushes up into the tower—her sanctuary; and wipes the spotless lens, seeking refuge from her angry thoughts.

A short time later, Caroline ascends the stairs and says, "Calm yourself, dear."

Stella responds, "He has created this problem, yet he continues to blame others. I can't live with him any longer, Ma. I refuse to live under his roof. I will not leave Hortons Point."

"Stella, you're angry now, and that's understandable. But we must wait for the Government's decision."

Stella sneers, "Are you really that innocent, Ma? He has a criminal record. Of course, they will let him go. He can't continue to hold a government position." Stella's harsh words pierce Caroline's heart, and her tears flow freely.

She says solemnly, "We must trust that the Good Lord will give us the strength to get through these difficulties. We don't know what the Lighthouse Service will decide."

As the sun sinks into the Sound, Stella prepares the lantern. Caroline, defeated, returns to the front porch and resumes rocking, the motion bolstering her against a flood of emotion. George does not return that night, and Stella is relieved to work on her own. She dozes in the watch room and is awakened around two by Caroline.

"Da isn't back. I'll take his shift."

"That's not necessary, Ma. I'll sleep during the day." Caroline retreats to bed.

When Stella comes down, Caroline has a hot breakfast waiting and has already tended the animals. Stella sits at the table and eats in silence.

When she's finished, she turns to Ma and says, "I am sorry for how I spoke yesterday."

Before she even finishes, Caroline comes over, hugs Stella's back, kisses the top of her head, and says, "This is a difficult time."

"Please, Ma, let me finish," Stella cuts her mother off and pulls away from her mother's embrace.

"I won't put you in the middle, but I spoke the truth yesterday. I cannot and will not live under that man's roof. I have lost all respect for him after what he's put this family through. I'm sorry, Ma, but I just cannot do it any longer."

"Stella, please, give it time."

"Ma, I don't know what I will do, but I am certain that I will not change my mind about this,"

Stella's steely tone is new to Caroline, yet she attempts to find a practical solution.

"Maybe you could move in with Lu and Eddie? They could use a hand." Stella is crestfallen at the idea,

"Yes, I suppose that might be an option, but Ma, I don't know how

I could live anywhere but at the lighthouse."

"Stella, we always knew the lighthouse was not a permanent part of our lives. Few keepers last as long as Da, uh, we have." she catches herself and corrects her words.

"Yes, that's true, but I grew up here. The lighthouse is the only life I've ever known and the only one I've ever wanted."

"All we can do is ask the Almighty to guide us through these difficult times."

"I wish I had your faith Ma."

"Just give it time," Caroline murmurs.

Caroline stays on at Hortons Point. She cooks and gardens and greets visitors through the busy summer season while Stella retreats into her nighttime routine of tending the light. She sleeps during the day and upholds full responsibility for the night watch as Da does not return. Stella sees little of Belle or even Lu and Eddie, who come out most weekends with their crew. At times the days drag, and Stella relishes their slow passing wanting her familiar routine to stay the same, but feelings of dread about the Lighthouse Service's pending decision hangs over them.

On Friday, the fifth of September, an official envelope arrives. George has not returned, and though they know he is staying at the cottage on Prince Lane, they haven't discussed it. When Stella gets up, she sees the unopened letter on the table, gingerly picks it up, and brings it to her mother, out in the garden.

"Open it," she demands.

Hesitating, Caroline says, "But it's addressed to Da."

"Open it!" Stella repeats.

"Stella," Caroline continues, "You promised you wouldn't put me between the two of you."

"Ma, this doesn't just affect him; it affects all of us." Caroline walks back into the cottage and sits down at the table. She places the envelope down and sighs.

"I'm not comfortable opening his mail."

"But we don't even know when or even if he'll be back," Stella says— pushing the letter closer to her mother and taking a seat across from her.

"Ma, we have to see what it says. We need to know where we stand." Caroline sighs, picking up the envelope.

She tears it open, takes out the letter, and passes it to Stella, saying, "You read it. I can't."

Stella takes it and reads it aloud:

Lighthouse Service Board

Federal Government

Hortons Point Lighthouse

Southold, New York

August 30, 1896

Keeper George Prince:

You are hereby informed that the Lighthouse Service Board finds you guilty of 'Public Drunkeness and Dereliction of Duty.' As a result of these charges, you are dismissed from the Lighthouse Service and must relinquish the Head Keeper's position at Hortons Point on 11 September 1896.

Your replacement, Captain Robert Ebbits, will arrive on-site on that same date to assume full responsibility as Head Keeper. Supervisor Wiggins will be present to oversee a smooth transition. You must attend to your duties until that date when you will vacate the quarters, leaving all official documents, tools, and household goods owned by the Federal Government at Hortons Point.

The Lighthouse Service requires that you leave the property on the eleventh with only your personal effects and not return in perpetuity.

Respectfully,
The United States Lighthouse Service
Board of Commissioners

Stella places the letter on the table, tears in her eyes. She looks up at Caroline, who says, "We suspected this might happen."

"Yes, but we didn't know who would take his place," Stella says, heartbroken—tears now flowing freely.

Caroline looks at her daughter as it dawns on her for the first time and says, "You didn't think . . . you would get the post?"

"I hoped. After all, I am doing the work."

"Yes, we know, but the government doesn't know that."

"They do know."

"What do you mean?" Caroline asks.

"Why else did they discontinue the assistant position when Lu and I finished school? They expected us to do the work."

"I see your point. I hadn't thought of that. I guess that might be true, but Stella, you couldn't handle all the work on your own."

"There are other women keepers. We've both seen reports in the *Keepers' Periodicals* of other women who take over when their husbands become ill or die."

"Yes, but they generally have children who help them. Caroline searches for the right words to avoid upsetting her daughter further, "I don't think any of the women are unmarried; that would not be proper," Caroline reasons.

Rising from her chair, Stella says, "I'm going for a walk."

Caroline folds the letter and returns it to the envelope. Not sure how or when to break the news to George since he hasn't been back to the lighthouse since he and Stella argued. Eventually, Caroline brings the letter to him in Southold; George reads it coolly, as though he'd anticipated it all along and doesn't care what it says. George stays away from the lighthouse leaving Stella to see to it by herself. Stella is dismayed by how much work is needed to bring the lighthouse up to standard for the handover. She pushes these thoughts out of her mind knowing she is working as hard as she can.

CHAPTER 20

September 1896

Taken Aback -
Sails pressed back into the mast from a sudden change of wind.

Stella continues performing her duties at Hortons Point right up to the day Captain Ebbitts and his wife Amanda arrive. Ma packed and cleaned the keeper's quarters in preparation for their coming. Since Stella hasn't removed her personal items, it makes sense for them to move into the Goldsmiths side of the cottage, at least for the time being. Caroline greets the couple with her usual warmth and sets about showing Mrs. Ebbitts around while Stella takes the Captain up to the tower. When they spot the Lighthouse Service's ship, the *Mistletoe*, offshore, he asks Stella to wait until Supervisor Wiggins arrives. They go down and assist their son, Robert, as he unloads the carriage with their personal belongings at Mrs. Ebbitt's direction.

Although George returned for the first time that morning, he stays out of sight in the office, updating the Keepers Logbook from the notes Stella meticulously collected during his absence. When Mr. Wiggins arrives, the men join him in the small office to review the ledgers.

George, impatient to be off, pays short shrift to the task saying, "I'm sure the Captain knows how to do this; he's been in service for years," referring to the fact that Captain Ebbitts had been the keeper at Cedar Island Lighthouse in East Hampton before coming to Hortons Point. Stella, hovering just outside the office, perks up when she hears this. She didn't know Captain Ebbitts had lighthouse experience and is relieved to learn that he does.

After the brief meeting, the men return to the parlor. Caroline offers them something to eat.

Supervisor Wiggins refuses on their behalf and says, "I'd like to speak with Miss Prince."

Stella is surprised but composed, turns to the Supervisor, and says, "How may I be of service, Sir?"

Captain Ebbitts smiles and says, "Now that's the right answer."

Stella cocks her head to one side, puzzled by the exchange.

"Looks like you're gonna get what you want after all," George snarls at her, then turning to Caroline; he gestures with his arm towards the door, saying, "Mrs. P., we're leaving." Caroline is startled by his directive. She hesitates, looking at the group standing in what has been her parlor for the past 25 years.

"I . . . I don't understand," she stammers.

"You don't have to understand. Let's go," George barks as he holds the door open.

Caroline walks over to Stella, puts her arms around her, and whispers, "Please come."

"You go Ma. I'll be fine."

Caroline follows George out of the cottage. She obediently climbs up into the wagon, and George yells to the horses, "huh." They take off at a brisk pace, leaving behind the life he destroyed without even a look back.

Inside the cottage, Supervisor Wiggins turns to Stella and continues, "As I started to say if you should so wish, Captain Ebbitts has agreed to allow you to live at Hortons Point with the understanding that you will continue on in your role as a helper...unofficially, of course." Stella gasps pulls out a chair, and sits down hard, shocked at this turn of events.

She looks at Captain Ebbitts and says, "Are you and the Mrs. comfortable with me staying? I see you have a son who might aid you?"

Captain Ebbitts sits across from her at the table.

"The Mrs. and I would be most grateful for your assistance. My wife is not one to take on much outside of the home, and our son is here only to help with the move. He is a seaman shipping out of Sag Harbor, so he will not live here."

"Oh! I see!" Stella says, astonished by this turn of events.

"Now, of course, Miss Prince . . . " Supervisor Wiggins continues, "This is an unofficial position and, as such, does not include financial compensation. However, the Lighthouse Service has agreed to include provisions for three adults; and of course, you will continue to live in the cottage as long as Captain Ebbitts and you agree."

"After the hearty recommendation your father just gave you, I'd be a fool to refuse," the Captain adds.

"My father?" Stella asks incredulously. Even more surprised at this than the offer from the Lighthouse Service. Stella stands as a smile stretches across her face.

Captain Ebbitts stands as well and puts out his hand to shake it, "So am I to take that smile as an indication that you are willing to accept this new situation?"

"Yes!" Stella says, taking his hand in both of hers.

"We are delighted to have you here and hope you will become part of our family," Mrs. Ebbitts says to Stella.

Stella turns to her and says, "I am so very grateful to you both and the Lighthouse Service." she continues turning to Supervisor Wiggins. "I am proud to accept this opportunity."

"Ok, then. Since we are all in agreement, Miss Prince can familiarize you with the specifics of this lantern. I need to get back," Supervisor Wiggins continues and heads to the door.

He turns, tipping his hat, and says, "Captain, Mrs. Ebbitts, Miss Prince, good day." Stella looks around, stunned.

Mrs. Ebbitts breaks the silence saying, "Isn't he the gentleman?"

Stella mumbles, "I've never seen that side of him before."

Captain Ebbitts walking towards the door to the tower, turns to Stella and says, "I guess we better head up top. I expect you have much to show me."

"Of course, Captain," Stella responds. "And I expect there is much I can learn from you, sir."

Mrs. Ebbitts calls to them, "Don't be too long. Stella's Ma made us venison stew and biscuits. I'll keep them warm till you're ready."

Climbing up behind Captain Ebbitts, Stella's mind is reeling; she can't quite believe her good fortune as she repeats under her breathe, "I get to stay . . . I get to stay!"

❀

Stella shows the Captain her routine at the lighthouse. His take-charge approach is unsettling to Stella as he tackles many of the less routine tasks with vigor. Though Stella understands the need, she is uncomfortable with his critical assessment of the lighthouse's condition. Stella doesn't point out that the more strenuous jobs were George's responsibility due to some misguided loyalty she feels to her father. Although she is a strong young woman, she has never taken on the most physically taxing tasks.

One afternoon, Captain Ebbitts enumerates a long list of projects that he wishes to complete to get the place up to par. Mrs. Ebbitts notices Stella's defensive posture and general discomfort during the Captain's monologue.

Trying to ease the young woman's obvious distress Mrs. Ebbitts says, "Captain, you do set a high bar." Later in private, she suggests that the Captain need not be forthcoming about how rundown Hortons Point appears.

Captain Ebbitts listens to his wife's suggestion and says, "I expect this young lady is tougher than most."

"That may be," Mrs. Ebbitts responds, "but you are criticizing her life's work."

"No one would expect a woman to do these jobs."

"Nevertheless, please be aware that this is a big change for her. She always lived with her parents, and as challenging as that might have been, it is the only life she knew until we came along."

In a nod to his wife's observation, the Captain limits his comments to how well, 'Miss Stella', as the Captain has come to address her, sees to her responsibilities.

His praise makes Stella even more uncomfortable; she is not used to this type of attention. For Stella, keeping the lighthouse is her duty. Captain Ebbitts' proposes that he and Stella alternate days rather than split the night shift in half.

He suggests, "Since you may wish to attend services in Southold, I think the following schedule will work. I will take the full night's watch on Saturday, Sunday, Monday, and Tuesday, and you can do the watch on Wednesday, Thursday, and Friday nights." He continues, "This way, you can spend Saturday night with your family, if you wish" . . . he trails off, registering her look of dismay.

Stella responds with conviction, "I prefer to stay at Hortons Point. I am here to assist as you see fit, but please know I can do more tower coverage."

"I know you are used to hard work, and there may be times when I will need help, but I think this schedule will serve us both." Stella excuses herself and writes to Ma and Lu about the changes, feeling ill at ease.

Stella spends Saturday afternoons giving tours, gardening, baking, and canning, depending on the season. At first light on Sunday mornings, she walks to Prince Lane to attend services with Ma and then stays for the church social after. Stella is unaccustomed to having so much free time and feels lost with her reduced role.

Caroline finds joy in every aspect of her four grandchildren's lives, though Stella is never comfortable with the noisy antics of Lu's active little ones. However, as the months go by, she comes to appreciate the opportunity to spend time with her mother and is always pleased to see Lu, though she spends as little time as possible with her father. When Lu and Eddie can't come to Southold, Stella and Caroline sometimes travel on Waitley's boat to Sag Harbor to stay with them. Stella always makes arrangements for return passage, so she is sure to be back at Hortons Point before it is time for her watch.

Captain Ebbitts proves himself up to the demands of the Head Keeper at Hortons Point. The Captain develops schedules that outline their responsibilities and keep the lighthouse in better condition than Stella can remember. In the fall, he repairs and whitewashes the fence and the exterior of the tower. During the winter, he whitewashes the inside of the tower and paints the stairs. The Captain reglazes the lantern every six months. They both polish the brass weekly and clean the lenses and the windows each morning and more frequently as needed. Captain Ebbitts does the most physical jobs though he does appreciate her assistance. She now sees how little George did during his time as the keeper, and the lighthouse is in better condition than Stella can remember.

On the other hand, Mrs. Ebbitts prefers to sit on the front porch and rock. She struggles to move her considerable girth and requires assistance to step off the porch. She is uncomfortable in the heat, spending most summer days sitting and worrying about the weather. She is not one to take on any work outside the cottage, and Stella cannot remember her ever climbing down the stairs to the beach or up to the top of the tower. Mrs. Ebbitts is content to remain within the square footage of her side of the cottage and front porch. When the harvest is abundant, she helps Stella put up fruits and vegetables. But most of her 'help' is done from the front porch, where she can sit and shell peas or husk corn.

Much to Stella's surprise, Mrs. Ebbitts is a capable seamstress. She told Stella this skill was born of necessity as she makes her own clothing since ready-mades do not meet her considerable physical requirements. She offers to sew Stella a new dress. Stella appreciates the offer and picks out fabric at Uncle Henry's store. In the store, Aunt Jennie questions Stella about the changes at Hortons Point. Stella reports that the Ebbitts are capable caretakers, and she is quite happy in her new situation. Aunt Jennie, never one to pass up an opportunity to find fault, reminds Stella just how improper it is for a single woman to be living with a family other than her own. Stella struggles to refrain from snapping back and is relieved when Henry comes out of his office and greets her. He comments that she is "the very picture of health," much to Jennie's chagrin.

Walking back to the lighthouse, Stella wonders if she hasn't put on a few pounds, what with the lighter workload and the heavy meals Mrs. Ebbitts prepares. Stella shrugs off these thoughts, content that though her frocks seem to have gotten tighter, they are pretty old, and Mrs. Ebbitts doesn't mind sewing new ones for Stella. She even remade one of her own that she said never fit her right. The Captain, on the other hand, is an industrious worker. Despite his substantial size, he efficiently performs lighthouse upkeep. Stella is quite proud of how well cared for the lighthouse and property now looks under his meticulous care.

CHAPTER 21

1898

Nantucket Sleighride -
the dragging of a whaleboat by a harpooned whale.

Early in the summer of 1898, Caroline and Stella are taking in the view and cool breeze on the front porch when Uncle Henry stops by to ask a favor of Stella. After greeting both women, Henry explains.

"Edith is planning a 16th Birthday party for a group of young people." he says somewhat sheepishly, "and she wishes to include you, Stella. It will take place at Conways Inn on Saturday, August 13th, and she would very much like you to lead the young people on a tour of the lighthouse. I think the main reason she selected Conways is the proximity to the lighthouse and, by extension, you," he continues.

Stella feels trapped. She has no desire to participate in what is likely to be an awkward social obligation. Summoning her courage, she responds, "I'm not sure . . ."

Henry cuts her off, saying, "It will mean so much to Edith. She does look up to you."

Reluctantly, Stella agrees, "I guess that will be fine. I wouldn't want to disappoint."

Henry returns to his wagon and, tipping his hat, says, "Thank you, Stella, and by the way, George Terry will bring the boys." Stella shakes her head, dismayed.

As Henry pulls away, Caroline smiling, says, "When will I get to meet the mysterious Mr. Terry?"

"Trust me, Ma, there's nothing mysterious about Mr. Terry."

Captain Ebbitts insists on taking her watch on Friday night before the party.

"You and Mrs. Ebbitts pamper me so. I won't be fit to live with if this keeps up." Stella remarks in response to his offer.

"Yes, Stella, sometimes, I forget. You are not a lady who likes a fuss." Upon rising Saturday morning, Stella takes extra care with her grooming. She puts on the new frock Mrs. Ebbitts made and struggles to see herself in the small mirror that hangs next to the stove.

Mrs. Ebbitts applauds with pleasure when she sees Stella in the new frock. She approaches her, gushing with praise of how pretty it looks, then asks her to turn around while she fluffs out the skirt.

She steps back and exclaims, "You do look handsome, my dear." Though quite uncomfortable with the attention, Stella appreciates the pride Mrs. Ebbitts takes in her workmanship and thanks her with a generous hug.

"It fits just right," Stella says and hugs Mrs. Ebbitts for a second time.

"You are such a dear. I am quite happy living here with you and the Captain."

"Why, we couldn't manage without you," Captain Ebbitts comments, coming in the front door.

He continues, "I think your charges are arriving."

When Stella and Mrs. Ebbitts join the Captain on the front porch, they hear a clamor of young male voices.

Stella and Mrs. Ebbitts sit on the porch and watch as they come to a stop. George Terry stands and tips his hat, causing the wagon to jerk as the horse pulls forward, and he loses his footing, nearly falling off. The young lads in the back laugh uproariously at the mishap, then bound down. George has the boys lineup in front of the porch and tells them to introduce themselves as proper young gentlemen. They quiet down, removing their caps, and each, in turn, states his name with a slight bow to Stella and the Ebbitts.

George comes up onto the porch, and taking Stella's hand in his own, says, "It is a pleasure to see you again, Miss Prince." Stella blushes, and the boys hide behind their hands, snickering. George turns around and gives them a stern look that quiets them.

"You are looking well." he continues. He approaches Mrs. Ebbitts and, tipping his hat, says, "I don't believe I've had the pleasure." Stella introduces George while the boys' race over to the bluff. He turns and calls them.

"Do not go down to the beach. We've come to go up in the tower." Catching himself short, he turns to Stella and stammers, "I-I didn't mean to presume."

"Of course," she says, "but perhaps we should wait for the young ladies to arrive."

"And here they are," Mrs. Ebbitts says as an elegant carriage full of equally noisy occupants approaches with Uncle Henry and Aunt Jennie sitting in front behind the horse. Uncle Henry climbs down and assists Aunt Jennie while the youths, drawn by the young ladies' arrival, help them disembark. Edith is introduced to Captain and Mrs. Ebbitts.

She curtsies and says, "Thank you for allowing us this special treat. We are excited to learn about the lighthouse and the work you do, Cousin Stella," she says, turning to Stella.

"I'm uh, glad you all could come," Stella responds awkwardly.

Turning to Uncle Henry for guidance, Stella says, How shall we organize this?"

Edith chimes in, "We all want to go up to the top."

"Of course, darling," Aunt Jennie says, having placed herself in the porch rocker Stella vacated.

"But I don't think you all can go up at once." Turning to Mrs. Ebbitts, she says, "Our Edith is quite the social butterfly. She just has so many friends and such a big heart she wants to include everyone in her 16th birthday celebration."

"Hm," Mrs. Ebbitts mutters.

Uncle Henry says, "We'll divide up into two groups." Stella, he continues, "You young folk divide yourself how you wish, and Cousin Stella will lead the way for the first group while the rest of you can enjoy the view from the bluff."

Turning to Mr. Terry, he says, "I'll go with the first if you can wait and go with the second?"

"Of course, sir," Mr. Terry responds affably.

As Stella waits for the first group, she hears Aunt Jennie comment to Mrs. Ebbitts, "Isn't he a nice young man?"

Mrs. Ebbitts, not one to hold back, queries, "Young?" Peering closer in George's direction, she continues, "I wouldn't call him young."

"Never-the-less," Aunt Jennie continues, "He seems ready to settle down."

"I should hope so. Some of those sailors never quite realize there's a time in life when staying in one place is better for your soul than roaming from port to port. My Captain realized it early on. Of course, he had me and his sons to draw him back from the sea. Does he have a wife?"

"Of course not," Jennie responds sharply, "Why would he be out here watching out for a parcel of young boys if he had his own?"

"He looks old enough to be the father of one of them." Mrs. Ebbitts retorts.

Jennie replies, "Stella's no spring chicken herself."

Mrs. Ebbitts now realizes there's more to this foolishness than just indulging the whims of a spoiled young lady. Jennie has her mindset to get Stella married. She wonders how Stella feels about this and if she's even aware of their scheming.

As the first group noisily descends the circular stairway, Edith bellows from the watch room window, "NEXT!" Jennie looks up, horrified at her daughter's lack of decorum but unable to think of a way to address it short of shouting back, refrains, for now, hoping no one else will remember this faux pas in all the excitement.

After the second group emerges, a bit overheated from standing inside the glass-enclosed tower, Henry suggests Stella ride with Mr. Terry. Stella climbs up into George's wagon.

He lifts the reins for the horse to start when one of the boys yells, "Wait, we're not all on yet." George glances back as the last of the young men climbs on. He calls,

"All set?" then turns the carriage around in the front yard and follows Henry to the Inn.

The rest of the day goes by in a rush of activity as they enjoy an elaborate meal then gather to play games Edith has planned. George and Stella sit together at a table for two on the side of the room. They are often interrupted by eager or awkward party guests with questions. However, they do manage small snatches of conversation between interruptions. George comments that he hopes his manners aren't too brusque as he's unaccustomed to dining with a lady.

Stella, chuckling, says, "I am no lady, sir. I have dined with sailors, shipwrecked passengers, and government workers. Your manners are no worse than many I've observed."

He asks after her parents, and she says, "Though she misses living with her mother, they visit often." She mentions the change in her work schedule, which allows her more time to herself than she had in the past. And she is happy to spend time at her sister's.

Stella inquires about George's living situation. He tells her that while he is comfortable in his home, he misses the camaraderie of being on board ship.

She asks if he will return to the sea, and George tells her, "No, that part of my life is behind me. Being at sea is a young man's game—full of hardship and danger."

After cake, Stella wanders outback, where George and Henry get the horses.

George comes over and says, "What you are looking for is inside."

"Oh," Stella states, eyebrows lifted in surprise. "I, um, didn't realize."

"I know," he says, sharing her surprise at indoor plumbing. As Stella heads towards the Inn, she glances back at George with appreciation, again struck by his gentle manner and unexpected warmth. There may be more to this man than she credited him.

After Sunday Services, Stella complains to her mother about the foolishness of such an elaborate party for a 16-year-old. Caroline gives her a warning look and reminds her, "We can never repay Uncle Henry his many kindnesses."

Stella looks down guiltily and says, "But Aunt Jennie . . ."

Caroline's stern look stops Stella as she says, "Let's remember this is the Lord's day, and we owe him all that is good in our lives." Stella recognizes that discussing this with

Ma will not get her anywhere. She will write to Lu, who she knows agrees with Stella regarding Aunt Jennie and her airs.

Hortons Point
Southold, NY
August 14, 1898
Darling Lu -
Sorry, we were unable to get together today after Services. The Reverend was quite eloquent this morning, and Ma's work had the

sanctuary gleaming —filled with the loveliest roses.

As I'm sure you recall, I was invited to chaperone cousin Edith's 16th Birthday party. I don't understand the reason for this sort of thing, but I agreed as Uncle Henry made a special trip to request my assistance, and of course, I could no more refuse him than bite off my tongue. He explained that Edith continues to have a great interest in the lighthouse and the work I do though I can't imagine why since she certainly does not need a livelihood.

Once again, Mr. George Terry accompanied the young gentlemen, if you can call them that judging by their loud and boisterous behavior. I know Aunt Jennie had a hand in that arrangement. They all came to the lighthouse, and I started my usual tour when Edith took over all but giving the talk herself.

After they all went up to the tower, we headed over to the Conways Inn. The Inn is expanded, and I doubt even Eddie would find much of what he knew from his years there. We had a private party room and a meal so extravagant I wasn't sure I could eat it all, though I did manage. They served fresh fish and beef and a three-tiered cake. When I told Mrs. Ebbitts about it, her eyes opened so wide I thought they might pop right out of her head.

I must confess I overheard Aunt Jennie tell Mrs. Ebbitts that Mr. Terry may be my suitor. I was horrified to think of such talk getting about. They arranged for us to sit at a table for two off to the side, and if I'm honest, which of course, I must be with you, my dear sister, he is pleasant. We did manage a bit of conversation, and he asked after each of you. Fortunately, he did not bring up the whole affair with Da. I am obliged for his discretion.

Suffice to say. I'm glad the entire event is behind me.

Your loving sister,

Stella

Before the post comes, just to add, we did have an unfortunate event here. On Monday morning, the Captain found his cow dead. It had wandered out of the barn during the storm late Sunday night and was struck by lightning. Poor thing.

Stella considers adding something about her feelings towards Mr. Terry but finds she does not have the words. Even though she is closer to her sister than anyone, she really can't let herself put down on paper the unsettling feelings that thinking about him stirs in her.

❁

During the night of November 26, 1898, Stella is woken from a sound sleep by the howling wind. She sits up and looks around in unaccustomed darkness. The lantern is not lit. Stella rushes out of bed and stumbles down the stairs to the Ebbitts' parlor. The Captain builds a fire while Mrs. Ebbitts huddles on the hay mattress as close as she dares. The wind is so loud; they don't hear Stella enter until she touches the Captain's shoulder, startling him.

He turns and, with great concern, says, "This is a bad one, Stella."

"Is it snow?"

"Yes, but the wind is blowin' a gale. The tower is shaking. I prepped the light - best I could, but I had to come down for my safety. The lantern won't stay lit."

"I'll go up," Stella says, ever mindful of their responsibility to keep the light burning.

"No, Stella. I don't think that's wise. If it were safe, I'd go myself. We should stay close to the fire. When there's a lull, I'll check." Stella glances around, unsure of what to do. While she accepts the Captain's authority, it feels wrong to abandon the tower under any circumstances.

"But what of the ships on the Sound? How will they steer clear of the dangers in our cove?"

"Sad to say, any ships out in the Sound tonight will be fighting to stay afloat. The safest course would be for them to head out to sea where they would hope to ride out the storm away from obstacles."

"If you're sure, there's nothing I can do? I'll go back to bed."

"You'll be safer bedding down here with us." Stella is surprised by this suggestion.

Mrs. Ebbitts pokes her head up from under the quilt by the stove, "You can join me here if you'd like."

"Um, I'll go back to bed." Stella walks back through her side of the house, sorely tempted to check the tower, but she returns to her room and huddles under the covers, trying to get warm and block out the roar of the wind. Her teeth begin chattering with the cold, making sleep impossible. Feeling defeated, she gathers up her quilt and walks back down the stairs returning to the Captain and Mrs. Ebbitts. While the room feels cold as she enters, it is warmer than her side of the house. She wraps up and sits in a chair that Captain Ebbitts pulled up by the fire. Stella dozes off- and on till dawn. When she wakes, she is confused by her surroundings. Realizing where she is and that the Captain is no longer in the room, she stands and heads to the tower.

As Stella approaches, the Captain comes through the door slamming it behind him and shakes his head with a sorrowful look in his eyes.

"How is it? she asks, "We'll need to keep the lantern burning all day."

"That's not possible. The wind hasn't let up, and the snow is blowing sideways right at the glass. A thick coating of ice is covering the windows."

"What can I do?"

"We need to keep ourselves safe and as warm as possible through the worst of the storm. Rest now, so when it subsides, we will be ready to take action." Stella returns to the Ebbitts side of the cottage, where Mrs. Ebbitts prepares breakfast.

"We must keep our strength up," Mrs. Ebbitts says.

After two days of unceasing winds, Stella startles, woken by the quiet. The Captain is already in the tower.

Mrs. Ebbitts asks, "Stella, want something hot before you go up?"

"Not now; I need to see what I can do to help," Stella replies.

When Stella gets up to the tower, she sees that the Captain has lit the lantern, but the light glares off thick layers of ice and snow-covering windows surrounding the lantern room. It is impossible to see through the glass even to identify familiar landmarks. Stella tries wiping the inside of the glass, hoping the friction will speed melting on the outside and at the very least clear away condensation.

The Captain says, "I don't think the beacon is visible. I have to go outside and remove the ice." Stella is alarmed. She knows that the metal stairs and gangplank around the outside of the tower are slippery. The Captain tries to force the door to the balcony open, but it is frozen shut.

"We'll try again later," he says, resigned to the situation.

"How can I help?" Stella asks.

"Keep wiping. Rubbing the inside might hasten the ice melting. I'll go tend the animals." Stella is glad for time alone in the tower and rubs the insides of the windows. The constant movement helps keep her warm in the frosted lantern room, and as she relaxes into her work, she is mesmerized by the lacey patterns of sunlight shining through the ice.

As the sun grows stronger, the ice around the door gives way. The Captain ties a rope around his waist. Then tentatively steps out onto the balcony, where he secures the other end to the railing. He carefully walks around the tower, holding the railing with one hand and stopping every few steps tapping the ice, careful not to crack the sturdy glass windows, then rubs them with a rag that he's dipped in kerosene to melt the ice.

Several days later, news of the many hardships her fellow North Fork residents faced during the storm reached Hortons Point. Mail could not get through, and the steeple on the Methodist church toppled. Although no lives were lost on land, no less than four ships met their peril during that fateful storm.

The only noticeable change at the lighthouse is that the fence in the front yard blew down the bluff, but Stella is starting to see things differently. As a child, she always felt safe as she performed her duties at the lighthouse. But this storm shook her up. Maybe because she's not living with her family, she felt trapped. For the first time, she wonders about the wisdom of her decision to stay. She is worn down by the cold and dampness that seems to reside inside her bones. She is never warm. Even in the heat of summer, she feels the damp building in her bones. She has lived here for 27 years, but her bond to the lighthouse is fading.

CHAPTER 22

Winter 1898–1899

Breach, a Full - a whale's leap, clear of the water.

While continuing her dedication to maintain the lighthouse, Stella contemplates her situation. She is 31-years-old. Not elderly, but by the standards of the day, an old maid and her aching joints make her feel like an old woman. She cannot perform much of the work needed to maintain her beloved lighthouse. Her job requires endless trips up the stairs carrying the heavy oil cans. She jokes with Lu saying, "she's considering getting a cane like Grandmother Merrill." In a series of letters to her sister, Stella sorts out her thoughts, and with Lu's support, concludes that she needs some time away.

Captain Ebbitts has the running of Hortons Point well in hand. And if she travels during the winter, she figures he can sleep during the day to recover from the all-night shifts that will be necessary. So rather than hibernate for the winter like so many of the creatures around her, Stella sends out inquiries to friends and relations to see where they might suggest she visit. Eddie proposes she visit his 'Mam' in Ireland, and Aunt Jennie expounds on the wonders of New York City, but neither catches Stella's interest.

Although Stella has stayed with friends and family in the past, she yearns for a more independent adventure. She comes across an ad in the *Brooklyn Eagle* for a women's boarding house, 'For Ladies of Good Moral Character and High Ideals.' Intrigued, Stella sends a letter to Mrs.

O'Brien, the proprietor, and learns that the rate is $4.00 per/week. Stella writes to Lu that she can't imagine how she could pay that kind of expense. Lu speaks with Ma of Stella's unhappiness and desire for adventure.

On a crisp January day, Ma walks to the lighthouse with a surprising proposal.

"Stella," Caroline says once she'd settled in around the fire and warmed her hands a bit, "You might know that Grandmother Merrill is very proud of your work."

"Yes," she has written me on several occasions, "and, curiously, she includes money in the post."

"Yes, I know, dear. Grandmother and Pop worked hard at the store for many years, and they are relieved that my brother has taken over. Between the store and Pop's Real Estate, They are quite comfortable now in their old age."

"I'm glad for them, but why are you telling me this?"

Caroline leans across the table and, taking Stella's hand, continues, "Grandmother Merrill wants to give you a gift to help finance your adventure."

"But why?" Stella stammers.

"I shared with Grandmother your wish to spend time on your own away from Hortons Point, and as much as she will worry, she agrees that it might be good for you to get away."

"What about the other grandchildren?"

"Well, everyone else has followed a more traditional path. Marrying and starting families while you have taken this unusual step of staying at the lighthouse. She even said that she's sure if you were a man, the Lighthouse Service would be required to pay you for your work."

"That may be true, but ..."

"Stella," Caroline says, raising her voice over Stella's feeble protests,

"You should have a break. I don't know any other woman who works as you do, and I think you deserve some time away. The Good Lord will watch over you, my dear."

"The good Lord and you, I expect. Not to mention Grandmother!"

Smiling, Caroline says, "I'm excited for you. Please make your plans and write to Grandmother to let her know we've spoken. She'll be looking for your letter, and I'm sure will welcome frequent updates when you set out on your adventure." Stella stands and hugs her mother. Her eyes fill with tears as she feels uncomfortable with the unusual sensation of being singled out.

Stella escorts her mother as far as the North Road, enjoying the warmth of the winter sun on her face. Upon returning to the cottage, she writes Grandmother a note thanking her for her generosity. Stella sends a letter to Mrs. O'Brien, confirming her interest in booking a room at her Boarding house for the month of February 1899. She will travel by train on the Long Island Railroad and requests the specifics in her reply, but before mailing it, she must get approval from Captain Ebbitts.

Over dinner that evening, Stella relays her plans. The Captain looks none too pleased, but Mrs. Ebbitts says she will try to help out as best she can in Stella's absence. All three know that Mrs. Ebbitts has never climbed the stairs to the tower. While Stella's trip will be inconvenient, the Ebbitts realize they have no real claim on Stella's time and resign themselves to her trip.

Stella sends a flurry of letters over the next several days letting all know of her plans. After much internal debate, She even jots a note off to Mr. Terry. Since Edith's party, he stops off at the lighthouse with some frequency. When he receives Stella's letter, he offers to drive her to the train in Greenport. Stella accepts his generous offer and promises to give him plenty of notice once she figures out the train schedule.

She spends the holidays at Lu and Eddie's and is livelier than usual. At

Lu's urging, she invites George Terry to join them for New Years Day. He arrives, bringing several dishes that he prepared. They spend a pleasant afternoon with her family, and she accompanies him on the ferry back to Greenport later that day. He drives her to Hortons Point so she can cover the lighthouse. Although she doesn't usually work on Monday, the Captain has asked her if she could be back so he and the Mrs. can spend a few days with their son. She is more than happy to accommodate so he can have some family time, knowing her adventure is fast approaching.

She books a room from Wednesday, February 1st through Tuesday, February 28th, and writes it down for the Captain and Mrs. Ebbitts, and of course, her mother. There is even a phone number where she can be reached in an emergency. Uncle Henry recently installed a phone at the store for public use though there are few other phones on the North Fork; one can call into the city. Stella writes George Terry giving him the date and time of her departure. She plans to take the 5 a.m. train from Greenport that travels to Brooklyn, where she will disembark at the foot of the Brooklyn Bridge at 9:30 a.m. Mrs. O'Brien wrote that the Ladies Boarding Home is three blocks from the Long Island Railroad terminal at 178 Bergen Street between Hoyt and Bond. She further directs; Stella to enlist a carriage-for-hire who will bring her to the house.

Rather than write back, Mr. Terry visits to tell her he will pick her up at three a.m. on February first. The couple sits on the front porch in companionable silence, observing the view of the Sound on this unseasonably warm January afternoon. Mrs. Ebbitts joins them and fills the quiet space with her usual chatter.

George takes this as his cue to leave, and rising, says, "So I'll see you on the 1st?"

"Why don't you stay and take your meal with us, Mr. Terry? We've plenty."

"Thank you, ma'am," George responds, "but I best head back. You never know when the weather may change, and I'd prefer to be back in my snug home before dark."

The month of January is a whirlwind of planning. Stella packs and rearranges her trunk several times before she's satisfied with its contents. She feels she owes gratitude to the Ebbitts for their many kindnesses and attends her duties with even more fervor than usual. Although Stella receives no remuneration for her work at the lighthouse, she knows she is critical to its efficient operation. Stella is glad that Captain Ebbitts is willing to spare her during the arduous month of February, when the beacon may need tending day and night due to harsh weather conditions.

On the morning of her departure, Stella is filled with anticipation. George drives her to Greenport, where she boards the Long Island Rail Road train and enjoys an uneventful trip. When she disembarks in Brooklyn, she is taken aback by many people rushing about. The street is packed with horse-drawn carriages, and even a few motor cars are zipping by at terrifying speeds. Stella never saw a motor car before though she'd heard of their growing use. The horseless carriage—quite a sight! She can't wait to write and tell Ma all about it, but first, she must get her bearings. Following the directions from Mrs. O'Brien, she sees a line of carriages, she raises her arm, and an enterprising driver rushes over and assists her into a carriage, then takes her ticket and runs to get her trunk. He loads it onto the back, and they take off with a jerk through the packed streets to 178 Bergen St.

Stella can't take her eyes from the carriage windows, stunned by the multitude of vehicles and people rushing about. Just as she leans back in the firm leather seat to catch her breath, the carriage pulls up in front of a tall red brick building attached in a row to similar structures. A robust woman who she assumes must be Mrs. O'Brien waves the carriage over and shouts orders to the driver. He opens the door for Stella, who is a bit overtaken by the warm welcome from Mrs. O'Brien. As they walk up the tall stairs, the older woman asks about her journey and impressions of Brooklyn and if she'd like tea and biscuits, all in a great rush.

Stella politely refuses, saying, "I'd like to see my room if it's not too much trouble?" Mrs. O'Brien leads her up a grand curved stairway in the center hall just inside the front door. Stella gapes at the numerous portraits on the walls and unique objects that decorate the vestibule and stair landing. At the top of the stairway, Mrs. O'Brien explains, the rooms on the left belong to Misses Jones and Hartwell.

"They're schoolteachers," Mrs. O'Brien tells Stella, "lower grades. They love children, but one can't help wonder if they will ever have their own."

Then turning to the right, she opens the door and, gesturing with her arm for Stella, says, "This is your room. I hope you will be comfortable. If you need anything, Willomenia, our housemaid, will be up to assist you.

"Oh, I'm sure that's not necessary," Stella responds, uncomfortable at the idea of someone helping her unpack.

"Our mid-day meal is at noon, but if you want anything sooner, please come down." Stella looks around the small but well-appointed room. The window looks out on the street with views of brownstones on the other side. She presses her face against the glass and tries to see if she twists her head to the left or right is she able to get a glimpse of the River or even the newly completed Brooklyn Bridge but no luck. Notwithstanding the lack of a water view, she is pleased with the cozy room she will call home for the next month.

As promised, her room has a small coal stove. Stella is delighted that it is lit and warms her hands. A quick knock at the door startles Stella, and a petite young girl enters. Her unruly hair escaping from the scarf on her head and her dirty apron the worse for tending to the coal stoves.

After a perfunctory curtsy, she says, "I'm Willomenia. I'm here to see that you've what you need."

Stella is startled by this abrupt invasion, and gathering her wits about her, she replies, "Everything is satisfactory."

Willomenia continues, "I will bring ya fresh coal each morning and stoke the stove mornings and evening, so you should be comfortable." She flutters about the room, fluffing the curtain as if Stella's looking out has, in some way, disturbed them.

Stella replies, "I'll have no need for your assistance with that. I am quite familiar with the workings of a coal stove, having tended one since I was a small child in the watch room."

"Watch room?" Willomenia looks at Stella with confusion.

"Yes, the watch room is where the keepers stay."

Willomenia shrugs, and Stella continues, "At the lighthouse. I work at a lighthouse."

"You work?" Willomenia's confusion appears to grow with each of Stella's statements, "In a lighthouse?" she exclaims. "I never heard no woman working at no lighthouse. That's men's work."

"Generally, men do perform the work of a lighthouse keeper, but I have been the keeper's helper since I was a child."

"Hmm, I never heard such a thing," Willomenia replies as she makes a hasty retreat. Despite Stella's protestations, Willomenia comes in to check on the fire as she assures Stella that it is part of her job to see to the guests' needs. She and Stella form an uneasy truce as the former is comfortable in her role as a servant, but the latter draws no comfort from being waited on by paid help.

Stella spends the first week exploring the area. Although she misses the view from the lighthouse, she is excited to discover her proximity to the East River, which is just on the other side of the train station. The majesty of the Brooklyn Bridge also captures her interest. She learns that it is the largest steel and cable suspension bridge in the world, a true wonder of modern engineering. Each day she ventures a little further, growing comfortable with the sights and sounds of people rushing along the pedestrian promenade and the busy ports below. From the middle of the Brooklyn Bridge, she stops and admires the unimaginably tall buildings of Manhattan, and chuckles, recalling the dispute she had with Anna about how tall the buildings in the city are compared with the lighthouse. She finds a postcard of the Manhattan skyline and mails it to her, writing,

'I believe you were correct!' Best Regards, Cousin Stella.

After the evening meal, she sits in the ornate parlor and writes letters and postcards. She even splurges and purchases two stereoscopic post-cards of the Brooklyn Bridge. Sending one to her nieces and nephew and the other to Edith, though she expects Edith has seen the bridge in person, she knows she will appreciate receiving the interesting photo that appears to move. Stella writes long letters to Ma and Lu about all she's seeing and doing, but as the initial excitement fades, she realizes she misses everyone back home, but perhaps most of all, she misses the sounds of nature and the rhythm of life by the sea. She wonders about their weather and if they've had much snow.

Stella is most intrigued by the other two guests, Miss Jones and Miss Hartwell. They are both public school teachers, one lower and the other upper elementary, and though they hail from different parts of the coun-try, they were drawn to Brooklyn by the desire to see more of the world. Miss Jones grew up outside Chicago, so she has some familiarity with the goings-on of big cities. On the other hand, Miss Hartwell hails from a small town in Mississippi, "Tupelo?" She says as if asking a question hoping the listener might have heard of it. She has the sweetest accent, and Stella could listen to her speak all day long. She's sure the children in her class are quieted just by the sound of her voice, particularly compared with the harsh sounding accents they are accustomed to living here in Brooklyn. Stella finds herself pausing when speaking to shopkeepers, trying to ascertain the precise meaning of their speech, which is too fast and too sharp sounding for her ear. She can't imagine how challenging it must have been for Miss Hartwell when she first arrived. Some evenings, Mrs. O'Brien shares stories about her husband, who worked on the Long Island Rail Road. His untimely death led her to open their home for ladies of good reputation. She speaks with pride about her ingenuity in response to the tragedy that led her to rent out rooms. She is proud to provide a safe and clean place for women staying in the area, whether temporarily or for work.

Stella enjoys the conversations shared around the dinner table each evening. The women are fascinated when Stella describes her life at the lighthouse. Miss Jones asks Stella to consider coming to school one afternoon to tell the children about her experiences as a lighthouse keeper. At first, Stella declines the offer, but when Miss Hartwell chimes in, saying how much the children would enjoy meeting a woman who has such an unusual life, Stella agrees to accompany them back to school on Friday after their mid-day meal.

On Friday, Stella enjoys telling the schoolchildren about her work at the lighthouse, but sharing the stories reminds her how much she misses it. She lingers until the school day ends and joins Miss Jones and Miss Hartwell on their walk home. It is most pleasant to spend time with others, even these new friends, but she comes to realize she is lonely even when surrounded by so many people.

They rush home in the cold, gather close to the parlor fire, and report to Mrs. O'Brien about the children's excitement at meeting a real lady lighthouse keeper. Stella is pleased and proud listening to their telling of her success with the children and how one little girl came up and gave Stella a big hug saying, "I want to grow up to be a lighthouse keeper, just like you."

Stella is surprised when she receives a brief note from George Terry.

He writes that he is still working at the store in Orient, that the weather hasn't been too bad, and that he looks forward to her return. That sounds just like him, she thinks with a smile. As the weeks pass, Stella acknowledges a growing longing to return to the familiar routines and dependence on the forces of nature that are part and parcel of a lighthouse keeper's life. She misses watching over the changing tides, but she misses her family most of all.

On her last weekend, Miss Jones and Miss Hartwell take her into Manhattan. They walk across the entire span of the Brooklyn Bridge, and Stella is thunderstruck as they join the noise and commotion of the busy Manhattan streets. Although she had taken in the view from the safety of the bridge during the past week, she couldn't stop staring up at the tall buildings surrounding them. The ladies each take one of her arms and escort her along the crowded sidewalks and across the streets bustling with horse-drawn carriages, streetcars, and private automobiles.

Stella yells over the noise, "I have never seen anything like this! Who are all these people, and why are they rushing so?" Stella's companions smile and nod, affirming her reaction. They encourage her to keep moving so they can get to their destination.

They are going to a rally supporting a woman's right to vote. Elizabeth Cady Stanton makes a fiery speech, and her fervor works up the crowd. Stella is mesmerized as the former President of the National American Woman Suffrage Association asserts the need for NY State to allow women the right to vote as Wyoming did back in 1890, nine years before. Even though the NY legislature received a petition with 600,00 signatures in 1894, they continue to deny the bill's passage. This is a startling new idea for Stella. While a little taken aback by the boisterous crowd, she wonders if she and all the other women could vote, would they also be allowed official titles, like president, minister, or even a lighthouse keeper? She knows that her mother and sister are more capable of making informed and rational decisions than her father.

After the speeches, the crowd disperses, and the three new friends have dinner at an elegant French cafe where Stella tries both frog legs and escargot for the first time. She is unsure about the former, but the latter is "deliciously indulgent," dripping with butter as Miss Hartwell exclaims with such pleasure that they order seconds to share. They return on the elevated Brooklyn Manhattan Train. Exhilarated by the day, Stella presses her nose to the window, trying to take in the sites as they rush past the moving train. Mrs. O'Brien is waiting, asking them about their day in the big city. She wants to hear everything about Mrs. Stanton's speech.

Stella spends her last day in Brooklyn, packing. Mrs. O'Brien has her trunk picked up early Tuesday morning, so it can be loaded onto the 3 p.m. train from Brooklyn Station back to Greenport, where she will arrive before 7 p.m. if there are no delays. George Terry has agreed to meet her train. She feels rejuvenated by the trip and looks forward to returning to the rhythm of her familiar life, assisting Captain Ebbitts and maintaining the lighthouse.

She dozes on the long train ride. Waking as they pull into Jamaica Station, she looks out the window; but is disappointed that it's not Greenport. Finally, she arrives, and George is waiting. They greet awkwardly, but George hesitates to release her hand when he assists her into the wagon. She appreciates the warmth of his touch and is gratified by his thoughtfulness as he brings a warm coverlet to wrap her in for their ride back to the lighthouse.

He asks, "Do you want to go to your mother's house?"

She hesitates for a moment and demands, "No, George, bring me to Hortons Point."

Realizing she may have sounded abrupt, she reaches over and touches his arm. He halts the horse and looks down at her. Despite her usual sense of herself as a capable woman, she notices how safe and protected she feels with him.

She says, "I hope it's convenient for you to drive me directly to the lighthouse? I didn't mean to presume," She adds.

"Not at all. I just wanted to give you a choice. From the sound of your letters, I thought you might be a bit homesick."

"I was," she responds, "but Hortons Point is my home." George shakes the reins, and as the horse moves forward, Stella looks up beyond the trees to catch her first glimpse of the bright white beacon calling for her return.

Once they leave Greenport, the only sound is the rhythmic clopping of the horse on the packed dirt road. The familiar salt scent and cold off the Sound fill her senses as they approach Hortons Point.

"I've missed this. It's so different. There were just so many people in Brooklyn and New York City! Where do they all come from?" Stella says as she speaks with uncharacteristic animation. Stella realizes she hasn't asked how George has been.

She says, "I'm sorry to go on so, but it was such a unique experience."

"Yes, I see you are excited. You know," George continues, "I've traveled the world onboard ship. I've even been to New York City. At least to the seaport."

"Oh, I hadn't realized. But of course. I'm sure you've seen many things in your travels. I'd enjoy hearing more about that, sometime, but right now, I'm just excited to be home."

"I'm glad you're home too, Miss Stella. I hope this trip didn't give you a longing for city life."

"Oh, no," Stella states, "I would never want to live anywhere except Hortons Point." In the dark of the country night, Stella doesn't notice George's shoulders drooping when she expresses her desire to always live at the lighthouse.

Stella goes on about her adventures in Brooklyn. She speaks of her new friends Miss Jones and Miss Hartwell and explains about attending a rally for Women's Suffrage. He glances down at her and shakes his head from side to side.

Stella bristles and says, "What is it? You don't believe women should vote?"

In his agreeable manner, George responds, "I can't say I've given it much thought. But if you feel so strongly about it, I guess I could be convinced."

As they turn up the road leading to the lighthouse, Stella falls silent. George looks down and sees glistening tears in her eyes in the reflection of the beacon's light "are you cold?" he inquires.

"No," she whispers, "just happy to be home." They pull up in front of the cottage, and George assists her down from the wagon, then unloads her trunk. She walks to the bluff and gazes out, listening to the sounds of the pounding surf on the rocks below, content to be home at last.

❋

Stella resumes her quiet life at the lighthouse. Though she encourages the Captain and Mrs. Ebbitts to take a break, they are reluctant to leave her for more than a night or two. This is a strange turn of events; when throughout his tenure at Hortons Point, her father never had any problem leaving his work to her. Captain Ebbitts has the lighthouse operation in hand, which leaves Stella feeling that she is not needed. In the spring, Stella plants a more extensive garden. She is eager to do her part and contribute despite working only three nights a week.

Stella feels productive during the busy summer season, but as the coolness of fall approaches, thoughts of another cold winter find Stella considering another trip. At her mother's urging, she writes to a few of her cousins who now reside in Jersey City and Staten Island, two places she never visited. After receiving welcoming responses, Stella informs the Ebbitts of her plan to travel in November and December. She will stay with family in Jersey, then Staten Island for Thanksgiving, then back to Brooklyn to Mrs. O'Brien's in December.

George Terry accompanies Stella to services each Sunday morning, where the local churchwoman comment on his frequent attendance. Stella finds their interest intrusive and often rails about it on the walk home. George's calm and sober presence is a balm to Stella's ranting. Ma is relieved that George Terry takes her daughter's ill humor in stride and refrains from weighing in when she is in a pique.

When Stella shares her travel plans with George, he listens in his respectful manner, but on their walk to services the following week, he brings up his hopes for them to share a life together when she returns. Stella stares off into the distance, uncomfortable with his pronouncement, and says, "George, though I have grown to care for you, I've never even seen your home in Orient." She sees Belle and her crew just ahead and hurries to join them, leaving George on his own to wonder if he has spoken out of turn.

Stella is excited and warmed by the welcome she receives at each of her destinations. But on December 24, she is pleased to return home to George, who is again waiting at the Long Island Railroad station in Greenport. Stella invited him to accompany her to her parent's home to celebrate Christmas. As they wind their way through the growing darkness of the streets in Greenport, George comments on the holiday revelers, and Stella responds that it is much quieter than Brooklyn.

"Does this mean you've developed a liking for city life?" George asks.

"Not at all," Stella responds. "Although, this may be the first time I'm not searching for the beacon."

He looks over at her and asks, "Does that concern you?"

"No, but it does feel strange. Maybe I'm just coming to trust that Captain Ebbitts has it under control."

"Yes, he appears to," George responds and points north where the lighthouse's beam pierces the dark sky. They travel down the Main Road to Southold and turn onto Prince Lane.

The following day Uncle Waitley takes them over to Sag Harbor, and they enjoy a pleasant day at Lu and Eddie's home. Stella is excited to see Lu and feel the embrace of her family's warmth, but she becomes restless after the large afternoon meal. George watches as she heads out to the front porch and looks north as though she could see the light from here. He asks Waitley if they can leave, and the family gathers their things and walks back to the dock. As soon as they get to her parents' cottage, Stella asks George Terry to drive her to Hortons Point. George, ever accomodating, nods and makes polite goodbyes to all, thanking them for including him.

By the time they are on the North Road, the sun has set. As they get closer to Hortons Point, the glow from the beacon fills Stella with a sense of peace and security. The Ebbitts are pleased to have Stella back and invite George to spend the night, but he says he's been away too long. Stella walks him out, thanking him for sharing her life. He steps close to her and takes her hands in both of his. She steps back. He accepts this indication of her discomfort, climbs up onto the wagon, and drives off.

CHAPTER 23

1900

Gamming - visiting, as practiced by whaleship crews at sea.

Like most people living on the North Fork, Stella's life is not impacted by the new century as she continues in her routine at the lighthouse with the Ebbitts, who all but adopt her into their family. Stella and George Terry continue to spend time together, deepening their connection. Their Sunday walks to services stave off some of the loneliness she feels with only the Ebbitts for daily companionship. Stella is also beginning to feel her age. When she turns 32 on October 17th, she doesn't expect anyone will even wish her a Happy Birthday. She is delighted when she sees Mrs. Ebbitts has prepared a special mid-day meal, her favorite a roasted hen, and just as they sit down to eat, they hear a horse outside. The Captain rises as if he'd expected as much and lets in George, who comes bearing a gift of a warm hand-knitted shawl that Stella wraps around her shoulders. Stella appreciates his deliberate manner and steady presence in her life. She is tempted to give him a peck on the cheek but refrains feeling self-conscious in front of the Ebbitts.

On Saturday, Stella goes to Southold to stay at Lu's. She is surprised that Lu and her brood are waiting to celebrate her birthday. On Sunday morning, George accompanies Stella to services, and when they return, he proudly presents a Birthday cake he baked.

"So much fuss over my birthday," Stella says. But she gives him that long-overdue peck on the cheek, and he beams for the rest of the day.

On the Tuesday before Thanksgiving, the Ebbitts pack up and leave Stella in full charge of the lighthouse. They are looking forward to spending the long weekend in Greenport with their son, although they are concerned about the prediction for bitterly cold weather. Stella assures them she has seen it all and will handle whatever 'Father Winter' has in store. She intends to go to Southold for Thanksgiving services, but the weather is so icy cold she finds just tending to the animals in the barn is all she can tolerate.

Stella spends Thanksgiving alone and wrestles with doubts about her choices. She wonders, not for the first time, what it would be like to be the wife of George Terry. She can't imagine bringing this up with the reserved yet kind man she has come to rely on, so she writes to Lu to get her opinion.

As ice spreads inside the windows, Stella retreats to the watch room, wrapped in layers of her warmest clothes. She eats little and drinks less as she doesn't have the energy to build a fire in the parlor. When the coal burns down, the watch room cools, and she wakes and adds coal, then dozes close to its warmth. Even climbing the stairs seems like too much trouble, but she forces herself to bring up oil for the lantern and coal for the little stove. She does the minimum: keeping the lantern burning and the lenses clear of soot.

Monday morning, Stella wakes to bright sunshine. After extinguishing the beacon, she returns to her cozy next in the watch room, pulling the covers over her head until she hears the Ebbitts horse and wagon crushing the ice coming up the path to the front of the house. Stella sits up, consumed with guilt for allowing the cold to affect her. She unwraps from her little cocoon and climbs into the lantern room to take in the glorious sunshine that sparkles off the ice-covered landscape. Captain Ebbitts calls up to her as he climbs up the stairs in the tower. He takes

THE LADY LIGHTHOUSE KEEPER

in the collection of blankets and wraps and surmises that Stella has been sleeping there.

"Looks like the cold might have been too much for ya?" he says. Stella's eyes widen, and she shrugs her shoulders like a recalcitrant child. "It's ok; I didn't mean to make you feel bad. That was a mean cold spell."

"Sure was."

"You didn't keep the fire burning in the parlor?"

"I guess it got away from me," she admits.

"You go down and see if the Mrs. needs a hand." Stella gathers up the pile of blankets from the floor and climbs down. When she enters the Ebbitts parlor, Mrs. Ebbitts looks up, startled to see that Stella is quite disheveled.

She rushes over and gives her a warm embrace, asking, "Are you alright? You look a sight."

"I guess the cold got the better of me. I've been sleeping in the watch room."

"During the day?" Mrs. Ebbitts inquires.

"Um, yeah. I just felt so tired fighting the cold."

"Bet you haven't had a good hot meal either."

"No," Stella replies, realizing that she can't remember when she's last eaten. Come and help me get this fire going, and we'll get the kettle on for tea. I brought some hardy turkey soup. We can heat that in no time." Stella is grateful for the kindness, warmed by their understanding as much as the fire

❈

Early in the winter of 1902, Edward Scott passes away from complications of pneumonia. His tragic and untimely death leaves Lu understandably bereft. She is a young widow with four children to raise; Carrie, now 14; Eliza, age 12; Agnes is 9; and the youngest, John, only 7.

Caroline and Stella rally to Lu's side, spending even more time with her, but ultimately, Lu realizes she must move her family back to the North Fork. Lu has a new home built on Prince Lane on the site where their home burned down. She assures her heartbroken children a lightning rod will be installed next to the house. They will grow up surrounded by her family, living just one house away from her parents.

The two older girls, Carrie and Eliza, are none too happy about the move. They grew up on the South Fork and look down on the North Fork as the place where the poor relations live. They are sad to leave their friends and school life behind. Lu puts a quick end to their complaining, reminding them that both she and Stella left school at 11 and 12 years of age and took on adult responsibility. Carrie and Eliza, on the other hand, will attend a fine private school, 'The Academy', where they will have more opportunities than she and Stella could have imagined.

Having heard through her mother of the girls' complaints, Aunt Stella steps in informing the girls, tongue-in-cheek, that they are more than welcome to spend as much time as they like learning the family trade of lighthouse keeping. She assures them that now that she is getting older, Captain Ebbitts will welcome the help of such young and robust assistants. The girls' shutter at the idea of working at the lighthouse. They are all too familiar with the lonely life of a wickie, awake and tending the lantern through the cold dark winter nights and in the summer heat. Though they love Aunt Stella, neither of the girls understands why she has dedicated herself to such a demanding job, and they do not wish to follow in her footsteps.

✴

At Lu's urging, Stella attends a play with George Terry. She is uncomfortable dressing up and going out in the evening. Lu comes over and helps fix her hair, and Ma loans Stella her best shawl that Grandmother

Merrill purchased in New York. When George arrives, Stella walks out of the bedroom and is greeted by his warm smile. She feels awkward being the center of attention and rushes them out. She comments on the warm spring evening ripe with the scents of budding flowers. As they walk west along the Main Road, they catch glimpses of the sunset. The closer they get to the Hall, the more people they encounter, most of whom appear to be going to the play as well. Uncle Henry approaches with Aunt Jennie on his arm.

The two couples greet each other, and Aunt Jennie takes Stella's arm, saying, "Isn't this exciting. I'm so looking forward to this performance. Anna is so jealous she can't attend."

Turning to George, she continues, "Anna, our eldest daughter, is married. There are many advantages to marriage, you know." Reaching over to take Henry's arm, she says, "I highly recommend it."

Now beet red, Stella looks toward George, who takes her arm, tips his hat, and says, "I hope you enjoy your evening." he then moves on, guiding Stella through the crowd.

"That was rather rude . . . don't you think, Henry?"

"Now, Jennie," Henry responds, "let's not spoil the evening. I think you just might have come on a little strong for our Mr. Terry."

"Me? Come on, strong? Well, I never." she says.

Henry chuckles to himself, muttering under his breath, "There are times . . ." Just then, Jennie spots their friends and goes over to chat, rescuing Henry from further censure.

The play engages Stella and George, and they find much to discuss upon its conclusion.

As they stroll towards Prince Lane, George's mood changes, and he says, "I would never want to see something bad happen to you."

Surprised by his serious tone, Stella responds, "That's why the Woman's Suffrage Movement is important. Women should have the right to vote."

"Yes, I can see that women are capable of making legal decisions though I can't say as I've known many women," he pauses and sighing says, "except you, Stella. And I know you are as capable as any man." They stop in front of her parent's house, and George continues, "Stella, you and I have known each other quite a few years now. You know I own my home in Orient. I'd like you to come and see it." Stella looks up, registering the seriousness of his tone, "That would be nice," she murmurs.

George continues, "It's important to me that you like it. You see, Stella," George takes Stella's hands in his own, "I think we should marry." George looks down into Stella's eyes with genuine longing. While George has given this a great deal of thought, it's a bit of a shock for Stella. Although she has thought about marrying and leaving Hortons Point, she doesn't know if she could? Now? At her age? And his? After all, she's 35 already, and he must be over 40! She's never heard of anyone marrying at such an old age and certainly not for the first time.

Stella says the first thing that comes to mind, "How old are you, George?"

Startled, he says, "I'm 47. But my Ma always said I was a late bloomer." Stella chuckles. "She would have liked you, Stella. I wish she could've met ya." With a quick release of breath, she composes herself and says,

"I need to discuss this with my mother and sister. You know Lu just lost Eddie, and she's grieving."

Disappointed, George says, "Of course," and backs away. Without another word, he gets on his horse and rides back to his tiny home in Orient that he hopes someday to share with Stella.

Lu's tragic loss upends any talk of Stella and George's future. Stella recognizes how much her sister needs her and doesn't mention the exchange for several weeks. Nevertheless, George is undeterred by the awkwardness of the marriage proposal. He continues in the same pattern escorting Stella to services on Sunday, waiting for the next chapter of their lives to begin.

❈

Another year passes with no talk of marriage, Stella falls back into the familiarity of her routine at the lighthouse. When George picks her up on Sunday mornings to bring her to services, they discuss the week and Stella's complaints about Hortons Point. George takes this as an indication of her desire to accept his offer of marriage and suggests they plan a family gathering at his home in Orient. Stella has never been to his house and has only been to Orient once in her life.

The morning of the visit, Da picks up Stella. Lu and Ma ride on the front bench, so Stella climbs into the back, happy to squeeze in with her nieces and nephew. It will likely take an hour to get to George's home on Navy Street with the full wagon. However, it is a pleasant journey east on the North Road. They pass the turn to Greenport and are enthralled when the road narrows, and there is water on both sides, Gardiner's Bay to the south and the Long Island Sound to the north. After a short stop and stretch, everyone settles back into their seats and continues east. At the buttonwood tree, they turn right onto the road leading into the tiny village. Grand whaling captains' homes line the roadway. They pass the small general store where George works, see Orient Harbor on the right, then turn left onto Navy Street.

Da spots George halfway down the block, standing in front of his modest home, chatting with a neighbor. They pull up, and George assists Stella and the girls out of the wagon while Da helps Caroline and Lu off the bench. Stella feels awkward being here with George in this unfamiliar setting. He introduces everyone to his neighbor, who has remained— curious to meet George's intended.

She turns to Stella and says, "So you're the lady lighthouse keeper I've heard so much about."

Stella blushes, and Lu always quick says, "That's our Stella. She's the best lady lighthouse keeper in NY State."

Stella looking baffled at Lu, says, "Aren't I the only lady, lighthouse keeper?"

"Only one I know of, so your standing is secure," Lu exclaims.

They laugh, and George says, "Please come inside. My cottage is not so grand as the lighthouse, but it is a cozy home." George extends his arm to Stella, leading them into the tiny one-room cabin. Ma and Lu follow behind while Da and John tend to the horse in the back. The girls begin to chatter about the small size of the home. Ma comments on the well-kept gardens, and Lu points out the large sassafrass tree blooming with bright yellow flowers. Lu turns and, with raised eyebrows, sends them that don't be rude look, used by mothers to contain their children.

"I bet this is beautiful in the fall," Lu comments.

"Yep," George replies. And the girls giggle at his brief response, only to receive another pointed look from their mother. They gather around a small table next to a blazing wood stove with a pipe that extends through the ceiling. Next to it is a ladder that protrudes through the hole.

"That's the sleeping quarters," George explains, pointing to the ceiling. The girls hide giggles behind their hands as the adults sit down on the few chairs and the children find a spot on the floor.

George wipes sweat from his brow, and Caroline says, "You've made a cozy fire."

"I know how Stella hates the cold, so I built it up for your visit," George replies, looking at her with longing.

Stella blushes, and Lu says, "What's cooking; it smells wonderful."

"I made a goose with all the fixings." Lu and Ma squeeze behind a half wall blocking off one side of the room where they see a sink, a small cook stove, and shelves that line the walls.

Ma looks out the window over the sink and says, "how pretty your yard is."

George suggests they eat outside at the large wooden table under the grape arbor with benches on each side. Da brings out a few extra chairs, and they enjoy the excellent dinner George prepared.

"At least it's cooler out here." young John exclaims, sweat rolling off his brow.

A wealth of deserts follows supper as Stella presents her homemade German Stollen, and Caroline uncovers the bumbleberry pie she'd made. Lu unwraps the chocolate bark candy she bought for the occasion. Oohs and aahs are forthcoming as the deserts are consumed with relish.

Da says, "We better get goin'." Amid small groans, they express their thanks, and with George looking on both sad and relieved to see his guests depart. Lu offers Stella her seat on the bench, but Stella demurs, happy for the warmth and cuddles packed in the back with her nieces and nephew for the long, bumpy trip home.

In the morning, George comes to Prince Lane to accompany Stella to services. They discussed yesterday's visit, and she thanked him for his kindness in having them. After services, George and Stella walk down to the water for a private talk. She has not revisited their conversation regarding his proposal and feels she has been negligent in letting so much time pass.

Uncomfortable at raising the topic, she finally dives in and says, "George, I would like to accept your offer of marriage . . . " He smiles hopeful as she continues, "But, I must say that having seen your home yesterday, I could not consider living in a one-room cabin." George is crestfallen at her pronouncement.

He steps away, then responds, "If I were to build you a larger home, might you consider my proposal?"

Surprised at his willingness to take on such an undertaking, Stella says, "Yes, I think I would, but . . ."

George puts his hand on hers, imploring, "Another but?"

"I think a small one this time," she says, smiling.

"Ok," he responds. "It's just that when we all visited yesterday, I saw the need for . . . Um, I'd like a two-seater outhouse." George smirks. And Stella continues, "Like Lu had in Sag Harbor."

"That's easy. Not that I see the necessity, but I will build that first."

CHAPTER 24

1903

Riprap -
A loose arrangement of broken rocks or stones placed to help stem erosion.

Captain Ebbitts keeps up with the demands of maintaining the lighthouse, systematically addressing the aging building's upkeep with regular whitewashing, repairing cracks, and tending the cistern on a schedule of his own making. Stella assists with the daily and weekly routines of cleaning and polishing, but she cannot perform the heavier jobs. Mrs. Ebbitts shares her concerns that it may be too much for the Captain as he is now 60-years-old.

Not for the first time, Stella wonders if she were not the helper would the lighthouse service hire a male assistant. Stella redoubles her efforts attending to all she can, but this only serves to highlight the many responsibilities that propriety and brute strength prevent her from performing. When Captain Ebbitts' son visits, he puts him to work on the heavier jobs. While he doesn't appear to be slowing down, Stella continues to worry that she is not pulling her weight. She appreciates that her room and board are in-kind payments for her work, but the fact that the government does not pay her a salary only increases her feelings of inadequacy.

Early in the evening on May 7th, Stella hears a crash then shouting from the base of the tower. She races through the passageway, the smell of paint fumes increasing as she gets closer. Stella is shocked when she sees Captain Ebbitts curled up on the concrete floor, moaning in pain. Stella yells for Mrs. Ebbitts and crouches next to him, trying to ascertain the nature of his injury. She rolls him onto his back and sees a bone protruding from his right thigh.

Mrs. Ebbitts comes in and cries out, "Oh, my! Oh, my! What shall we do?" The Captain reaches up to comfort his wife then groans in pain. Stella orders Mrs. Ebbitts to run over to the Conway's to get the doctor. Mrs. Ebbitt dashes out the door faster than Stella has ever seen her move.

Looking to make the Captain comfortable, she rushes inside and gets blankets and a bottle of the local brew from his desk drawer. Then quickly returns to him. He is still conscious but only barely. Stella places a blanket over him and another under his head. Propping him up, she offers a sip from the bottle. He takes a few drops, grimaces then his head falls back.

Stella notices night is falling and realizes she must get up the painted steps to kindle the lantern. She sees that the ladder the Captain was using has a broken rung. Unwilling to take the chance, Stella is duty-bound to climb the wet stairs. She holds up her skirt as best she can to avoid getting wet paint on the hem and makes the climb up the 28-step circular stairway. Stella realizes her efforts were for naught as the wet paint drags down her skirts. She hikes her dress up in one hand, continues up the two 7-step ladders to reach the tower, and kindles the lantern before total darkness descends.

Mrs. Ebbitts returns and howls when she sees the Captain remains on the floor at the base of the tower. She strokes the Captain's forehead and asks, "Can't we move him to the bed?"

"I think we'd better wait for the doctor," Stella suggests, "But, maybe we should move his bedding to the parlor, so after the doctor examines him . . ." Stella trails off.

"I'll see to that," Mrs. Ebbitts says, glad for something to do. Alone with the Captain, Stella offers him more spirits. He takes a sip then waves her away.

Several hours pass in this manner before the doctor arrives with two workmen from the Conways. He asks them to bring in more lamps to illuminate the small space at the foot of the stairs but realizes there is no way to attend to the injuries under these conditions. The doctor pours a small quantity of chloroform onto a rag and places it over the Captain's nose.

The Captain struggles, managing to push the rag away from him, and says weakly,

"Do not amputate." The doctor puts the cloth back over his face, and he stops struggling.

Mrs. Ebbitts screams, thinking that her husband has succumbed. The doctor directs Stella, "Get her out of here."

He stabilizes the Captain's injured leg tying it to a broken broom handle. The doctor instructs the two men to lift him through the door they'd removed for that purpose. Then, exercising great caution, they carry the moaning man to the bedding in front of the fire. The doctor asks for clean rags and boiling water. He administers more chloroform, then cleans the wound, sets the bone, and stitches the Captain's skin closed.

Mrs. Ebbitts paces, clutching her sides; Stella tries comforting her with a cup of tea. Reluctantly, the older woman sits down hard in the chair. Stella adds a bit of 'spirits' to the tea to help calm the woman. Having done all he can, the doctor joins the women.

Stella rises, and Mrs. Ebbitts looking as if she's aged ten years in this one night, croaks, "Will he survive?"

The doctor places his hand on her shoulder and says, "He's a strong man. I've done all I can for now. He needs to remain quiet. Only give him liquids if he wakes. A little spirits wouldn't harm him," he continues with a wink at Stella. He hands her a bottle of chloroform and says, "If he becomes agitated, put a few drops of this on a cloth and hold it over his nose. It will quiet him. I'll be back tomorrow."

As the doctor walks out, Mrs. Conway arrives prepared to lend a hand with a basket of supplies, including another bottle of spirits. Realizing that it will be a long night, she is ready to tend the patient as needed. Mrs. Ebbitts is crying at the table with Mrs. Conway at her side, stroking her hand and listening as she relays the evening's events.

Finally, Mrs. Conway says, "Stella, please come down and check from time to time if you will." Stella nods, grateful for her help, then extracts herself from the room and returns to the lantern.

Mrs. Ebbitts begins to wail again, "If it weren't for our Stella, my Robert could have perished."

"Now, now Amanda, no need to fuss. Let's see what we can do to make him comfortable." Stella comes back and relays the doctor's instructions pointing out the bottle of chloroform on the table. Then she exits, glad to escape the drama. When Stella opens the door to the passageway, the smell of paint is overpowering. Her shoes stick to the damp stairs as she climbs the tower.

Stella is unaware of the days passing. Sleeping little, she assumes full charge of the light and assists the Ebbits in whatever way she can. George comes on Sunday as usual and is alarmed to learn of the Captain's plight and to see how worn down Stella is. Stella dashes off a note to her mother that George delivers, informing her of the unfortunate events and asking for assistance.

On Monday, Caroline arrives with a basket of supplies along with Carrie to help out. Once her mother settles in, Stella gets her first real sleep since the accident.

Carrie wakes her saying, "Grandma wants to know if you can get up and light the lantern? She's not sure she remembers how." Startled and groggy, Stella looks around and realizes it's already twilight.

"Did I sleep all day?" she asks, surprised at how tired she still feels.

She dresses for the night's work and heads down the stairs, first checking on a sleeping Captain with Mrs. Ebbitts dozing in the rocker on the other side of the fireplace.

Caroline has a warm meal ready for Stella, but she says, "Sorry, I need to go up and get the lantern-lit."

"I understand but come right back down." she continues, "Carrie, maybe you could go up with Aunt Stella and help?" Reluctantly, Carrie troops up behind Stella. She does not wish to learn how to light the lantern, but she feigns interest as Stella ignites the wicks.

"It's a shame John isn't older," she says.

"Why?"

"Cause he's a boy, and this is man's work."

"He is only a boy still, so I guess we two will just have to forge ahead," Stella responds, too exhausted to discuss women's abilities with her niece.

"Do you think you could sit in the watch room while I go down and have some supper?" Stella asks.

"Um, I guess," Carrie says. "But what do you want me to do?"

"I just want to eat and check on the Captain. If you see any change in the lantern, call me, and I'll come right up."

"But what if you don't hear me?" she asks, unhappy at being left alone in the tower.

"Hmm, I remember a little girl playing tag who could holler loud enough to be heard throughout the neighborhood. I'm sure I'll hear you."

"Aunt Stella," Carrie says in horror. "I was a child then. I'm a lady now."

"You are a young lady with the same lungs that you had then. Just use them if you need me. Ok?"

"I guess," she says, plopping down on the little stool next to the stove.

Stella goes down, drawn by the smell of her mother's cooking, and realizes how hungry she is. She sits down across from her mother, who has just returned from tending the Captain and Mrs. Ebbitts.

"How is he?" Stella asks, not even looking up from her bowl as she takes several mouthfuls of the delicious stew.

"I think he's making headway. He wants to speak with you."

Stella starts to get up, and Caroline says, "You sit down and finish your supper. Whatever he has to say can wait." Stella, comforted by her mother's taking charge, sits and eats. They share a much-needed laugh that Carrie, the eldest of four, might have trouble making herself heard. Stella goes to the Captain.

He asks her to pull up a chair alongside his mattress, so he can see her face and says, "First, I have to thank you."

"No, she cuts him off; you have nothing to thank me for."

"Let him talk," Mrs. Ebbitts interrupts, all decorum set aside by the extreme situation they find themselves in. Stella looks up and returns her gaze to the Captain's pained face.

"I want you to know I'm going to beat this thing, but in the meantime, I need your help."

"You know I'll do anything."

"I know I can rely on you, but it's long overdue for the Lighthouse Service to acknowledge your role here. I'm sending them a letter; about what happened and the fact that you need to be promoted to 'Official Keeper' while I'm laid up."

"I don't know what to say." Stella looks up and, with tears in her eyes, asks

"Do you think they will agree?"

"They better." Mrs. Ebbitts says.

"I need to get back to the tower but thank you. And I'm glad you are getting stronger, Captain. You don't have to worry. Whatever the Lighthouse Service's decision, I will keep the beacon lit." Stella leaves the parlor and goes up to the lantern room. Carrie is still sitting next to the stove, where she left her. Carrie looks up, relieved at Stella's return.

She stands and asks, "Can I go down now? I'll come back up, but I didn't eat either."

"Of course, you can, Carrie. I didn't mean to leave you without dinner."

"I'll come back up when I finish. Maybe I should learn the family business. At least for the time being."

"Thank you," Stella says, smiling at her acquiescence.

Captain Ebbitts' injury requires him to be immobile for months. Stella attends to the lighthouse's daily responsibilities and sleeps during the day. George Terry spends every weekend at the lighthouse. While he can't assume any of the official duties of manning the lantern through the night, he does take over much of the daytime chores, allowing Stella to catch up on her sleep. Lu and the children also come out and stay for days at a time, tending the garden and seeing that Stella and the Ebbitts have regular meals.

Lu is still mourning the loss of her beloved Eddie and often becomes teary. Stella writes to Ma, asking if it is in Lu's best interest to spend so much time at Hortons Point. Ma walks out the next day to speak with Stella. She says how important it is for Lu to keep busy and feel needed. Lu knows the work at the lighthouse, and Stella needs help.

Ma continues, "Of course, Lu's loss looms large in her life; she needs to move forward. She's too young to succumb to her grief, and her children need her."

Stella takes her mother's advice and turns to Lu for help at Hortons Point. In particular, Lu enjoys giving tours of the lighthouse to guests. This was always her favorite part of working there, even as a young girl.

Stella gladly relinquishes this time-consuming responsibility to Lu.

In early June, Stella is pleased when an official government letter of 'Commendation to be Acting Assistant Keeper' assuming full charge of Hortons Point Lighthouse, by order of President Theodore Roosevelt. The only new responsibility for Stella is the daily recording in the *Keepers Log*. She is nervous about this and spends considerable time studying what previous keepers wrote.

The Keepers' Log is a legal-sized leather-bound book with lined pages. On the top of the page, keepers write the month, and then in the extreme left column, the date is noted one line for each day. Next to the date, wickies log the weather. On the right side, notations are made, such as descriptions of shipwrecks, rescues, and lighthouse upkeep. Stella enjoys reviewing the comments made by previous keepers, such as her father's notation on March 6, 1883, 'A government inspector arranged to have a kerosene light put in to replace the lard oil.' Stella remembers how much more soot was released when burning lard oil, nor does she miss having to melt the coagulated lard on the stove and the malodorous odor of pork that hung throughout the house. She smiles over Captain Ebbitts's comment on August 12, 1898, about losing his dear cow that had gotten loose at night and struck by lightning. Feeling encouraged, in her best schoolgirl script, Stella dutifully notes the weather each day. However, she does not make a single additional comment during the 11 weeks that she logs the weather.

In late July, Captain Ebbitts' son makes him a lap desk that he can use to write correspondence when propped up even though the injured leg still must be kept immobile. Stella stops in to check on the Captain, and he asks her how the logging is going.

Stella is a bit taken aback by the request, but she goes into the office and returns with the logbook and places it on the lap desk, saying, "I've done my best, Captain, but would gladly relinquish this aspect of the job should you feel up to the task."

"I'll take a look, and we'll discuss how to move forward. If that's alright with you?"

"Of course," Stella says curtly as she exits the room.

Mrs. Ebbitts calls to Stella's back, "Won't you join us for some griddle cakes, Stella?"

"No, I'm going to sleep. I'll check in with you later," closing the door behind her may be harder than necessary.

The Captain and Mrs. Ebbitts exchange concerned looks, and she says, "Hope you weren't too harsh on the girl. I fear she's wearing herself out. Although, it's good that Mr. Terry is spending so much time here. He's proving himself a reliable man in her life. You'd think her father would step in—even if only for the shortfall."

"We're all the better for George Prince's lack of interest. Stella is a strong woman. Quite exceptional in her ability to take on man's work. I think she's fortunate for Terry's interest in her."

"And he for her interest in him," Mrs. Ebbitts says protectively. "If it weren't for her stepping in, where would we find ourselves?"

"Quite right," the Captain acknowledges.

"Now, if you could remove this heavy book, I've been smelling your griddle cakes and not had a bite to eat."

On August 1, 1903, Captain Ebbitts resumed journaling in the daily log. The doctor brought him a wheelchair. He can get through the front door and out onto the porch with assistance. He spends much of the day enjoying the breezes off the Sound and the occasional visitor. He logs the weather conditions, happy to resume his work, even if only in this small way. He enjoys the weekend guests and regales them with stories of his days at sea from his perch on the front porch.

On September 25th, 1903, Captain Ebbitts noted in the *Keepers Log* that the supply vessel Armenia brought supplies of oil, coal, and dry goods to last for the next three months. As the chill of late fall arrives, Stella is exhausted. Maintaining the lantern every night and tending the animals and garden proves too much even with her family's help. There are so many larger jobs that Stella cannot perform.

Stella dreads the cold and dark of winter that will lengthen the time the light must stay lit. Mrs. Ebbitts cooks, cleans, and cares for the Captain, but she doesn't go up into the tower or do any outside work. While the Captain is making steady progress, it is slow, and of course, he cannot manage the stairs. With the total weight of tending the lantern resting on her shoulders, Stella considers that it is too much to handle on her own.

A small unexpected bright spot lightens Stella's mood when a reporter from the *Brooklyn Daily Eagle* comes out and interviews the Captain about his fall. The story appears the following week, and in it, the Captain places all credit for the smooth operations at Hortons Point on Stella, explaining, 'Miss Prince is the very one who found me after my fall. Her swift and efficient response probably saved this leg here." He continues gesturing to his still immobile leg. "She is in full charge of all lighthouse duties. I take my orders from Miss Stella.'

By early December, the Captain makes a remarkable comeback standing with the aid of a wooden crutch his son made for him from a sturdy branch of an oak tree. He begins to hobble around the cottage and even takes short walks outdoors with Mrs. Ebbitts at his side. On several mornings, Stella finds him at the bottom of the circular stairway, looking up as she comes down from her night watch.

She assures him that all was fine that night, but after the third morning, she asks him, "Do you want to give it a try?" gesturing toward the stairway. The Captain nods then hops up the first step leaning down on his crutch. Stella stands behind him as a shield in case he should slip. Slowly, with frequent stops, they climb the 28 steps. He stops when he reaches the landing. Although out of breath, he looks up, eager to tackle the ladders.

Stella shakes her head from side to side and says, "Maybe you best sit here and rest before we go back down."

"I'd love to continue up."

Stella sighs, shaking her head no, and says, "Maybe next time?"

"I think I can make it," the Captain responds forcefully.

A loud bellow from below echoes in the stairway, "Captain! Stella! Where you be?" Stella and the Captain exchange looks of alarm as if caught with their hands in the cookie jar.

At the same time, they call down, "We're here." Mrs. Ebbitts at the bottom of the stairs harrumphs loudly.

"And what are you up to?" in a tone generally saved for naughty children.

"I'm coming down now, dear," the Captain says.

"I'll be right here waiting."

Stella helps the Captain back to his feet and steps in front of him on the circular stairway. She gathers her skirt so it doesn't get in their way and reaches for his arm.

He shakes his head no and says, "I can do it." Slowly he descends the steps leaning heavily on the railing on one side and the crutch on the other, while Stella backs down ahead of him.

At the bottom, his brow drenched in sweat, he looks Mrs. Ebbitts in the eye and says with conviction, "I must return to my post. I'll try again tomorrow." He makes his way through the cottage and plops down in the chair by the fire, exhausted from the effort.

He continues to climb up each morning. After a few weeks, he accompanies Stella up in the evening and goes down on his own after checking that they are squared away for the night. He climbs back up each morning and assists with wiping off the night's soot, then draping the windows with the black cloth to protect the lens from the sun. Stella is uncomfortable with his assistance but recognizes that he needs to regain his strength if he is to return to his job.

By Christmas, the Captain insists on taking watch as long as Stella sleeps by the fire in her parlor with the door open so that she will hear him should something come up during the night. Not satisfied with that arrangement, Stella finds an old ship's bell down in the basement and brings it up for the Captain to ring should he need assistance. Stella is accustomed to sleeping during the day and being awake all night. She doesn't sleep that first night, but she stays downstairs until first light out of respect to the Captain.

When she goes up, the Captain is wiping down the windows, "Morning, Captain," she says, "How's it feel to be back on duty?" He beams at her and nods his head in a slow, rocking, assent pride in his broad smile.

"Some days, I had my doubts," he says.

"A lesser man mightn't have done it, but here you are."

The Captain looks over, taking her measure, and says, "And a lesser woman wouldn't have been able to do the job. Thank you for your service." Stella smiles, though uncomfortable with the attention. The Captain continues, ". . . not that you're done here. I'm just glad the government finally acknowledges your work."

Stella nods and says, "Guess we better go down for breakfast; the smell is making me hungry."

"I'm right behind you." As Stella climbs down the ladder, she looks up, checking on his slow labored steps. Using his arms to support his weight, he hops down the ladders; then, continuing backward, he grabs his crutch and descends the stairs. Delicious smells draw them to the parlor, and they sit down to enjoy eggs and potatoes cooked with salted pork in front of the roaring fire.

"Looks like a banquet set for a king," the Captain says.

CHAPTER 25

January 1904

Mill, to - To turn when a whale makes a sudden change in direction.

George Terry joins them for a quiet Christmas dinner. Later that evening, Captain and Mrs. Ebbitts tell Stella that they want her to celebrate the New Year with her family. They insist she take a break and assure her they will manage. Mrs. Ebbitts explains they need room as both their sons will be staying with them. Understanding that the Captain will have help, she agrees.

In addition to pitching in at Hortons Point, George is building the 'real' home Stella insisted she wanted before marrying him. After dinner, he informs her that the house is nearing completion and invites her to see it. He adds, "I will accompany you to your family for New Year's, and we can inform them of our plan to marry."

Stella's eyes widen in surprise. Her first thought is that his pronouncement feels presumptive and almost impudent, but she realizes that the truth is George has patiently waited for her decision. During these several years, he's become her steady companion, supporting her work at the lighthouse while building them a 'proper home' as she requested.

Stella, speechless, nods her assent. George takes both her hands in his and pulls her to him. He kisses her forehead. At first, she pulls away, tensing at the physical closeness, but the familiarity of his presence overrides her discomfort. Stella leans in, and he places his hand under her chin and kisses her on the mouth. She gasps, unaccustomed to the pressure of his mouth against hers, but she soon relaxes, then rests her head on his shoulder, feeling the pleasure of his muscular body against her own.

The next day Stella sends a letter to Lu and Ma telling them they will join them on New Year's Day and will have an announcement. She receives letters from them by return post expressing their joy about the good news. Stella remembers her reluctance to see Lu wed and is relieved that Lu is happy for her. She reminisces about their many years at the lighthouse, from her father's harsh demands to Captain Ebbitts' accident; they have weathered it all. Stella is still apprehensive about leaving the lighthouse and living in Orient as Mrs. George Terry. But, she expects the Lighthouse Service will hire a proper assistant, a man, to take her job when she leaves.

George Terry comes Friday morning to pick up Stella. He sets up the lantern for Captain Ebbitts, with a full oil can of kerosene and coal for the watch room. Mrs. Ebbitts insists they both sit and enjoy a hearty breakfast before setting off on the cold, bright morning. As they are about to pull out of the lighthouse property onto the road, George stops the horse and, turning to Stella, presents her with a small diamond ring. Stella is speechless as he slides the ring onto the finger of her left hand.

"This makes it official," he says and notes the tears in Stella's eyes. Stella reaches over and kisses him on the cheek as he jerks the reins, and the horse sets off to Southold.

Before they pull up at the cottage, Stella slips the ring into her pocket and says, "Let's tell them after dinner."

"If that is what you wish," George acquiesces. Stella is grateful that George Terry is by her side. Though he is a man of few words, he has proved himself a steady companion, and she believes they can build a comfortable life together. She hopes this is a solid bedrock for an enduring marriage. She and George don't have the kind of passion that Lu and Eddie sustained throughout their marriage, but perhaps she is better suited to the steady, quiet life that George has to offer.

Though several years after his death, Lu continues to pine for Eddie. Though no substitute for Eddie, George Terry does his best to provide the children with a male presence. Of course, the children miss the love and laughter their father brought into their lives but are adjusting to their new home and benefit from the support they receive living close to their grandparents and extended family.

After supper on New Year's Day, all gather around the fire; Stella remains standing and taking George's hand; she says, "Excuse me, every-one, if we could have your attention for a minute?"

All eyes turn to the smiling couple, and George looking at Stella for support, continues, "We are pleased to announce we are going to be married." Stella slips the diamond onto the ring finger of her left hand and admires it while the family cheers, then they gather close, taking turns hugging the couple, wishing them well.

They sit, and as it quiets, little John says, "What's all the fuss? I thought they were already married!"

Laughter follows as he climbs up on Uncle George's lap and reaches over and hugs Aunt Stella.

✤

Long Island Traveler-

November 1904—Orient, NY

Tongues wagged as Mr. George Herbert Terry

rebuilt his one-room cabin into a two-story home.

Being a single man who lives a sober and solitary life, it was said:

"He has the cage; he must have a bird in view, but who is it?"

The village gossips had their answer when on:

Thursday, October 11th,

Mr. Terry returned to Orient with his bride,

Stella Maria Prince Terry

The former Lady Lighthouse Keeper from Hortons Point.

The town's folks extend a warm welcome.

"May their joys be great, and their cares be small."

That evening Mr. & Mrs. Terry enjoyed a boisterous

serenadeby their neighbors.

✤

OBITUARIES

In order of their passing:

Lucy Merrill Prince Scott—Born 1869–Died Feb. 12, 1914

After many months of suffering, Mrs. Lucy (Prince) Scott passed away on Thursday of last week at her parents' home, where she had received the utmost care from them and her physician. Her four children, her sister, and many friends did much to cheer and comfort while her disease made its inroads, but nothing could stay its progress, and the young widow passed on to her reward. She was a faithful member of the Methodist Church. On Sunday afternoon, the Pastor, Rev. H. Marsland, conducted her funeral. Mrs. Scott is buried in Willow Hill Cemetery.

George Stayley Prince—Born May 24, 1842–Died April 13, 1922

George Prince, a twice-wounded Civil War Veteran, was the lighthouse keeper at Hortons Point for 27-years. He died in his home in Southold on Thursday, April 13th. Mr. Prince was 80 years of age. He was one of the first to enlist from the area in 1863 and enrolled with the Sixth New York Cavalry, participating in the Battle of Gettysburg. His name is inscribed on the Gettysburg Monument. During the battle of the Wilderness, he was wounded and sent to the West Philadelphia hospital. After recovering, Mr. Prince re-enlisted until the close of the war. New York State gave him a medal with his honorable discharge. On Saturday, funeral services were held at the Presbyterian Church, with the Reverend William H. Lloyd officiating. Interment was in Willow Hill Cemetery in the Merrill family plot.

Stella Maria Prince Terry—Born Oct. 17, 1867–Died Feb. 23, 1928

Mrs. Stella (Prince) Terry, wife of George Herbert Terry of Orient, died Thursday morning, February 23, in Southold, NY. Mrs. Terry, who was 60 years old, had been in failing health for over four years. She spent her last months in her family home on Prince Lane under the care of her mother. Mrs. Terry was well known as the only 'Lady Lighthouse Keeper' to serve at Hortons Point, where she lived for 37 years. After marrying George Terry, she moved into his family home on Navy Street in Orient. Mrs. Terry was a faithful member of the Methodist Church in Southold until she married, then she joined the Methodist Church in Orient and remained an active member there until her death. Mrs. Terry was a strong supporter of all activities as long as her health allowed. Interment was in Willow Hill Cemetery, where she joins her sister, Lucy Scott.

Caroline E. Merrill Prince—Born May 11, 1847–Died June 12, 1936

Funeral services for Mrs. Caroline Elizabeth Prince, who died early last Friday morning at her Southold home, were held in the Southold Methodist Church last Sunday afternoon. The Pastor, Reverend Ross Linger, officiated. Since her youth, Mrs. Prince had been a faithful member of the Methodist Church and was always a regular in her attendance. She is survived by her four grandchildren, Miss Caroline Scott of Southold, Mrs. Eliza Jacques of East Orange, N.J., Mrs. Agnes Fountain of Riverside, Cal., and John Scott of Southold, two great-grandchildren, a brother Harry Merrill, of Greenport, and a sister, Mrs. Thomas Mason of Bellaire. She is buried in Willow Hill Cemetery in the Merrill family plot. With her husband George Prince and her daughters Stella Prince Terry and Lucy Prince Scott.

IN CLOSING

So that is Stella's tale as I interpret it. I hope she would be proud of the work I've done, resurrecting her life's story from the bare historical bones, but I suspect the public attention might make her uncomfortable.

Nevertheless, whenever I drive by Willow Hill Cemetery on the Main Road in Southold, I call out to her:

"Stella—I'm telling your story!"

HORTON POINT TODAY

Horton Point is a homely lighthouse, set on the northern edge of the rural community of Southold, on the North Fork of Long Island, NY. Its plain, solid white stucco exterior belies the importance of the work it continues to perform, warning vessels sailing on Long Island Sound to steer clear from the sand bar and glacial boulders jutting out of the surrounding waters. Horton Point and the property where it sits are community treasures maintained by the Southold Park District. Thanks to a group of local history buffs, the former keepers' quarters now house a nautical museum, restored in the 1990s with generous donations from local families. Professional staff from the Southold Historical Museum curates the exhibits, and volunteer docents interpret them for guests. Part of the restoration required the Coast Guard to return the light to the tower.

In 1933, the beacon was fully automated and electrified. It continues its nightly duty: exhibiting its characteristic flashing green light at 10-second intervals identified on naval charts as 'GR—10S' and only requires twice-yearly inspections by the Coast Guard. If a bulb burns out, it drops down, and a new one replaces it automatically.

If you wish to learn more about the factual history of Stella and other women lighthouse keepers in the late 1800s, please check out the narrated virtual exhibit at Southold Historical Museum's website, "Stella—The Lady Lighthouse Keeper of Horton Point." https://www.southoldhistorical.org/virtual-tours

ACKNOWLEDGEMENTS

My search for Stella Prince began when I read Don Bayles's informative book, *Horton Point Lighthouse and Historical Museum*. His detailed account of the lighthouse's history inspired me to learn more about the only woman to serve there. I turned to other published works about woman keepers—*The Lighthouse Keeper's Wife, The Lighthouse Keeper's Daughter, Women who Kept the Lights,* searching for Stella's story, but there was no mention of Stella.

My fellow docents urged me to contact Dan McCarthy, a Southold library researcher, for more information about Stella. He became my go-to guy for the historical detail that is the backbone of the book. Dan located obituaries and newspaper stories that included engaging tidbits such as Stella making the honor roll, traveling, and significant events in the family. Dan found it all! I owe a deep debt to his skill and persistence.

The professional archivists at Suffolk Historical Society guided this fledgling researcher to the original journals kept by Henry and Edith Prince, providing insight into day-to-day life in the 1890s. I am also grateful for the remarkable Helen Wright Prince (1912–2013), who collected and organized the Prince family journals and documented the historical record *Descendants of Captain John Prince and Their Place in Local History*—rich with factual and anecdotal information. Many thanks to the librarians at Mattituck Laurel Library who located the real obituaries, rich with details of how the Prince family lived and died.

Thanks to—Amy Folk, our local historian, who shared her knowledge, expertise, and time. We met at the office (Uncle Henry's store!) at Southold Historical Museum and at Oysterponds Historical Society and shared photos of Stella in later life. She reviewed the original *Horton Point Keepers Log Book* with me, translating the fading handwriting of the various keepers who served during Stella's time there.

It was sheer serendipity when the home Stella lived in with her husband went up for sale, and the owner allowed the realtor to give me a private tour of the house, which retained many original details and a few artifacts from Stella and George's life there.

I am grateful for the consistent support of the Cutchogue Writers Group—Bonnie, Carolyn, Heide, Jeanne, Julia, Kelly, Ken Lauren, and Nancy. And of course, for Parnel, who not only organized this group but agreed to be one of my beta-readers and then spent many hours on the phone with me during lockdown—upgrading my words to more accurately reflect the period and culture of the North Fork—essentially taking this suburban girl and schooling her on the norms of agricultural life.

Thank you for the patience of my beta readers, Laurie, Michelle, and Erna—who carefully read my overblown manuscript that was two times as wordy as the book you now hold. I couldn't have done it without each of you! And to my fellow lighthouse docents and many friends who encouraged, listened, and commiserated with me through this three-year voyage of research, then writing, then editing, then publishing.

I am indebted to my three pre-publication reviewers, Elnor DeWire, Deanne Witte-Walker, and Rosemary McKinley, who read and critiqued the manuscript enriching it with their expertise.

Thanks to Helene Munson, editor and publicist, extraordinaire, whose energy and insight guided this neophyte author through the laborious process of completing the manuscript and finally getting it published!

And, of course, for my sons' encouragement to overcome obstacles and fresh ideas for the plot to reach a younger audience. Particular mention to Desiree who located a Birthday postcard that Lucy sent to Stella making the sisters come alive for me with the simple message and her signature 'Lu.'

Last but certainly not least to my husband, who listened to my many frustrations and challenges and provided unwavering support and encouragement even in the face of my nightly complaints as I read other authors' books and said, "This is so good. My book will never be this good." To which he would respond, "Stop comparing your first draft to someone else's published book."

He was right! It's better now! I hope, dear reader, you agree.

GLOSSARY OF TERMS

The following terms may be unfamiliar to the modern reader but were common in the late 1800s.

ablutions—the act of washing oneself

ambles—to walk slowly

beholden—to be in someone's debt

"Bonnie Lass"—Irish colloquialism describing a beautiful baby or young child.

Buttonwood tree—a sizeable spreading sycamore tree with thin bark that scales off in small plates and has ball-shaped fruit heads.

chaperone—an adult who accompanies a younger person or group, most often an older unmarried family member.

churlish—rude or impolite

consternation—dismay or worry over something unexpected.

'Declamation Speech'—a dramatic oration—an artistic form of public speaking

deportment—a person's behavior or demeanor.

dismayed—distressed

dory—a small, flat-bottomed rowboat with high sides.

edifying—educational

emboldened—to make confident

fortnight—a period of two weeks

frock—a women's or girl's dress

Hortons Point—since the early 1900's Horton Point is referred to without the 's.'

kindle—to light a fire

Lighthouse Service Board—the government agency that oversaw US lighthouses' building and maintenance until the early 1900s, renamed the Lighthouse Commission in 1906. The Coast Guard Service took it over in 1939 by order of President Franklin Delano Roosevelt. Keepers and their families generally referred to these overseers as 'the government.'

malodorous—an unpleasant smell.

partake—to participate or share as in a meal.

plaintively—sadly or mournfully

pram—a baby carriage

put up—late 1900's term for canning/jarring fresh fruits and vegetables to store for the winter

promontory—a high outcropping of land—a bluff

queasiness —nauseous, upset stomach

repast—a meal

reverie—to daydream or go into a trance

samp—cracked corn kernels that are dried and stored in the cellar. This hearty grain expands when added to water or broth though it does not have much flavor; it does stretch the meal to feed a crowd and can be added to stews, oats, or eggs.

satchel—a small soft-sided suitcase after the Civil War may be referred to as a carpet bag

scullery—a nook off the kitchen used for storage, a guest room, a birthing, or a sick room.

Spirits/local brew—alcoholic drink generally homemade

'The Little Corporal'—an illustrated monthly magazine for young people published from 1865–1874—with moral themes in short stories and poems

Trudges—to walk slowly with heavy steps typically due to exhaustion or harsh conditions

Wickies—a colloquialism for lighthouse keepers as they were the keepers of the wicks.

Zouave Uniform—a uniform worn by a particular unit of the Union Army during the Civil War. The image of a child dressed in this uniform was on every cover of 'The Little Corporal Magazine.'

QUESTIONS FOR DISCUSSION GROUPS

1. Many people have romanticized ideas of lighthouse life. Did you before reading "Stella …"? Have your views changed because of the book's portrayals?

2. Do you think Stella and Lucy's childhoods differ from other children of their day? Do they differ from children of today? In what ways?

3. Discuss Caroline's role as wife/mother/community supporter. How does it differ from women today?

4. How impactful was George's drinking on his family? His attitude towards work? His ability to hold a job?

5. How did the Captain and Mrs. Goldsmith impact the Prince family. Was the Captain too tough on George?

6. Discuss the roles Uncle Henry and his family played in Stella's life. Can you recall similar influences in your family when you grew up and in your own children's lives?

7. Compare the roles of Eddie Scott and George Terry in the Prince family.

8. What do you think of Stella's decision to stay on when George was fired? Her response to Captain Ebbitts fall? Her decision to leave the lighthouse?

9. How does Stella's extended courtship with George Terry compare with modern relationships?

10. What do you think about George Terry expanding his home to accommodate Stella's wishes. Does this seem out of character for their relationship? Where there 'grand gestures' in your own dating life?